His Destiny

by

Sheila Kell

HIS Series, Book Five

Cover Art by *Lea Schizas*

The Wild Rose Press, Inc.
PO Box 708
Adams Basin, NY 14410-0708
Visit us at www.thewildrosepress.com

Publishing History
First Edition, 2024
Trade Paperback ISBN: 978-1-5092-5847-5
Digital ISBN 978-1-5092-5848-2
Previously Published Cunningham Publishing 2017

HIS Series, Book Five
Published in the United States of America

Dedication

To my dad, Jay Cunningham. We may not have had the years together, but we still have the love.

Chapter One

The person who invented maternity pants was a freakin' genius. Kelly Williams struggled to fasten her blue down jacket, covering her bulging belly again. If only they'd invent a good maternity jacket that was as comfortable as her jeans, she'd be a happy camper.

At five months pregnant, she already felt as big as a house, especially since she'd had to abandon the clothing she typically wore. Although the initial joy of being pregnant and shopping for all the cute maternity clothes excited her, the thrill was quickly wearing off. She missed her short, tight-fitting dresses.

"Kelly, I don't like leaving you like this. I wanted you to fly home with me for the wedding. In your condition, you don't need to be traveling alone."

Barely keeping from tightening her gloved hands into fists as her ire rose, Kelly instead reached out and clasped the hand of Brian Platt, her fiancé. The man didn't know the first thing about pregnant women if he thought she couldn't travel by herself. Pregnant women could do most anything. Sure, they shouldn't lift heavy items, but the airport has people who work for tips to do that and more. She squeezed his hand. "I'll be fine. It's only a week. Besides, you're the one who's going home early."

Walking beside her, with his leather messenger bag strapped across his chest and his wheeled luggage in his hand, he grimaced. "I know, sweetheart. Something's come up, and I need to talk with Dad."

She loved Mike Platt. Growing up, he'd been like a father to her, maybe since she and Brian had been tied at the hip most of their life. As his high school sweetheart, she'd spent plenty of time at the Platt ranch, escaping the craziness of too many siblings at her family's home. "How is he?"

Brian shook his head. "It's hard to tell. He's still weak and his cough is really bad. The doctors still don't know what's going on."

Her mind wondered if part of his undiagnosed illness might have something to do with his other son leaving without a word. Then she shook it off. He'd always been a strong man and while his son leaving might make him unhappy, it wouldn't bring down his health. Nibbling on her cold lip, she worried about her own family. Her father was about a decade older than Brian's father.

As she thought of her father, she knew she still wasn't ready to face her family. She'd put off her and Brian's wedding as long as she could. Being five months pregnant shortened her timeline. Her parents would expect her to live up to the values they'd instilled in her since childhood, so she felt the pressure to conform. A fist clenched around her heart at her failure.

"Kelly, did you hear me?" Brian asked, breaking into her thoughts.

She shook her head. "I'm sorry, no." Smiling up at him, she asked, "What did you say?"

Leaning down, he dropped a quick kiss on her lips. "Just that I love you and can't wait for you to be my wife."

At the crosswalk, they looked both ways and began to cross, then proceeded to the parking lot to get Brian to the airport.

Her heart pained her. She loved him. She did. She just wasn't *in love* with him despite wishing so hard that she was. She hoped it would be enough. Guessing it had to be, she whispered, "I love you, too."

Brian's hand was ripped from hers when something pushed into them. Knocked to the street, her belly tightened. Her heart constricted in panic when she reached to support her baby as she landed on her side. *Oh God, please let Ashley be okay.*

Taking deep gulps of cold air, her lungs burned as she fought for each breath. She pulled herself into a sitting position, looking around, dazed. Her pulse pounded in her ears, blocking her ability to hear, let alone think.

A woman rushed to her side with a phone to her ear, talking. Kelly shook her head, fighting the loudness, trying to concentrate on the woman. Pulling the cell away from her ear, the woman asked, "Are you okay, honey?"

Kelly focused on the woman's moving lips, letting her words register. It took her a minute to assess whether she was injured. There would probably be a few scrapes and a bruise or two that she couldn't see dressed as she was, but she appeared okay. But, the baby. "I think so…" Her heart picked up speed once more. Fear wove its way through her body. "But my baby…I'm not sure about the baby."

The woman patted her on the shoulder in a gentle, motherly fashion. "Don't you worry none. There's an ambulance on the way. My name is Ethel. What's yours?"

On autopilot, Kelly nodded as she looked around, taking stock of all that had happened. "Brian," slipped from her lips. Where was he? What the hell had happened?

The woman clucked, offering her a sympathetic smile. "I'm afraid your husband is pretty bad off. There was an EMT on the sidewalk. He's working on him until the ambulance arrives."

Her gut clenched, nausea climbing up her throat. She had to go to him. Putting her hands down to help her stand, she ignored the tears blurring her vision. "I have to see him."

The woman's hand touched her shoulder again, but this time it pushed her down with a force she wouldn't have expected from a woman who couldn't be more than five-two, with heels. "No. You need to remain here. You don't need anything to upset you and that baby."

My baby. Wrapping an arm around her stomach, she brushed away an escaped tear and then craned her neck to see Brian. He was so far away from her. She shook her head, loosening more tears. She looked on, straining to see what was happening through her blurred vision, but he was surrounded by men, some stood, and some knelt, but all blocked her view.

Turning back to the woman by her side, she tried to smile and remember her name. Ester? Ethel? Ethel. "Ethel, what happened?"

"Oh, a car plowed right into the two of you on the crosswalk. Pulled out of a spot and gunned it. Your husband pushed you out of the way at the last minute."

Kelly blinked slowly, not bothering to correct her

and appreciating the directness of the woman. She couldn't handle anyone's emotions but her own.

Brian had saved her from getting hit. She gulped as worry gnawed at her every nerve. "Did the driver stop?"

Ethel pursed her lips. "No. The bastard kept driving."

A hit and run. The thought shook her, bringing back with it some semblance of herself. The news helped shake off some of the shock. *Son of a bitch.* They'd both looked both ways to make sure it was clear to cross. *Dammit.* Her frustration raised her pulse rate, and she reminded herself to remain calm for little Ashley's sake. "Did someone get his license plate number?" The police could run it and find the asshole who hurt them. *Hurt.* That had her looking again toward Brian. She couldn't sit here while he was injured. He needed her by his side.

Struggling to her feet, a burst of determination pulsed through her. She thanked the woman for her kindness but told her she had to see Brian. As sirens neared, she closed in on where he lay. His leg was bent at an odd angle, and that relieved her a little as a broken leg healed fine. Then she looked up his body, and her blood froze. With her hand to her mouth, she held back her gasp. Brian bled from his head. And she meant really bled. That couldn't be good. He appeared to be laboring to breathe.

Oh God.

The EMTs jumped out of the ambulance and spoke with the man she guessed was the EMT on the sidewalk while they worked. As they did, she heard Brian ask about her. Pushing her way through, she steeled herself.

She needed to stay strong for him. They could fix him. This was the twenty-first century with modern medicine.

She made it by his side when the EMTs lifted the gurney. They stopped for a brief moment, and she grabbed Brian's hand.

"I love you," he gasped. "If I don't make it,"—pain masked his face—"take care of our little girl."

Kelly's belly tightened again. Their baby kicked under her jacket. Relief at that small wonder rippled through her. Their baby was okay. "Don't say anything like that. You'll be just fine." Despite her determination to remain strong, her voice wavered.

"Ma'am, we've got to go," an EMT told her.

Not wanting to let go, but knowing she had to, Kelly dropped Brian's hand. "I love you."

After the ambulance departed with Brian, she stood frozen, fearful of what would happen. She didn't want to lose him. Ethel approached her and offered her a ride to the hospital. Normally, she'd give an emphatic negative answer to a stranger, but she shook so badly that she couldn't drive safely. She knew this, so she accepted the ride with a police officer agreeing to meet her there.

Later, as she sat in a corner alone in the hospital waiting room, she remembered her last words to Brian.

Guilt plagued her. Anxious to finally marry and have a family, Kelly had settled for Brian, her high school sweetheart, when he'd come to Baltimore several months ago to win her over. Only he hadn't truly been her Mr. Right, and things hadn't turned out as she'd expected. They were having a baby, and she'd been reluctant to actually wed because she wasn't *in* love with him.

No longer able to sit, she stood and walked down the hallway. When she found a women's bathroom, she slipped inside and, after making sure she was alone, at least for the moment, she pulled out her cell phone. Cycling through numbers, she found the one she needed and hit the Call button.

"Hello," Mike Platt answered the phone. "Kelly, is that you? Do you have an update?"

Pain for Mike, heartache for herself, and devastation for her unborn child swirled through her. She closed her eyes, preparing to devastate Brian's father.

Before she spoke, Kelly rested a hand on her belly and promised to give her little girl all the love she had. She thought she'd shed all her tears already but was wrong. As tears streamed down her face, all she thought of was that her fiancé was dead.

Chapter Two

Kelly Williams, investigative journalist for *Baltimore's News First* newspaper, parked her car, her nerves on edge about her visit to the North Branch Correctional Institution. Coming here alone was not only foolish but dangerous. With ominous clouds in varying shades of gray—from almost black to dirty white—hovering heavily in the sky, she stepped out of her vehicle, winter boots plopping onto the snowplowed parking lot with a crunch.

She took a moment to inhale deeply, relishing in the fresh scent, although laced with a dampness promising more snowfall. The air didn't have the cleanness of the Montana air she'd grown up with, but a calm settled within her, easing her tension. Jacket snapped in place, gloves and hat on, she grabbed her identification from her wallet and moved to hide her purse in the trunk.

She shoved her keys in her pocket after using the remote to unlock the trunk. Next, she deposited her purse, then slammed the trunk shut before she had time to register why she had Brian's suitcase still inside. It had been a month since his death.

The gloom of the facility sent a shiver slowly snaking up Kelly's spine and branching out to her fingers and toes. She tugged her black cashmere scarf up higher and moved forward, remembering her goal of obtaining a new twist to a story she had previously covered. Adrian Copeland had been convicted of property insurance fraud and providing false statements to the insurance commissioner. She had followed his story closely and received high praise for her news coverage.

Oddly enough, Adrian had contacted *her,* pleading his innocence, and that he needed her to help clear his name. It seemed strange that he'd asked for her as she had written about his crimes and the overwhelming evidence against him. *Why me?* had bounced through her mind since she'd received his phone call.

Adrian had reportedly hired William Darling, a seedy, conniving arsonist, to torch his businesses for the insurance money. William had testified against Adrian, though, with the promise of immunity for his testimony. Both men disgusted Kelly. Dishonest, crooked, and greedy only began to describe what the criminals stood for. Adrian received eleven years of prison time. Despite his testimony, William received a worse sentence from someone other than the justice system. A man named Jason Brock had murdered him with a single gunshot to the head.

Jason and Adrian appeared to have been placed in the same correctional facility. Both asked to meet with her today, and Kelly's curiosity was piqued to the highest level. What a story this would make!

With the bits of dirty snow and ice crunching under her boots, she made her way to the prison entrance gate. After having her identification scrutinized, going through doors and gates that had to be unlocked for her, and one unwelcome search, Kelly finally realized what she was doing. She stood inside an actual prison. Her body quivered at her predicament. *What am I getting myself into talking with a murderer?*

Kelly's fear dissipated when she saw Paul Lintz—an old friend of hers who worked in the facility as a correctional officer. He greeted her with a smile, then looked at her sternly. "I'm not happy about your being here. I take it your boss and the warden are friends since not only did you get a private room, but you're seeing two prisoners." He paused. "Two men that you should leave alone." With a sigh and a reluctant wave forward, he continued, "But, come on."

Her damp rubber soles squeaked as she walked down the corridor, and the sound echoed off the walls. Outside of legal representation, the meetings had been an unusual request, but she wouldn't balk at how it had happened. With a smile, "I imagine so," was all she managed in reply.

"You going to tell me why you're meeting with someone you had the pleasure of exposing in your articles?"

She cringed. According to Adrian, there was new information that the courts refused to consider. How could she pass that up? Instead of explaining it all to Paul and admitting how much she relished in the thought of having a new twist to the story, she shrugged and smiled. "I'm just curious."

"Hmph." Disbelief wrapped in his voice. "Well, I'm not comfortable having you alone with them. Especially a murderer like Jason, but I don't get a choice. I'll be right outside the door."

Being alone with Jason Brock wasn't something she looked forward to either. The man had admitted to killing William Daring. Her heartbeat thumped hard against her rib cage at the thought of being closed in a room with a convicted murderer. She couldn't stop her mind from screaming that she was taking a huge risk for a story.

After inhaling a deep gulp of air, Kelly stood straight and steeled herself against the unrealistic notion of what could happen. There was no reason he'd attempt to kill her, especially in here. Paul ensured her all was safe for visitors. She trusted Paul with her life.

She had to put Jason's crime on the back burner in order to remain objective and focused. He claimed to have heard William's last words before he shot him in cold blood. Something that Adrian Copeland felt should be made public. Damned that investigative journalist mind of hers. Of course, she had to know.

They arrived at another locked door, and Paul looked down at her. His brows furrowed. "Be safe. I'll be right outside."

He inserted the key into the lock, turned it, and preceded her into a room with a small table and two metal chairs. She inwardly sighed. Before she had much time to reflect on how the government should do something to liven up the room so visitors weren't reminded of the oppressive environment, the door opposite them opened. Dressed in a prison jumpsuit, a man entered with a guard. Only then did she notice Paul had stepped in front of her. Not blocking her view, but letting Jason Brock know she was protected. A fat lot of good that did when the two of them were alone.

But when Kelly sized up the murderer, she almost laughed. Jason Brock, a thin man, stood only about five foot nine. Her body immediately eased. This was a dangerous murderer?

Believing what criminals said was a tough call since some would say anything to get their sentence reduced. Jason, however, wasn't asking for that. He claimed to just want to set the record straight. To clear Adrian's name. That made this even more intriguing. What exactly had Jason and Adrian discussed behind closed doors? Her blood surged, energizing every cell with a dash of euphoria at that thought. A new investigation always invigorated her.

She scooted around Paul and stood behind a chair. "I'm Kelly Williams. You wanted to meet with me." She raised an eyebrow at the prisoner.

"I ain't talking with either of them in here." Jason motioned toward Paul and the guard.

Shoved forward by the guard, Jason moved and dropped into the seat at the table. After the guard cuffed him to the table, the guard turned away.

Paul touched her forearm to gain her attention. She turned back to him. "Remember," he said, "I'll be right outside the door." He glared at Jason, then turned and walked out of the room, as did the guard. The closing of the two doors seemed so final, it gave her a moment's hesitation, and nervousness attempted to gnaw at her. Kelly shook it off and sat in a chair.

She leaned back. "Now, I must remind you that I am neither legal representation or a private detective. I'm an investigative journalist for *Baltimore News First*. I may or may not look into your story. The confidentiality level is yours to decide. Before we begin, are there any questions on that? Are you clear there are to be no expectations from this meeting?"

Jason nodded and grumbled, "I understand."

When he didn't say anything else, she began her

interview. "Why are you coming to me with this and not the police?"

The man's shoulders sagged, taking a pitiful stance to a whole new level. So much for the big, bad murderer she'd built up in her mind. "I did tell them, but they didn't believe me."

That figured, considering his status as a convicted felon. "So, why me?"

He looked bewildered. "You were the one who worked hard on the story of Adrian and William. I thought you'd want to know the truth."

Excitement sliced through her veins, leaving a tingle in its wake. They'd supposedly already had the truth. "What truth is that?"

"William said Adrian didn't hire him."

Her breath caught. She should've expected this since Adrian also wanted to meet, but it still came as a shock. And not so believable. Recovering, she responded dryly, "And, you came forward with this after you met Adrian? Makes it a bit hard to swallow."

Jason shook his head. "I came forward with it because he doesn't deserve to be in here if he didn't do what they say."

Interesting. When to trust the word of an unscrupulous arsonist? Did he tell the truth during the trial or when he had a gun to his head? Truly, both were difficult to believe. William had been a career criminal who could've lied under oath. Then, with his life on the line, he said Adrian didn't do it. But why change his story?

Narrowing her eyes, she wondered what was in it for Jason. Absolutely nothing, as far as she could tell. His sentence was for murder, and he'd made a deal with the prosecutor for a shorter stint in prison. "What's in this for you?" she asked bluntly. No sense wasting her time. The hope was he answered honestly. She almost laughed out loud at that thought.

"Nothing except peace of mind. I have a family, and I know what it's doing to them while I'm here. Adrian has one, a grown child, and his son doesn't deserve the pain and anguish of his father being locked away for something he didn't do."

Touching, but still, she remained skeptical. That was what kept her sharp in her field. Needing to know more about this man, she changed tact. "What happened? Why'd you do it?" Kelly had read what had been available on Jason, but something inside—some instinct—told her that it hadn't been what came from his heart. That, she wanted to hear.

A heavily burdened sigh escaped the man. "I'm a carpenter. Times were tough, and I'd been out of work for close to six months. My wife, two girls, and I were about to be put out of our home. Heck, we'd barely had enough to eat." He swallowed hard, his Adam's apple bobbing with the effort. "Every day I went out to find work, and every day I failed. Then one day I found an envelope in my car—my locked car—with a thousand dollars and a note that I had a job if I wanted it." Leaning forward, he dropped his head low to reach his chained hands. "If only I'd known."

While he took a moment to recover, Kelly assessed his body language. The man was troubled, possibly filled with guilt. Maybe he regretted what he'd done and what his family was now dealing with due to his incarceration.

She was about to speak when he looked up and

continued, "I had no choice. I took the money to the bank and bought ourselves a little more time under the roof of a house I helped to build. Nothing happened, but I was nervous since I didn't wait to see what job it was before I spent the money. Two days later, I found out. A second note appeared in my car, with another grand, telling me exactly what I needed to do and that it would pay me ten thousand dollars."

He shook his head. "I went home, realizing the first money had only delayed the inevitable—unless I did this job, I'd be a victim myself. It turned my guts inside out. I couldn't return the first grand. It was already spent. So I knew I had no choice. That night, I kissed my wife and girls goodnight, then grabbed our gun and left the house."

"You found William at his apartment?" That much she remembered.

Nodding, he continued, "Yeah. All I could think about was my sweet babies and wife about to lose their home and criminals like William roaming the streets. The note told me I needed to kill William because he torched some businesses and more were to be set on fire." Jason shook his head.

"William pleaded for his life and asked why he was getting knocked off. I told him someone wanted him dead for torching businesses. William laughed in my face. Although I never mentioned a name"—Jason stared boldly at her, pleading—"I didn't know any. He said that he promised to keep lying about Adrian hiring him to do the jobs. When I said there were supposed to be more, he laughed and said that was doubtful since his boss only wanted to ruin Adrian. Now that he was in jail, it didn't matter."

Jason shifted in his chair. "Then he laughed again. Laughing like I was some idiot or something. I was so confused that I didn't notice when he reached for the gun. There was a struggle, and well, the gun went off. I ran. Hadn't thought of fingerprints. They wouldn't have had them on file if I hadn't had a drunken fight while in college."

Jason closed his eyes. "I'm so sorry I ended that man's life. Criminal or not, he didn't deserve it. Now, my family's no better off than they were before, and I can't help them." Jason's voice broke near the end of his sentence.

"But why come forward now?" Kelly asked.

"I can't bring William back. I can't change what I did. But, if I can get an innocent man out of jail, well, then at least I accomplished some good in my life."

Before she could formulate an appropriate response, a knock sounded on the door, and Paul stepped into the room, scanning the table and Jason before looking at her. "Time's up."

Kelly nodded and watched a second guard unlock Jason from the table and walk him from the room. Her thoughts spun on whether to believe him or not. Even if she did, how would she prove his innocence? The police had ignored this new information. Why shouldn't she follow suit? What reason would he have to lie, though? Did Adrian promise him money in return for helping to set him free?

Releasing someone the DA convicted of a crime would go against their office's record, even if they actually found the guilty person or persons, so why put themselves out for a known criminal? She guessed justice wasn't always served.

Biting the inside of her mouth, she lost herself in thought. It was no secret that her articles bolstered his guilt. She'd never actually accused Adrian in her articles, but she'd put a great deal of circumstantial evidence out there. She'd been so positive he was guilty. Could she have been wrong all along? Kelly flinched. She'd listen to Adrian—truly listen and not patronize him—to see what came of this new information.

No sooner had she made her decision when Adrian was led into the room where she'd met with Jason. At fifty-three, Adrian was still a striking man with his dark hair that was mostly gray and dark brown, almost mysterious-looking eyes. Although thinner than Kelly remembered him, he still had an appealing figure for a man.

Assuming a standoffish, professional persona, she didn't stand for his entry but only nodded. "Mr. Copeland." She gestured to the chair across the table for him to sit, hoping the slight tremble in her hand didn't show. After sliding onto the chair, he leaned his forearms on the table, clasping his hands together before being cuffed to it by the guard.

After being left alone, he spoke. "Thank you for coming, Miss Williams. Did you speak with Jason?"

The eager, hopeful look tugged at her heart. *Stay strong.* "I did," she answered. "But, I'm not sure what you want me to do about it. And, I'm not printing a story with just his confession, and I see no way to corroborate it. In fact"—she leaned back in her chair, keeping herself far from him—"I'm surprised you contacted me about this."

His eyes widened. "You're perfect. If anyone can

prove me innocent, it's you. I know from experience that you don't let go of a story, and you'd want your own evidence to prove I didn't do anything illegal."

In an instant, her hands shot up in a surrender movement. "Whoa. I'm not going to prove you innocent. I'm not the police."

"But you're a professional who prides herself in getting it right." He nodded. "Yes, I looked into you. And"—he stressed the word—"I think you want to get this right. It's got to be getting to you to know I might be innocent."

Damn him. It was. Not that she'd tell him. "If the police don't believe it, why should I?"

"Because the police won't admit they were wrong. They only listened to that bastard William who lied." Anger lanced so strongly through his words that she felt it in her bones.

Still reeling from the onslaught of the vehemence in his statement, she questioned, "Why not hire a private investigator?" That was what she'd have done. She almost shook her head. No, she'd probably have gone to the press also. Yet, she might be biased based on her profession.

"And pay them how?" He raised his eyebrows. "They took everything my ex-wife—the bitch—hadn't already taken. My son is struggling to pull it all back together. I won't take from him. Besides,"—he smiled confidently—"I think you'd do a better job."

She probably would, if she made the time. Releasing a small sigh, she nodded. "I can't promise anything, but I'll listen."

Relief washed across Adrian's face. "That's all I ask. And, in return, I have some information I overheard that you might want to hear. About the death of your fiancé." He smirked, and her stomach lurched.

Kelly's nerves tightened. Her confidence and strength instantly washed away.

Later, as she made her way to her car, still reeling from the interview, she tried to process what Adrian had told her about Brian's accident. His death. Part of her doubted the validity of his statements, but she wanted to know who had taken her fiancé's life so needlessly.

As she approached her vehicle, Kelly noticed the trunk was open. Hadn't she closed it? She picked up her pace. Once at the back of the vehicle, she swallowed hard. An icy chill slid down her spine. Kelly looked around at the sound of squealing tires, wondering if that was her thief escaping.

Unsettled, and dreading what she'd find, she reached down and slowly lifted the open trunk lid so she could see inside. A quick glance confirmed her purse had been stolen. There'd only been one other thing in her trunk, and it was also missing. Brian's large suitcase that had been stowed there until she could deal with its contents. Deal with the memories associated with it.

Although angry at losing her purse, she shook her head in disbelief. Now, who the hell would want Brian's clothes?

Kelly slammed her trunk closed and entered her car. Once seated, she blew out a deep, long sigh. Emotions, mainly hormone-induced, spiraled out of control. Her eyes tried to produce tears, but she held them at bay. Jason. Adrian. Brian. Information overload. But, there was one other person that entered her mind, as it often did on occasion whenever she reflected on her life. Trent McKenzie. The only man she ever truly was in love with. Deeply.

Where was he now?

Chapter Three

Sitting on the secluded beach on the Gulf Coast, Trent McKenzie and Jamie Michaels laughed at all they'd done while traveling. Once he'd recovered enough to leave the hospital after surviving the bomb blast where he'd saved a little girl's life, Trent had prepared to hit the road on his bike and never return. Too many painful memories and problems awaited him in Baltimore.

As for Jamie, she'd been his constant companion these last few months. Initially, he'd balked at having company on his pity party tour, and that was truly what it had been planned to be whether he'd officially called it that or not. That had been Jamie's label for it. The woman believed in speaking her mind—no matter how blunt. But then, he'd learned why she'd been so insistent on joining him on his travels.

Jamie, a nurse at the hospital where he'd been recovering from burns and wounds inflicted during the bomb blast, had approached him on more than one occasion about riding off with him. He'd brushed it off as a joke. On the day before his release, though, she'd tried one last time. "Trent," Jamie had said softly, "I know you planned to go off alone, but you don't really need to be alone. And, I don't want to be alone any longer."

"Jamie—" he'd started. It had shocked the hell out

of him. She'd been a great nurse caring for him but hadn't acted as if she cared more than nurse-patient. Granted, as a red-blooded male, he'd noticed her beauty. She was attractive with long dark hair she kept tied back and her deep, laughing chocolate-colored eyes. No matter her good looks or her constantly cheerful attitude, he wasn't ready for a romantic relationship. He might never be again. Hell, who would want him as fucked up as he was on the inside and especially on the outside?

As for his trip, he hadn't kept it a secret that as soon as he'd recovered enough, he was taking his bike to the road and going wherever it took him. Getting away from it all was the only thing he could think about that didn't rip his walls apart. As a grown man, he didn't need shit bothering him. Better to let it all go and start over elsewhere.

She'd put her hands up to stop his flow of words. "I'm not asking for that. I'm talking about companionship. Just give me a month of seeing what I can of the country. After that, I don't think I'll be up for much." She had paused, and he'd been ready to interject again and decline to have her as a travel partner. Then, she'd heaved a burdened sigh, and he braced himself for what he guessed he wouldn't want to hear. "You see, I'm dying of ovarian cancer."

That had stopped him in his mental tracks, and his heart had beaten rapidly for her. She'd seemed so full of life that he'd struggled to rationalize her words. It took him a few moments to regain his senses and ask more questions to find out further information, even if he didn't like the answers. He'd steeled himself. "What about chemo? Drugs? All the stuff they do to help save someone with cancer?" He knew not everyone survived, but it happened.

While she shook her head and her eyes glistened with unshed tears, his heart ached for a woman he didn't really know. A woman who'd tried her damnedest to cheer him on a daily basis. An impossible task.

"It's too late. I can try it all, but...." After she'd left that to hang between them, he didn't need to ask anything else. She'd answered him. Either way, she'd die soon.

He'd swallowed hard. How could he deny a dying woman her final wish when it was in his power to grant it, but only his selfishness stood in the way? Thinking back on how she'd taken care of him, changing his bandages and keeping him company to the point where he'd somewhat looked forward to her visits, ate away all his self-absorbed thoughts. An aching need to repay her, in any way he could, had overtaken every thought in his head.

So, after he'd helped Devon on a quick mission, he and Jamie had taken off with no real plan in mind. Eventually, she'd given him a list of places she wanted to see—the Grand Canyon, Niagara Falls, and other major tourist destinations—and they'd seen every landmark that had been on her bucket list.

Only, he hadn't taken her back after a month. They'd both been so carefree—her not worrying about dying and him not worrying about his next move.

"I love this one." Jamie leaned her phone toward him with a photo of Trent at the Grand Canyon.

Smiling, he pulled out his phone. "Oh yeah." He flipped through some photos on his cell and found one identical to it with her in it. "I like this one." Proudly, he showed her the picture. They'd done that at most photo sites. When they couldn't get someone to take their photo together, they'd take them in the same spot on each phone.

"Wait. Wait." She pulled her phone back close and snickered. "I've got it." Producing a photo of the two of them in the same spot, she smiled brightly.

For some reason, it created fits of laughter between the two of them. They'd had a good time at each stop, when Jamie wasn't too weak.

"I'm glad we took that tour through Yellowstone instead of trying to find all those magnificent spots ourselves," Jamie said.

Talking him into ditching the bike hadn't been easy for her, but in the end, he'd acquiesced, and they'd joined a tour. Like her, he was glad they had. She'd enjoyed it so much.

"What was your favorite place?" he asked.

She appeared to think for a moment, then turned to him. "Here."

A lump formed in his throat and guilt hit him square in the chest because he'd never felt so alive as he did at the moment.

"I still say you can't surf, not that there were enough waves here to do it properly," she teased.

Trent laughed. "You've got me. I have no clue how to fucking surf. But," he said and winked, "I looked good doing it."

"I don't know about that. Taking as many headers as you did only made for plenty of funny videos."

"You didn't," he said aghast.

A big smile split her face, and she hugged her

phone to her chest. "I did."

Reaching out, he grabbed for the phone. "Give me that. I want those videos deleted."

Jamie giggled, and he decided to tickle her instead which increased the volume of her laughter. Once she began to hiccup and could barely get, "Enough," out, he stopped.

God, he was going to miss her.

During the travels, he and Jamie had never become anything more than friends. They'd become close enough that he'd poured open his heart and she'd listened. And she'd given her advice. Advice that always made sense, but his gut twisted too much at what she'd tell him. He just wasn't ready to let the pain go. He might never be. It wouldn't be fair if he did and lived as if his life hadn't been torn in two. Hell, each night he went to sleep, he'd be almost sick to his stomach at the fact he'd enjoyed the day. A day he didn't deserve to have attached to his life when he'd survived but Les hadn't.

Since they were on a secluded beach and it was only Jamie in sight, he'd removed his shirt to enjoy the sun. Because she'd nursed him in the hospital, he was never embarrassed for her to see his hideous back; she'd already seen the destruction the bomb blast had wrought that modern medicine hadn't been able to fix. It had been…freeing, sitting in the sun without hiding his torso. They'd raced in and out of the waves and relaxed on the sand underneath a beach umbrella. *Damn,* he thought as his mood continued to turn south. He caught himself before he plunged into a place he didn't want to be.

She's been good for my soul.

Trent had nearly blocked out the world by resting his head on his arms. The sound of the surf washed through him, leaving him relaxed and clear-minded.

"Promise me something, Trent," Jamie said.

Uneasy at what her request might be, he hesitantly responded, "I'll try."

Turning to him, she placed a hand on his cheek. Her touch soothed him. "Forgive yourself and your family and go home to them."

He jerked back so quickly, her startled look almost frightened him. "I can't promise that."

Forgive what? Senator Blake Hamilton, since Trent found out he was his real father?

He'd grown up on the grounds of the Hamilton estate and finally knew why. The man had wanted to keep Trent under his thumb while hiding his past affair with Trent's mother.

"I don't think I want to deal with"—he hesitated before spitting out—"my father." He scrunched up his face. "The word feels like sand sliding across my tongue."

"You'll have to make your peace with him at some point. Whether you forgive him or not."

"I'm damn sure not going to forgive him."

"What about your brothers? The Hamilton brothers are innocent in this, even though you say the oldest, Jesse, found out and kept it quiet."

With the weight of her statements, his shoulders sagged in despair. "They've been good to me. They've always been good to me. Growing up, they involved me in everything."

"That's good then." She cocked her head at him. "Isn't it?"

Leaning forward, he dug his hand in the sand and made a small pile before answering. "I don't know. I don't blame them, but calling them my brothers after a lifetime of wishing they were…I just don't know."

The sun began its rapid descent beyond the horizon, and they both sat, transfixed.

"Are you going to go back to work with them?"

Several years ago, the Hamilton brothers had started a business—Hamilton Investigation & Security, or HIS as it was commonly called, where they pooled together the talents of military and law enforcement to make a top-tier crew of professionals that were in high demand. It paid so well between the private and government contracts that they could pick and choose their assignments. It seemed that lately, their time was spent chasing after men who were terrorizing women who'd ended up becoming Hamilton wives. Or, husband as with the men's foster brother marrying their baby sister. It was their little girl, Amber, who he'd saved.

"I don't know."

"You said they offered you a partnership," she said.

The sun slipped away completely, and they sat in the growing darkness, only lit by a full moon.

"I don't want it," he spat out.

Jamie sighed. "Fine. We won't talk about it."

They sat quietly for a few minutes before she spoke again. "We both know my time is close. Before I go, you have to promise me to at least deal with your survivor's guilt. It's what's eating you up, and I worry that once you don't have me to worry about, you'll never fully recover from it because you'll just run

27

whenever you can."

Her words were a punch to Trent's gut. How could he forgive himself for not finding a way to save Les? For being the one to save Amber instead of trying to stop the bomber?

Trent had trusted the Hamilton men to get them all out alive. He'd trusted himself. He'd failed, and the damn terrorist had blown herself up, taking Les's life with her.

In his mind, he didn't deserve to live after not saving his friend. "How can I ever forgive myself for not finding a way to help Les? To change spots with him? I don't know if I'll ever go back. I can't face them." The HIS mission may have been successful in saving Amber, but at a high cost. Les had been a good friend to all.

"Did your brothers say anything about it when you released yourself from the hospital and helped them rescue one of your brother's wives? Didn't they trust you?"

Flinching, he knew she was right about helping Devon—one of his half-brothers. God that word burned his tongue. "No. But that was different."

A coughing fit hit her, and he was reminded of her illness. His heart tore apart, knowing the end loomed. He'd never had someone he was so comfortable with as a friend except for Kelly Williams. And he missed her greatly. Kelly was the one person he knew who wouldn't judge him. At least he hoped. He couldn't take her censure.

"Trent, you're ready to face it all. The new family. The new father. And Les's friends and family," she rasped. "Promise me."

No way in hell was he ready to handle any of it. He'd rather just move somewhere and start over and forget about it all. No one person should have to deal with so much at one time. But there was only one answer to give at this point. He would have to lie to her. "I promise."

One thing Trent knew was that the beach would be their final stop. Jamie couldn't go on any further.

As the days went on, when she began to weaken, he took care of her as she succumbed to her disease. Not having any close family, she hadn't planned to burden them—or him. Yet, he couldn't deliver her home just so she could die alone.

The rifles discharging in her veteran salute startled him. Jamie had earned that respect as an army nurse with two tours in Afghanistan. He was glad he'd taken her home and arranged for it.

Jamie, I know that I promised you I'd go home, but I need more time. I can't face them yet.

With that thought, he turned from the funeral and silently left.

****

The soothing sound of the waves crashing upon the shore and then receding, leaving the sand coated with white foam, seeped into Trent's soul, attempting to cleanse all that was wrong in his world. Sitting on the sand, legs pulled up and forearms on his knees, he braved being shirtless because, from his experience with Jamie, no one came to this little parcel of beach. They'd wondered if it was privately owned and they were trespassing. Then they'd decided they didn't care. If it was someone's little chunk of paradise, they could come and toss them off the beach.

In order to remove his shirt, being secluded was important to him since the bomb blast had done a number on his back, butt, and rear of his legs. In recovery, he'd suffered through many skin grafts, but, in his mind, he still looked like a hideous monster.

The true problem he faced was his soul, not his skin. Jamie had called it survivor's guilt. That was what he'd been feeling, why he didn't deserve to be here, why his soul had been ripped apart and destroyed. Because had he not walked into the situation, his friend Les might've found a way out. But he had walked into the mix of things. Sure he'd saved Amber's life. Sure Les hadn't been in a position close enough to help; instead, Les had been closer to the terrorist. There'd been no choice. Had Les not stepped between them all and tackled the bomber, Trent and the little girl would also be dead. His picking up Amber, pulling her in his arms, and putting his back to Les before launching himself into the swimming pool, was how he'd been injured. It had hurt like hell. So much so that at times, he'd wanted to die.

God, he wanted to punch something, and punching the sand wasn't cutting it. *Slow, deep, calming breaths,* Jamie would tell him when he got himself into an emotional tangle. Hell, he'd come back here because of the peace he'd found when the two of them had been here. That calm wasn't coming his way today.

Inhaling deeply, the extra expansion of his lungs as he held his breath calmed him. Today, the air smelled like an ocean should—clean, wet with a salty tease.

Sadness for Jamie seeped back into his heart. She'd been so weak at that point that he'd been mostly carrying her. The doctor he'd made her see hadn't approved of her activity but told her that he understood.

Long before the shadow came over him, he'd heard the squeak of feet walking in sand, but not in enough time to don his shirt. Whoever it was might be so grossed out they'd go away. Hopefully, it wasn't screaming as they ran. Just going away would be nice because he didn't want company.

All along he'd wondered if his new family had known where he'd been. They probably had. Devon surely tracked his credit card activity or whatever shit he did to find someone. His damn secretive CIA computer-shit training was spooky.

Trent had been curious how long the Hamiltons would let him be before they intruded with what they thought was best. If this was one, he expected it to be the eldest Hamilton brother. Jesse always took control of everything. His pulse skipped at the thought that he had to decide whether to acknowledge his relationship with the family.

But the intoxicating scent that wafted over him and tickled his nose as someone sat down beside him told him it wasn't one of his newfound brothers. It was a perfume he recognized, as was the blonde hair flapping in the wind he caught from the corner of his eye.

Realizing who it was, he smiled at the thought of her visiting him, but cringed inwardly a little. She was someone he hadn't wanted to see his burned and scarred back, although he knew deep down she wouldn't comment on it. Wouldn't get sick looking at it. Wouldn't give him the fucking pity look. That was the one thing he really didn't want or need.

Still gazing over the sea, the two sat in companionable silence. This was a woman he'd once made a move on, only to be rebuffed. True, his heart hadn't been in it, nor was it broken now, but unbelievably, she'd chosen the youngest Hamilton brother over him. Playboy AJ. Hell, both men had been players. But Trent had even taken a bullet to protect her, and she'd still chosen someone else. *Women. They need to come with instruction manuals.*

He guessed it only made sense to send her if the Hamilton men were being pussies about approaching him. They'd want to bring out the big guns, and with him, Megan was it. Actually, Kelly was, but Megan was within their sphere. The question in his mind was why were they searching him out now.

Unable to stand the suspense any longer, he greeted her, "Hey, doll. Did you finally have that kid?" He should've slapped his own self for that stupid fucking question. Without even turning to fully look at her, it was obvious she wasn't pregnant any longer. Plus, he'd been gone long enough that she'd had the baby months ago or it'd be a world-record pregnancy.

She leaned back, propping herself up on her arms. "Yes. Not long after you left. You have a beautiful nephew—Alexander Jonathan."

Nephew? This whole family thing would take some getting used to—if he decided to do so. He'd been an only child all his life. Hell, he wasn't ready to deal with this crap because with the brothers came the father. A man he'd just as soon never see again in his life.

"Where's your keeper?" It amazed him that AJ allowed her to sit this close to him for so long. Her husband was a jealous and possessive shit, especially around Trent. He knew AJ didn't like when Trent flirted with her, but he couldn't help it—flirting was in his blood, and it took control of his actions far too frequently. He mentally shrugged. AJ would show up at any minute.

Through the salty breeze, a soft chuckle reached his ears. "He's at the hotel with Alex."

Utterly flabbergasted, he jerked his head to her. "He let you come here—alone?"

Tossing her head back, her hair sliding off her shoulders, she laughed. "Let? Like I allow him to dictate to me." Dropping her head to the side, she focused on him and smiled. He loved how it brightened her face. "When are you coming home?"

Home. He really didn't have a home any longer. Hadn't since his parents died. Roger McKenzie was his dad. The man had raised him. He didn't need a replacement father. Or instant brothers. He blew out a breath. He wanted to joke with her—have fun like they used to do, but he couldn't do that with this conversation. "I don't know that I am." *Sorry, Jamie. Maybe I'll make good on my promise one day, but not today.*

"Look," she said in all seriousness, "this is between you and Blake. Don't hold your brothers responsible for this. You've been a part of this family all your life."

"And we now know why," he bit out more harshly than she deserved. Good old fucking Senator Blake Hamilton kept him as his dirty little secret. Wondering how Blake actually kept it quiet all these years with opponents trying to unseat him in the senate, always digging up dirt, he almost missed her next words.

"Make peace, or not, with your father, but don't cut out the only friends you've had."

Knowing *his brothers*—there, he'd said it—

weren't responsible, didn't make it any easier to act like nothing had changed, except their title went from friend to family.

Water slipped toward them as the tide moved in and waves slid inland. Maybe he should've taken off his shoes instead of his shirt. Stupid thing to think about considering the conversation, but now that he had company, he'd certainly feel more comfortable that way. "I'll think about it."

"There's something else. It's the main reason I wanted to be the one to speak with you."

Curious, he appraised her and raised a brow. "Go on." His gut turned in warning that this could get interesting.

"It's Kelly."

Instantly his blood turned to ice with fear, and his entire focus became this conversation. "Kelly?" he questioned with a croak in his voice and his heart pounding.

Nodding solemnly, she continued, "Something's going on with her. I don't know what it is, and she won't open up."

Blood pressure rising rapidly, he took those damn soothing breaths Jamie told him to take as sweat broke out on his brow. "What kind of trouble? Is she safe?" he rushed out in one breath, wanting all the information yesterday so he could act.

"Honestly, I don't know that it's any trouble at all, Trent, but something has her spooked."

"I'll leave in the morning and drive straight through." *Kelly, baby, stay safe until I get to you.*

Shocked, she sucked in a breath. "Trent, that's sixteen and a half hours."

Shrugging, he was already calculating everything he had to do before he left. That long drive was nothing for Kelly's sake. Hell, if he didn't need transportation when he got back to Baltimore, he'd just hop on a flight and store his bike. "I can make good time on the bike. Besides, it's Kelly."

A knowing smile spread across Megan's face.

Let her think what she wanted. Kelly was special to him. Precious. And, not to be touched. He respected her too much. That didn't mean his dick didn't think differently whenever he was around her. But what was important now was making sure she was okay.

"Tell me more," he insisted, as the need to be by Kelly's side simmered in his veins.

Well, Jamie, you got your wish. I'm going to face them. At least my brothers.

Chapter Four

Men's clothing was launched into the air and onto the bed as a tall man bent on devious ambition pulled them from a large, black suitcase. Finding Sam Gibson had been luck and a godsend. A young kid had attempted to pick his pockets, but he'd caught the kid. Christ, the little thief had been only about ten years old. Seeing an opportunity, he'd had the kid take him to the boy's leader, Sam. Unsure in the beginning, Sam hadn't wanted to work with him. Mistrust and all that.

Hiring someone to lift something of Brian Platt's, he'd found himself immediately called boss. In the network of thieves Sam ran, they found one to steal the paperwork from Brian's hotel room. Unfortunately, the hotel staff caught him before he could abscond with the information.

Then Brian had been killed before the items could be acquired. That had been a misunderstanding of monumental proportions. Lift, then kill had been the directive.

"It's only fucking clothes!" he roared at Sam. His eyes zoomed around the hotel room with its Mediterranean flair in search of what he wanted. A wave of irritation grew inside him knowing what he desired wasn't there. "Where's the fucking messenger bag?"

"That was all there was in her car, boss." The slight

nervousness in Sam Gibson's voice surprised him as the thief master had always shown himself to be a confident man. "That's where she supposedly left everything after the police released it to her."

Turning his focus on Sam, he frowned at the criminal. Maybe he'd misjudged his ability to do this simple job. Discomfort radiated from the thief master's thin frame with a large, gold cross hanging from his neck. Sam's dark hair could definitely use a cut to sharpen the criminal's appearance. "What about her house? Have you tried there?" This man couldn't be that much of an idiot. How hard was it to search for something when you were supposedly one of Baltimore's best thieves? "I want those papers. She's had them far too long." He would say it's already too late—that everyone knew—but nothing seems to be happening on the property, and something would happen if anyone had read the information Brian had collected. Then he'd never get his hands on that land. That expansive plot in Reed Point, Montana, would make him wealthier than he ever imagined possible, all because he knew the truth about it.

This trip to Baltimore had been a spur of the moment, but necessary once he'd found out the current Montana landowner Mike Platt, Brian's father, was clueless about the findings, heck even about what Brian had done. He needed the elder Platt to remain ignorant, and that meant getting his hands on the paperwork Brian had in his possession before he'd died.

The man had had the perfect chance when he'd found out Brian had flown to Baltimore not so long ago, not only to pick up his bride-to-be for their wedding, but he'd collected the results of the survey personally. Hiring a Baltimore firm to do the work had seemed odd, but since Brian had been in the city frequently to visit the woman he was to marry, it made sense. Albeit inconvenient to the boss.

For the time being, he had to focus on getting those surveys and reports before anyone was any wiser. If Mike found out, he might put the property up for sale, and the price would be too high.

I have to control that property.

Almost forgotten, Sam shifted his stance. "Why did you wait so long to call me again? I mean, the man died weeks ago," Sam said.

He was furious at being questioned, but he managed to control himself mentally. Although he didn't have to explain himself to Sam, he knew he still needed the man and found himself explaining anyway. "I thought they'd sent Brian's personal effects back to his family, and it was too late. When no one acted on the information, I knew something wasn't right. A little bribe at the police station told me they'd released his possessions to his fiancée, Kelly Williams, right after the accident."

Sam raised his eyebrows. "Now that Brian is dead, shouldn't getting your hands on the land easier? Wasn't that the problem that the old man wanted Brian to inherit it?"

Feeling the need to punch something over the injustice of it all, the boss clenched his fists, but shoved them into his jeans' front pockets instead. "No. The old man is holding out for the kid now. He wants it to go to Brian's brat." Sighing, he released his grip on his palms, figuring there were crescents in the skin from his fingernails. "Believe me, I talked to him until I was almost blue in the face. He's set on this."

"You talked to him about this after Brian died?"

He drew down his brow and pulled memories from his mind—the conversation about the property with Mike. It was hopeless, unless he acted—maliciously. And, he needed Sam on his side, so he provided more information. "I had to find out if he knew about the survey and what he planned to do. You'd think he'd do the honorable thing and at least include his other son. But, no, he's still hung up on Brian," he spat. His distaste wasn't at Brian—he'd liked him—it was at the idea of waiting for a child not even born to inherit.

"I thought the old man was sick. Can he even last that long?" Sam queried.

"He's sick, but that old buzzard isn't going to die anytime soon. He's tough as nails. Plus, the idea of a grandchild seems to have put a second life into him."

"Hmph," the thief master said.

"Hmph is right." Pulling his right hand from his pocket, he rubbed the back of his neck in frustration. "This was supposed to be simple: get rid of Brian, so the old man had to change his will. Now, there's a fucking child to contend with," he mumbled to himself. Why the hell couldn't things work out for him the way he wanted without him resorting to something vicious?

"Can't you just get rid of Mike?"

Pissed he'd allowed himself to speak loud enough to be overheard when he'd just been thinking out loud, he narrowed his eyes at Sam, as if it had been his fault. Things were becoming clearer to him, and it wasn't necessarily pleasant. "I must get rid of all those who are in the will before Mike dies or all is lost as that child will inherit. Then who knows what the fiancée will do with the land."

"I'll get the paperwork, don't you worry. I'll do it personally," Sam said with a confident nod.

The boss shook his head and considered his only option. "She might have read it and is just biding her time until her child inherits. I can't chance it."

Sam cocked his head. "What're you saying?"

Straightening to his full height, he set his shoulders back in determination. Decision made, he issued his directive, "I'll be lying low for a while. Take care of the woman and find that paperwork before Mike sees it and gets other ideas. Get whatever she's working on now, too. She's messing in other business of mine, but doesn't know it yet."

"I don't kill women, boss."

"Then find someone who will—like you did with Brian."

Chapter Five

A week had passed since Kelly had spoken with
Adrian at the prison. A week to replace in the items
from her stolen purse. A week with so much to
consider. A week to decide what to do with the
information she'd received.

The thought of Brian brought moisture to her eyes,
but she forced back the tears. Her heart ached from
missing him. Despite the truth of her love being locked
away from him, he'd been one of her best friends, more
than that, he was the father of their unborn child. A
small part of her heart was glad she hadn't corrected his
belief that she loved him that deeply while he was alive.
Knowing that you were loved while you died had to be
better than the alternative.

Her mind still reeled that Brian's death might have
been murder. The need to know the truth flooded her
body with anger and so many more other fleeting
emotions, that she worried about her emotional well-
being. Allowing her mind to believe—without
evidence—that it hadn't been an accident went against
her normal journalistic instinct. Yet, after the suitcase
had been stolen, she couldn't let it go. Her mind
became invigorated with searching for the truth. There
had to be something there.

Focusing her gaze on the road she was driving on,
she continued to turn everything over in her mind. Her

brain just wouldn't freakin' stop working. As for the vandalism to her car, Paul had been just as livid as she'd been once her mind processed it. The security footage had captured a dark sedan, but there were no visible license plates. It had also shown a person— presumably a man due to their size—jumping from the passenger seat, quickly breaking the lock, grabbing her purse and Brian's luggage, and stowing it in the back seat of their vehicle, before returning to the passenger seat and driving away. Both the passenger and the driver had their heads and most of their faces covered. Winter weather was a bitch for identification. But what had increased Paul's ire was that the guard who was supposed to be watching all the cameras had been sleeping. Paul caught him red-handed.

With a pounding heart and nerves jumping up a firestorm, she'd taken Adrian's words that Brian's death hadn't been an accident to the police officers who'd handled Brian's case, but got nowhere. After requesting a complete copy of the accident file, she'd received narrowed eyes from the two officers, but they'd sent her through the proper channels, and she had what was a thin report of the hit and run that took Brian's life. They'd written it off almost as soon as it had occurred.

Unfortunately, she understood why they had come to that conclusion after she'd questioned the witnesses and found no helpful information to determine is it was intentional or identify the driver. By all accounts, the man sped out of a curbside parking space, which isn't unusual for that area. So, she was back to square one with nothing to point her in any direction, whether accidental or intentional.

She had no other option but to put the two incidents—Brian's death and his suitcase theft—down as coincidence. There was nothing to indicate otherwise. It was possible for someone to be in the wrong place at the wrong time more than once. Not likely, but possible. She'd been with Brian, then she'd been at the prison.

Finding no leads, she had to let it go or else she'd turn into a physical mass of knots of despair and woe. She choked back a sob that threatened to send her into an emotional upheaval.

Taking a deep breath, she turned her attention to what she could do something about. Oh, she'd never forget Brian's accident; she just had to wait until she figured out what she could do.

For the time being, she'd promised Adrian—since he'd told her about Brian—that she'd try to find something to help clear him. It was quite possible something existed, but he should've hired a private investigator as she also had other stories to follow. She did have a job to do.

A driver cut her off, and she slapped on the brakes and swore like a sailor on shore leave. *It's not like my yellow car doesn't stand out, asshole.* She knew she'd have to do better curbing her language when the baby arrived. There was too much to do before then, such as help Adrian.

Like a good little reporter, she'd taken the results of the meetings to her editor, Kristen, but had received a mixed response. Her boss had hoped for more from the man—something solid—not the word of a convict who admitted to murdering the person they were quoting. So had she, but they both knew that wasn't always the case in investigative journalism. Otherwise, there'd be almost nothing to actually investigate.

Releasing Kelly to chase after Adrian's innocence wasn't in her boss's plans, so she'd nixed the potential story. They wouldn't publish Jason's confession, and they wouldn't try to chase anything that would prove Adrian had been set up for his crimes.

On the other hand, Kelly had that tickling in her tummy—different from the baby feelings—that told her something was there and that she owed the man. Adrian had been very convincing in his assurance of innocence. Finally meeting him and believing herself to be a good judge of character, she wanted to help the man.

Maybe he'll learn who the driver of the car that hit Brian was. He said he'd try to find out and seemed hopeful in his success. But, she'd keep that on the back burner and not allow him to forget.

With blood pumping through her veins faster than normal, Kelly couldn't wait to get her teeth into the story. How great it would be to find the evidence when the police thumbed their nose at the confession. To free an innocent man. A man even she'd thought guilty. Yes. She planned to squeeze in the investigation between her current assignments, and when she had something, her boss would let her run with it— officially.

Adrian had provided her with three people who might want to see him in jail, financially bankrupt or both. Maybe none of the three had anything to do with Adrian's incarceration, but it couldn't hurt to poke around and see what she could discover.

One important thing she wanted to do first was

review the court transcripts. Since it had been a lengthy trial, reviewing them would take a while, but it was a start. Remembering back to the one day she'd sat in court, she knew to expect a show, even on paper, from the ADA who'd been out to make a name for himself so he could climb that proverbial ladder to DA.

She pulled into the parking lot and stepped into the cold. Dressed again for warmth, Kelly smiled at the security guard at the courthouse as she entered. Even though he continued giving a woman directions, a smile formed on his face.

At the records department, she strolled to a desk and set down a to-go cup of chocolate mocha beside a keyboard. The middle-aged Hispanic woman at the desk looked up at her and grinned. "Is that what I think it is?" Excitement lit the woman's features.

Kelly slid a chair from an empty desk, sat beside her, and nodded. "Of course, Esme. Only the best for you."

Meeting the woman by chance at a friend's party had been a blessing. Finding someone at the courthouse who would aid a reporter was challenging, unless it was from an employee whose information was unbiased. But, Trent McKenzie had been at that same party and introduced the two women.

A soft sigh slipped from her lips. There he was again, barging into her thoughts.

At first, she'd been jealous thinking Esme had been one of his women—ones he loved and left—but she'd discovered Esme was a happily married woman who'd met Trent when he'd been in the FBI.

Esmerelda, who preferred to be called Esme, narrowed her hazel eyes behind bright blue-framed eyeglasses. She casually slipped a few strands of dark hair behind her right ear as she spoke. "What do you want?"

"Just a small favor." Waving her hand, to insinuate that it was nothing important, Kelly smiled. "Aren't you going to try it while it's hot?"

The woman hesitated a moment as if judging between her desire for the beverage and the payment that would be required. Desire won over, and she reached for the cup, took a sip and sighed in what sounded like pleasure. "That's good stuff."

A few long moments passed before Esme spoke again. "Okay, what do you want?"

"Court transcripts for Adrian Copeland's case."

"Now, you know there is a procedure for that, and I'm not part of it."

"But, you can get them to me today. With their procedure, I could be old and gray by the time I receive them." Not quite accurate, but still, this was more expeditious. She pulled down her eyebrows and tried to incorporate sadness in her eyes in an attempt to make her face look as pitiful as possible.

Esme laughed. "It ain't that bad."

Happy her statements—and facial expression—worked, but not ready to leave it sit and wait for the woman to decide, Kelly continued, "Okay, not that old and gray, but still…."

"So, you want me to break established procedure, dip into a file I have no business in, and print it for you all for one hot beverage?" She cocked a perfectly shaped eyebrow.

Kelly fought to keep the grin off her face. This could be their written play—almost word for word—

whenever Kelly requested a file. Sometimes she wondered if Esme recorded the conversations for future use, either getting herself out of a jam or blackmail. Considering the woman, she decided no. It appeared to Kelly that the clerk enjoyed the banter. Hoping the appropriate sheepishness showed on her face, Kelly answered, "Well, yes."

They broke into fits of laughter.

Jesting aside, Esme sobered and asked, "What are you going to do with it?"

She shrugged. "I want to see if he's innocent."

"Hmph. Well, give me a bit and I'll get it for you, but I want something in return."

Unused to Esme asking for something, Kelly pretended to view her manicure and act like the question was normal. "What?"

"I don't want to be seen down in records asking for this, so could you see what my soon-to-be ex-husband just filed? I want to make sure he's not hiding assets from me."

That sounded easy enough, although she wouldn't be able to pick it up and bring it right back here if Esme didn't want anyone to know she had it. Kelly shrugged. "Sure."

Esme nodded. "Then give me some time."

The urge to hug the woman hit her, but she ignored it. They weren't that good of friends. "I'll be back in an hour." And she'd go to the records department and figure out how to discreetly give the information to Esme. Curiosity at what her friend's husband might be up to grabbed hold of her.

Her friend nodded in agreement. Kelly rose and left Esme to the computer she was already busy typing on.

After being disappointed that Esme's ex had only acquired copies of their registered assets, she'd slide into a busy courtroom while she waited. Maybe she'd pick up something to bring back to the news desk.

Esme took longer than an hour to pull the file since other work matters kept popping up for her to handle. Given the late hour, they agreed that Kelly would pick the transcript up the next morning.

The squeaking of her boots on the marble flooring followed her to the exit where a different security guard nodded a greeting to her. She smiled back and exited into the cold.

Clouds covered the sky and their dreary gloominess weighted on the area. Snow hadn't completely melted from the last front, and the cold dampness in the air told her it was time for more. Getting back to work and then home before the storm settled in overrode her curiosity of any story.

Pulling on her gloves, she walked briskly to her car. With years of practice, she'd become accustomed to moving quickly through the elements without slipping on her heels, but she truly enjoyed walking with the boots. A huge gust of wind knocked her in the face, almost halting her progress. Dropping her head, she trudged forward and jumped when a siren screamed in the distance.

An uneventful drive home, followed by a stroke of luck with parking near her apartment, had Kelly almost prancing to her front door. Her joyful mood came to a sudden halt when a tall, blond-haired man stood from his seated position on her front steps.

A slice of awareness glided over her as it always did when she saw this deliciously handsome man. It was a pity for womankind that he refused to be tied down since he evoked a similar reaction in all the women she knew. Looks, charm, confidence, he had it all. Searching for someone to replace him in her heart had led her to Brian and then back to loneliness. Yet, he'd never known she existed in that way.

Trent McKenzie, probably suffering from a freezing ass after sitting on the concrete steps, smiled at her as if it were any other day and he hadn't left without a word. Her heart thudded in her chest at the sight of him in his classic, black, leather jacket.

He opened his arms, and she flew into them, tears slipping down her cheeks. He'd come back! God, how she loved this man.

Their embrace was cut short when Trent separated them, and with his ocean-blue eyes, he looked down at her belly before gazing back into her eyes. "Good God, Kelly, you're pregnant!"

Wiping at the tears on her frozen face, she forced a smile. "Let's get inside and get warm." With her keys in her hand, she reached to unlock the door and stopped, her heart pounding in panic.

"What's the matter?" Trent asked.

She looked at the doorknob, noticed the telltale scratch signs, and unease scrambled through her blood. Glancing back at Trent, she swallowed past the fear lodged in her throat, then stepped closer. "These scratches weren't there when I locked up this morning."

"You stay out here while I check it out."

"Do you have your gun?" she asked, worried that someone might be in the house. "Maybe we should call the police."

"I'll be fine."
Famous last words she thought.

Chapter Six

He needed a swift kick in the ass after his open-mouth-and-insert-foot action. Shocked barely scratched the surface of the emotions that rolled through Trent at seeing Kelly's rounded belly tightening her jacket. *Christ. She must've married. Found the "Mr. Right" she'd been seeking.* Had she married that Brian guy she'd started seeing before he left? For some reason knowing the man was her "Mr. Right" didn't make him feel any better. He should be happy for her, but instead, it sent him an unexpected pang of longing and loss. Why hadn't Megan said something?

"Do you think they could've been made by your husband?" Trent tried to sound casual, but he thought he'd probably failed by her expression.

Sadness passed over her features before she schooled herself, but not enough that he could tell something happened. Something he would've known about had he been here. "I'm not married."

Well, hell. That answer only fed to more questions, making him forget the small problem of the lock. *The lock!* Snapping himself back to the situation at hand, he focused his mind. Reaching up, he checked the doorknob to find it locked. Turning back to Kelly, he managed not to take another look at her protruding belly. He reached out his hand. "Hand me the key."

That was when he noticed a shadow of fear lurking

in her eyes from the moment she'd mentioned the problems with the lock. His insides twisted into knots knowing she had even a slight amount of distress. She deserved all that was good in the world, not fright. "It might be nothing—someone who tried to break in and failed. Just in case, stay right here, and I'll check it out."

She nodded. With shaking hands, she placed the keys with her palm tree key chain in his outstretched hand. "There's a baseball bat beside the door."

His brows shot up in astonishment and intrigue. *A baseball bat?* At least she hadn't fought to follow him inside. Maybe being pregnant had given her more sense because the Kelly he knew would've pitched a fit to follow. The knot in his gut twisted tighter at the thought of her walking into danger. He had to focus but seeing her pregnant just stood out in his mind and blocking it out—even for a short term—was damn hard.

She shrugged, hard resolve in her gaze. "Living alone can sometimes suck."

When she placed a hand on her belly, a new situation confronted him—a pregnant Kelly with no husband. The bastard who knocked her up would step up and be a father. With none of her big brothers close, he readily accepted the task of seeing to her future. Trent would have to deal with that after he made sure no danger awaited her inside. Shaking his head, he turned back to her apartment, slipped the key in the lock, quietly opened the door, and slid inside to stillness and darkness.

Having been in her apartment numerous times, he didn't wait fully for his eyes to adjust. Nothing appeared to be disturbed, making him wonder if a potential thief had actually entered her apartment.

Passing through the living room, he skirted around the gray couch with its orange pillows. He'd never understood that but Kelly had told him orange was a creative color and since her desk was in the far corner of the room, she craved creativity. Whatever. Orange was for the fruit. *Her desk.* He swiveled his head to the desk nestled in the corner and dropped his brows at her laptop sitting there, unharmed.

He made his way in that direction when a figure bounded from behind the curtains. His pulse lurched high in his throat. With little time to protect himself, he was able to duck and tackle the intruder at the waist, knocking them both to the floor. The sound of something crashing to the floor and breaking barely penetrated his senses. He had a scrapper on his hands to contend with.

Rolling around, Trent held the dominant position of being on top but was thrown over quickly by his assailant. The man, now on top, held in place by Trent because he wasn't letting this asshole leave without the police, threw a punch, and Trent gritted at the sharp pain of the glancing blow to his jaw as he took advantage of the man's unbalance and tumbled them again.

The intruder tossed up a forearm that stopped Trent's fist from plowing into his face. Shifting, Trent used his weight to keep the man down and grabbed both arms, holding them to the floor. Getting a good look at the intruder, he wanted to spit in his face.

The intruder windmilled his legs and toppled Trent. They rolled, Trent holding him tightly and the attacker trying to escape. Once Trent was back on top, he didn't plan to lose control of the situation this time. No one dared harm his Kelly.

As soon as he rolled on top, a mind-splitting pain hit the back of his neck and shot through his body, and he unconsciously loosened his grip before he slumped over. The intruder crawled out from under him before Trent could recover his senses.

Dizziness washed over him and a bout of nausea assailed him. With his hand on the back of his neck and skull, he was helpless to do anything but watch the man leave. Looking behind him, he frowned at Kelly standing there with a baseball bat in her hand.

"Oh my God, Trent!" The metal bat clattered to the wood floor, and the noise resonated in his head like a trumpet being blown in his ear. "I'm so sorry. You two were rolling around, and I thought he had you pinned." She moved to his side as he tried to stand. Like she would be much use helping him to his feet. "Do you need an ambulance? Or to go to the hospital?"

How could she have so little faith in him? That kind of pissed him off. She should know he could take care of himself, with what he did for a living. Then again, this was Kelly. She had a mind of her own, and he couldn't fault her for wanting to help. But, dammit, she put herself in danger. His head hurt thinking this back and forth knowing he'd never settle on whether to be angry with her or proud of her.

After getting him settled on the couch, she made a big deal of checking the wound, which he could tell would be a goose egg and bruise. He tightened his jaw at how tender the spot was. "I'll be fine. No hospital." That was the last place he wanted to go. He'd have to be bleeding to death for him to voluntarily go back.

While she prepared an ice pack in the kitchen, he stood, swayed a bit, then checked the rest of the apartment and ensured the doors and windows were secure. They didn't need a repeat performance.

Returning, she handed him the ice pack, which he placed on his throbbing neck. Even though expecting it, he jolted at the freezing coldness when it made contact with his skin. Goosebumps dotted his flesh at the sudden drop in temperature around his wound.

"Trent, I am so sorry. I heard the crash, and I got worried when you didn't come back. I thought I was helping. I never meant to hit you." She fretted her hands as she spoke and he wanted to reach out and soothe her, but his damn head hurt too badly to do anything but sit there.

"Don't worry about it, Kelly. You should call the police."

"But, what if nothing's missing?"

"What the fuck does that matter?" Shock slapped him at her response. "The guy broke into your place and tried to beat the shit out of me. Don't you think the police should know?"

"Not to discount his deserving to pay for trying to hurt you, but you know the police as well as I do. Do you really think they'll catch him if nothing is missing for him to pawn?"

Sighing in resignation because he understood her, Trent knew she'd be set on this. He could push it, but she had a point. Although he wouldn't tell her that. He could describe their intruder, but that case would rank very low on the list for the officers who responded. It could actually take them from something more important. But wasn't Kelly's safety just as important as murders? In his mind it was, but probably not in the police department's.

So what that he'd almost had his ass kicked? No. He'd had it in control—until Kelly attempted to aid him.

A smile broke out on his face. She'd tried to help him. No woman had come to his rescue when he'd been in a fight. He didn't need it, but he kind of liked that Kelly had the gumption to do it. Although he'd have been pretty pissed had she been hurt. More than pretty pissed.

Thinking back to their current situation, he'd talk with Jesse about what had happened and take it from there. Unless something had been stolen. "Take a look around and see if anything is missing."

She glanced around the room, and her eyes zeroed in on her desk. After reaching it, she frantically searched the area, but when she saw him noticing, she acted as if nothing was amiss.

"Something missing?" With the laptop still there, he couldn't see what else a thief would've taken while leaving the computer. Which left him to wonder if it had been an actual thief. That put a new spin on things. Could they have been scoping out one of her stories?

"No."

He knew she lied because her eyes shifted when she answered, avoiding his direct gaze. As far as he knew, she'd never lied to him before. Why now? For something stolen? He was ready to turn her over his knee. That thought tantalized his body, making it tighten in places it shouldn't while they were dealing with the break-in.

"To me, nothing looks out of place, but you might

want to check the rooms. It's been a while since I've been here, and I don't know about jewelry."

Nodding once, she scooted off to her bedroom. With her out of the room, he poked around her desk and noticed nothing that struck him as odd. Something bothered her, and he'd bet his last dollar that man had escaped with something important to her.

Kelly returned to him waiting by the couch for her. "Nothing's missing."

Yeah, right. He'd tackle that later. "Now come here and give me another hug," Trent instructed as he opened his arms wide.

With a smile, she rushed forward and embraced him. The contact warmed his blood. It felt so good, even with that belly pushing into his as she tried to get closer. A barely noticeable cherry scent tantalized his nostrils, bringing back fond memories of their times together, like when he'd held her after a breakup with an asshole who'd just wanted to fuck her. Then there was the scent of—*Wait, a minute. This isn't right.* He held onto that for a moment and greeted her instead, "I missed you, Kelly."

"I missed you, too."

"Did you change perfume?"

She laughed against his chest. "Only you would notice that. Like it?"

Did he ever? He only hoped she hadn't changed it for the fucker who got her pregnant and didn't marry her. "I like it on you." And, it did fit her well as far as he was concerned.

"Megan gave it to me for Christmas."

Relief spiked through him at the gift Kelly's friend had bestowed to her. He'd never been jealous of Kelly dating. Okay, he couldn't lie to himself, he'd been jealous all right, but that was because he didn't think any of the men were good enough for her. Yet just the fact she may have been wearing perfume for someone in particular had that green-eyed monster surging through him. That made no sense considering she was his friend, not a lover.

They separated, and he wanted to grab her back and hold tight. Something had shifted in him and holding her seemed important…and necessary. He couldn't explain it and didn't want to try. He'd just missed her in his life as his friend…confidant. Yes, his best friend.

"You dyed your hair blonde."

She touched her hair and shrugged. "One of those things I just had to do. Some say it's pregnancy hormones in action. I say that it's about time. Like it?" She spun her head from side to side to show off her nearly shoulder-length hair.

The blonde did suit her, but he also loved her natural, auburn-colored hair. Peering intently, he decided he could get used to blonde also. Luckily, she could wear either color well. He nodded. "It suits you."

Blushing, she shifted another step away from him. "I've been dying for some hot chocolate. And you could use something while you hold that ice pack in place," she said on her way to the kitchen.

He caught himself watching the swish of her butt as she walked. Slapping himself wasn't good enough. He'd never noticed her in that way before. Okay, maybe the first time or two—before he'd come to know her. Since then, he'd fought the sensation that pulled at him to ogle her when they were together. Instead, he'd just give his dick a lecture when he knew he'd have to hold her.

Finding himself alone, he followed her path through the archway into a small kitchen. Again, her rear was to him as she pulled a half-gallon of milk from the refrigerator. He stifled a groan and not from his neck wound. She'd obviously fallen in love with some guy and gotten pregnant. Trent had no right looking at her like his next fuck.

If he ever had Kelly in his bed, she'd never be just a fuck. That he knew without a doubt.

"Kelly, why don't you have a pet? A cat at least?" There was no telling where his mind pulled those questions from. In all the time he'd visited her, he'd never thought to ask and the idea of her at least having a pet to battle loneliness cheered him. He'd witnessed the love she gave to two of the Hamilton family pets, Bob, the cat, and Dottie, the dog. He almost grumbled about Dottie. The dog still didn't like him. He wasn't a threat to her master, Kate. She was happily married to Jesse. Not that he'd ever tried to be with Kate to begin with. She'd been nothing more than a colleague at the FBI.

"The landlord doesn't allow them."

That answer didn't work for him. She deserved the companionship of a pet, plus didn't kids need a puppy or kitten while growing up? "We'll have to fix that."

A chuckle floated through the air from her. A sweet, melodic sound that settled soothingly in his heart. "You've met my landlord, Trent. You should know better than to think you'll change his mind."

That asshole hadn't even come to mind when he'd thought of changing her circumstance in relation to a pet. He saw her with a dog and a yard. There was no yard here.

"Are you having some hot chocolate?" She reached inside the cabinet for a mug.

"Sure." It'd been probably a year since he'd last had Kelly's hot chocolate and it sounded like a damn good consolation for his injury. His mouth watered at the fact that she warmed milk and used real chocolate. "Got any marshmallows?" he asked hopefully. The thought of the hot drink almost vanquished the forming headache. Almost, but not quite.

She laughed again. "Of course." Reaching into the pantry, she retrieved a bag of miniature marshmallows, then held them up to him with a beaming smile. "Just for you."

"If those are for me"—he captured her gaze in all seriousness—"you'd best check the date." They'd need a long-ass shelf life since he hadn't been here in about five months, and it had been much longer since he'd asked for marshmallows.

"Don't worry. They're fine."

When Kelly finished making the beverages, she handed him a bright pink mug with a flamingo. It said something about keeping calm. He raised his eyebrows at her, and she laughed. He loved that laugh. It touched his tortured soul and lightened the load he carried.

No problem had ever seemed too big with her. She'd been there when he'd decided to leave the FBI, start his own security firm, and then decide to join HIS. Her wisdom and welcome ear had made all the difference when he'd made those choices. Plus, she'd been a damn good nurse when he'd been shot. And, yet, he wouldn't consider unburdening himself now.

With a quirk of his eyebrow, he lifted the mug. "Let's exchange." He changed his mind after he read hers. "I'm a journalist, not a *female* journalist." Couldn't people have plain old mugs anymore without some stupid saying?

Settled in the living room, they carefully sipped their cocoa with an uncomfortable silence filling the air. It was damn odd for them, and Trent didn't like it one bit.

A rich warmth coated his tongue as he swallowed the beverage. With a perfect temperature, so it didn't burn, the heat slid down his throat to his stomach where it settled, bringing relaxation and calm to his world. Then, he almost laughed out loud watching Kelly try to cross her legs. Her slacks swished across each other halfway before her pregnant belly got in the way, and she settled stocking feet back on the floor. He did a double-take. When had she removed her boots? Great observation skills he had going on today. That belly of hers threw him for a loop bigger than he thought.

Drinking more cocoa, he contemplated the right way to ask a question. They had always been open and honest with each other. Hell, he'd shared stuff with her he had never shared with anyone else. Enough stalling. Taking a deep breath to calm his unexpected nervousness, he bit the bullet. "How far along are you?"

"Six months."

A slice of anger wedged itself at the base of his spine. "That means that you had to be pregnant before I left. Why didn't you tell me?" That was a bit presumptuous of him. She didn't need to tell him anything. Only, he thought their relationship had been closer than that.

She blew on her cocoa before she spoke. "You wouldn't see me when you were in the hospital."

He winced at the truth of her statement and his anger melted away. Refusing to see everyone at the hospital had worked to keep her away, someone who could've been good for his soul at the time. But it hadn't worked for the Hamilton men. They would barge into his room regardless of what security told them. Christ, he still had to face all of them. *One thing at a time.* "I'm sorry for that."

She took a sip and swallowed. Her slender neck with its lovely arch grasped his attention, and he wanted to kiss his way up and down it.

Stop that train of thought, McKenzie.

"I'm sure you had your reasons."

He snapped out of the sexual haze he'd almost been sucked into. *What had she said? Oh yeah, reasons.* Like wishing he could just die already. Between the pain of his injuries and the fact he *had* survived, he'd never wanted to see another day. He wouldn't allow his problems to rear their ugly heads when Kelly needed him. "What happened?" He shook his head and chuckled at the absurdity of the question. "Okay, not *that* what happened, but why aren't you married? You made no secret of the fact you wanted to remain a virgin until you married." He swallowed at the thought and worked hard at controlling the burst of anger. At himself, maybe? "He had to be pretty amazing or a shyster. If the latter, I'll kick his ass for you." *What did he have that made you give up what you'd held dear? Was he that much of a man?*

Expecting a chuckle at that statement, his gut twisted at her uncomfortable expression, and he hated he'd done that to her. He was putting his foot in his mouth again and again.

"I was getting married." She took a moment before continuing, "But, he died."

"But you still—"

"Had sex beforehand," she inserted, breaking off his words.

And thank the fuck for that. He'd have been ankle-deep down his throat with that one. Sure they'd talked about it before, but it truly wasn't any of his damn business. With Kelly, he always wanted to know everything.

"Yes, we slept together."

Kelly with another man made his insides clench into a fist. He had no right to her—never had, but somehow, he'd always thought she'd be the type of woman he'd marry—if he ever married. So much time had been spent screwing around. Plans for the future were never considered when it came to family. Hell, he was only twenty-seven years old.

"Where's the father's family? Why aren't you with them or your family for that matter?" he rushed out without really thinking the words before they left his big mouth.

She cocked an eyebrow at him. "You do know women can have a baby without their family around, don't you?"

He almost laughed, but bit it back since he'd been trying to hold out a serious tone for the discussion. She had him there, but still…. "I get that, but why when you can have help? You have a big family, and I'm sure they'd love to help."

"How's your neck?"

Automatically, his hand went to the ice pack that had almost frozen in place. At the size of the knot there, he'd been damn lucky she hadn't seriously wounded him. The woman packed a wallop. "I'll be fine. Thanks."

He let it slide that she'd changed the subject. Maybe he'd pushed too much too fast.

Sighing, she gestured toward his drink. "Do you want a refill? I'm getting one." After standing, she reached for his nearly empty cup without waiting for his response. He had no idea they'd emptied their hot cocoas so quickly. It was a testament to how good she made it.

Eyes tracking her movements, he realized he'd shoved his foot in his mouth again with his last question. By now he should be gnawing on his knee he had it so deep.

She stopped and turned, both mugs in hand. "Brian Platt was my high school sweetheart. I wanted to come to the big city, and he wanted to run the family ranch, so we broke up before college. I went one way and he went another. After graduating, I moved here."

"You introduced me to him, didn't you?" She had. He distinctly remembered meeting the man and feeling a bit threatened. At the time, he'd worried that meant something was wrong with Brian, something that would affect Kelly's happiness, but then the accident had happened and, well…he'd forgotten.

She nodded. "Yes, when he first came here, about eight months ago. Before he and I started seeing each other and…."

"Before I almost got blown to smithereens?" He tried to instill a bit of levity so she didn't have to say the words. It was only fair since she'd saved him from talking about her having sex.

She bit the corner of her lip, drawing his eye to where her white teeth nibbled on a place where he'd love to kiss her.

What the hell was wrong with him? He'd learned to control his urges around her a long time ago, but right now, he strongly wanted to hold her and enjoy her luscious body. Pregnancy and all.

"Yes."

An unexpected searing pain knifed through his heart. She had to have loved this man to agree to marry him and agree to—He swallowed against the lump that had formed in his throat. Agreed to sleep with him. She'd been so firm in that conviction. It was why he'd never hit on her. It was also probably why they were such good friends. The best of friends as far as he was concerned. It had to be similar for her as she'd shared things with him that he couldn't imagine her sharing with others outside her inner circle of friends.

Knowing it would take her time to warm the milk, he followed her into the kitchen. Leaning against the wall with his arms crossed over his chest, he watched her move about gracefully. Once she'd set the milk to heat on the stove, she turned the tables on him. "Where have you been?"

He didn't want to allow her to completely change the subject, so he'd stay vague for now. Later, they could talk about him if that's what she wanted. "Here and there. Most recently, the Gulf Coast."

Preparing the chocolate, she continued questioning him. "What brought you home now?"

Was that hope in her voice? It was something he

couldn't nail down. He answered the question, but she'd given him the perfect opportunity to turn it around on her. "Megan's worried about you. Why is that?" He knew, but he wanted to hear it from Kelly.

Not turning around, she shrugged. "I don't know why she's worried."

He leaned off the wall and stepped closer to her. Grasping her shoulders, he turned her to face him. "Really? Something about you acting like you're being followed everywhere you go? How about someone breaking in here and something missing that you're keeping secret from me?"

She was startled at his final question. He'd caught her, and she knew it.

"Kelly, you can't hide anything from me. Now tell me what the hell is going on."

Releasing a loud sigh, she dropped her shoulders in defeat. "I don't know what to think of it. Lately, I've felt like I'm being followed. There's no reason for it, just that odd feeling. It could be pregnancy hormones."

She paused and looked away, but he didn't take the bait and interrupt. He wanted the entire story.

"Megan probably told you that someone broke into my car." She paused while he nodded. "They took my purse along with a suitcase full of clothes." Pausing again, he guessed she was considering how much she would reveal. She could consider it all she wanted; he'd have the full story. "Today, someone broke into here, as you know, but he took a bag with some papers."

They were the damned oddest items to be stolen. Her purse he could understand. Thankfully, they could trace it if any of her credit cards were used. He'd contact Devon. She wouldn't get anything back, but it'd all be taken care of properly. The clothing and papers were unusual for a thief to swipe. However—"What's their connection?"

Looking down, she fretted with her hands. "Besides my purse, they were Brian's."

Fuck, what had that man gotten Kelly into? Anger at himself for not being there for her raged within every cell in his body. He didn't want to ask, but this seemed to be a day for that, so he opened his mouth to insert his second foot. "How did Brian die?"

With a firm jaw, Kelly looked him in the eye. "Hit and run," she said, and then added, "and it might not have been an accident."

Holy fucking shit. He should've come home sooner.

Chapter Seven

Trent rotated his sore neck and pain splintered outward as he hurried from his apartment after a quick shower and getting dressed. At first, he'd wondered who had cleared away the dust, making the place livable. Something inside him knew it had been Kelly. No one else would've been that thoughtful during his absence. Also, she'd been the only one with a key to his place. *And she hadn't said a word.*

Sleeping on Kelly's couch hadn't been as comfortable as it had in the past since he couldn't stop the pain that throbbed in his head and neck. He'd been damn lucky she hadn't broken anything when she'd hit him. Still, he chuckled a little at her trying to help. He wished he'd seen her wielding the bat. Maybe then he'd have been able to direct it to the right person. Since she'd told him it was there, he should've grabbed it first, so she hadn't had the opportunity. But, who'd have thought she'd rush in to assist because she worried about him?

The physical discomfort and the concern that someone would return to her place, had kept him awake most of the night. Oh, she'd tried to push him out the door citing the man had already stolen what he'd wanted and had no need to return. Oh, the naiveté. How little she understood criminals. As far as he and Kelly knew, she could've been the target all along, and Trent had simply interrupted things. His stomach clenched at the thought of her in real danger.

This morning, he'd been hard-pressed to leave her side before she left for work. Everything inside him screamed that she needed protecting. But, protecting from what? Someone obviously wanted something of her ex-fiancé's. Since it appeared that they'd finally taken everything she had of Brian's, there shouldn't be any more trouble.

He hoped.

Filled with a sense of unease in his gut, he shook his head. The paperwork must contain something important, or detrimental, to some unknown player. There was no doubt in his mind that it had to have been a pro who'd broken into her place since there had been the discipline to take only what was wanted and leave valuables behind.

And I missed him with the bag over his shoulder. Great fucking observation skills.

Then again, so had Kelly, but she'd been so focused on him after she'd walloped him, the thief probably could've picked her up and carried her away with her barely noticing until she lost sight of him.

That brought to mind the question she'd shared with him. Had Brian's death been an accident? So what that a murderer had told her that the driver that hit Brian had been hired to kill him? The man had chosen a hit-and-run, which was fucking stupid in Trent's mind as there was no guarantee the person would be killed. If the thefts were related—and he'd bet his most valuable collector baseball card they were—maybe the driver had been supposed to have acquired the stuff first and only meant to scare Brian instead of killing him.

Trent mentally shrugged. Anything was possible. He sighed in frustration. They wouldn't know unless they found the driver.

The problem was whether to believe the string of unreliable criminals.

Kelly had hit rock bottom with her investigation but was hopeful he might find out something. With all she'd shared, Trent hated to tell her that her hope was wasted unless the criminal network would actually ID the culprit. So he didn't tell her. Instead, he promised to have HIS look into it. A promise he shouldn't have made because he had no idea if he could keep it. He was only a team member, no matter what Jesse had said to him in the hospital. *"You're a Hamilton, and, as such, you're welcome to become a partner with your family at HIS."*

Booted feet on the ground, his warm motorcycle snuggled between his legs, Trent took more of the calming breaths Jamie had prescribed. Returning to HIS rattled his nerves. Images of Les's face before they made the move to save Amber swam before him.

Sweat broke out on his brow, and his pulse ratcheted up several notches. Black dots danced before his eyes. Forcing in another calming breath, he reminded himself he couldn't change the past, and he had to face the men, no matter their judgment. According to Jamie, he had to look forward and not back.

He could do this. Somehow he'd make it through everything. For Kelly's sake.

Finally stepping off the bike and settling it with the kickstand, he removed his helmet, shoved it under his arm and started for the front door of Jesse's home, where in the back he housed HIS headquarters. Trent had heard Jesse planned to install a separate entrance so everyone wasn't traipsing through the house at all hours. Trent figured that Jesse and his wife Kate had been caught messing around and didn't want it to happen again. Maybe it was like the time Jesse had caught AJ with a woman on the table covered in whipped cream and AJ holding a jar of cherries, ready to dress his dessert.

Trent chuckled at the story the team never let AJ forget, even though it occurred when he was still with the FBI.

Removing his black leather gloves, he slapped them across his jean-clad leg, ignoring the slight sting of the cold, before tossing them inside his helmet. Riding his bike down the beach where the weather had been so much nicer, called to him, but he squashed it. He needed to be here.

As his stomach rumbled, he hastened his steps. With his rush to arrive at headquarters that morning, he'd skipped breakfast. Kate's cooking sounded really good right about now. In the past, she'd made extra, just for the men, and he couldn't be more appreciative since he wasn't much of a cook.

Barely three steps inside the house, he was waylaid by a short, dark-haired girl.

"Uncle Trent!" Reagan, Jesse's seven-year-old-daughter from his first wife, jetted into his arms.

He froze at how she'd addressed him but quickly recovered when he remembered she called all the men of HIS "Uncle." Wrapping his one free arm around her small body, he smiled, joy filling him at seeing the little imp. "Hey, Rea-Rea," he said, using a nickname many of the men had begun to call the young girl. Damn if she didn't get cuter every day. Jesse would have his hands full when she got older.

Pulling back, a huge smile plastered on her face, she bounced a little. "When I call you uncle now, it's like when I call Uncle Dev uncle because Daddy says you're my real uncle, not just an uncle like all my other uncles that work with Daddy."

Head spinning at that many uncles spoken in one long sentence, he relaxed when Kate intervened.

"Leave your Uncle Trent alone, sweetie." Kate wore a frilly pink apron over a red sweater and carried a platter. She approached him with a welcoming smile.

He didn't have the heart to correct Kate because, honestly…she was right whether he acknowledged it or not.

"Okay, Mommy." Hearing Reagan calling Kate, her stepmother, Mommy, strengthened the joy behind his smile. He knew Kate's secret of not being able to have children of her own.

For some reason, women liked to share things with him they didn't with others. He figured he had some sign that only women could read that said, "Spill your guts to me, I won't tell anyone." He never did.

At Kate's words, and without a glance his way, Reagan tried to dart off, but Kate snagged the back of the little girl's blue long-sleeved T-shirt. "Take these"—she handed over the platter of breakfast biscuits in her hand—"and put them on the conference table. Then leave. Don't bother anyone."

Once Kate turned to him, he stepped forward to give her a hug and a kiss on the cheek. "Hey, doll," he drawled with his usual greeting. Working with her when they were both with the FBI had given him great respect for Kate. How she fell in love with Jesse was something he couldn't guess. Jesse was the biggest unrelenting alpha male he knew, and he hadn't been so nice to her when they met. Then again, she could be independent and stubborn when she chose. They came together like oil and vinegar. With a mental shrug, he thought, *To each his own.*

Kate reached for his helmet and eased it from his grip. "Let me take that. We installed a shelf just for them since three of the team rides now, even in this miserable weather." Nodding for him to follow her, she turned toward the back of the house and headquarters.

Following her across the large living room and down the hallway, he removed his jacket knowing the war room would be a comfortable temperature. Devon was a master at keeping it perfect for his precious computers.

When he entered the spacious room, a slight tremor entered his body. Squashing it, he reminded himself he had to do this. He'd promised Jamie he'd come back and tackle the ghosts before him. The ghosts interfering with his living a full life.

Kate settled his helmet on a shelf inside the door. "Here. It keeps them out of the chairs that Devon harps about our never sitting on." She rolled her eyes.

"I heard that," a deep voice rumbled from within the room.

Trent couldn't stop his chuckle upon hearing Devon's reply. Looking past Kate, he caught Reagan slip from Devon's lap as the man came to his feet behind a series of computer screens. And, on the conference table, sure enough, there was a plate of biscuits, which appeared to be stuffed with eggs and meat. His stomach rumbled again. Bless Kate and her need to cook.

With an outstretched hand, Devon approached. "It's good to have you back."

Of course, there was no surprise in his greeting. Since they'd sent Megan after him, Devon probably knew exactly when he'd arrived in town. Trent wouldn't tell them he wouldn't be back if it weren't for Kelly needing him. No matter what she thought, he knew in his gut that she did in fact need him. No one would harm his Kelly.

That jolted him.

It was the second time he'd thought of her as *his* Kelly. He'd let the first time slide because it could've been a fluke in his just returning to her friendship. Yet "his Kelly?" As in something other than just his friend? Hell, she was pregnant with someone else's child. That made her as far from his as possible. But it didn't stop his sudden possessiveness of her.

Gripping Devon's hand tightly, he only nodded his response before releasing his grip. Without shame, he walked to the table and picked up a biscuit.

"Some have bacon and some have sausage," Kate informed him.

He didn't give a fuck what they had inside. He needed food and something to prevent him from opening his mouth and saying something he might regret, like "I'm not ready to face my demons" before leaving with no help for Kelly. Biting into a biscuit, he glanced around the room as the delicious flavor of egg and, thank the Lord, bacon exploded across his taste buds.

With his focus on the war room, he squinted as he did another perusal. It appeared to be the same, but something was different. Unable to put his finger on it, he shrugged and took another bite.

Kate must've returned to the kitchen, leaving him alone with Devon who slid into a chair at the conference table, before he leaned back and watched Trent. Talk about suddenly feeling self-conscious as he ate.

Devon waited until he finished the biscuit and spoke before Trent could grab another. "Well? Is she in trouble?"

It took a moment to recall that the men knew Kelly. With Megan joining the family, Kelly had joined in on Kate's dinner parties. And, like Megan, she'd had to agree not to pursue any stories on HIS from any of its team members. A huge requirement Jesse had for all of their reporter friends.

Had they waited until they brought him home to find out what was happening with Kelly? Christ, she could've been in serious trouble, and they'd sat back. The need to vent his frustration was strong, but he shoved it back until he had all of the facts. Hopefully, he was wrong, and they had been behind her all this time.

That niggling feeling hit him. All what time? There still wasn't anything specific except thefts. Pulse pounding, he fisted his hands at this side, keeping a reign on his rising temper, and he answered Devon with his own question, "Did you think she was in trouble?"

Devon shook his head. "Not from what we could find out. She wouldn't open up to anyone, which is why we sent for you. According to Megan, you're her best friend."

A lump formed in his throat, making it painful to breathe. *Best friend?* Some friend he'd been leaving her while she was pregnant and unmarried.

One thought stuck with him. They'd sent for him because they couldn't get anywhere else. Which meant HIS was also worried.

Devon looked down at the table and began moving his fingers across it, like on a keyboard. Trent's mind spun. What the fuck? Had Devon lost it? Then the table came to life, and he really noticed it, and the difference he couldn't place. Hell, it was a different shade of wood. His observation skills since he'd returned were atrocious and he'd best figure it out because that could get him killed in their line of work.

Devon had threatened to get something high-tech that they all figured only he could operate. "New toy?"

A smile lit up the man's face like that of a kid in a candy store. He nodded to the center. "Take a look."

Trent moved in to see a HIS file on Kelly Williams. A small sense of relief coursed through him. They hadn't just left her out there all alone. Yet they hadn't been protecting her either, his mind countered. *They sent for you,* whispered through his mind.

Startling Trent since he hadn't seen him move, Devon stood beside him and leaned forward, his hand swiping at the picture of Kelly. Up popped background information. Before he could read through it all, Devon swiped his hand again, and a file of Kelly's recent articles appeared.

Gratification swam inside him. This information could be helpful and the fact they'd collected it settled his gut. Of course, Devon couldn't help collecting data on everyone. It was a compulsion. In fact, he imagined there was a file on him, and he didn't give a shit at this point in time.

So engrossed in seeing what Kelly had been up to in his absence, he didn't hear Jesse and a few others enter the war room. He did see them grab breakfast biscuits as they passed the table until the tray was nearly empty.

Glancing around, AJ entered with Matt, two more Hamiltons.

"Hey, man," AJ said before shoving a biscuit in his mouth. Typical AJ. He and Matt had grabbed the last two biscuits.

A smile split Trent's face. Relief at their camaraderie and not pummeling him with questions about his absence surged through him. He did miss them and all that went with it. A small weight lifted from his shoulders, and he welcomed being in their presence.

"It's about time you showed your sorry ass around here," Jesse said jokingly.

"Fuck you," Trent slammed back in the same joking manner. "If I had prettier faces to look at…."

"Hey, my wife is hot, so don't even try that shitty excuse," Jesse countered with a quirked eyebrow in challenge.

Trent couldn't resist poking the bear whose wife was his own Kryptonite. "Don't I know it," he said in a dreamy-sexy kind of voice, just enough to piss Jesse off at his praise of Kate.

"Fucker," Jesse said and presented Trent with his middle finger.

Laughter filled the room, and this is what had

drawn him to HIS. Not laughter per se, but working hard and having fun as a team. But yet, he still wasn't sure that this was where he belonged. Something was missing. Wait, no, someone—several in fact—were missing from the group.

"Before you ask, Jake has a team in the UAE guarding a prince. Actually making us money," Jesse said out of the side of his mouth.

"Where's Brad?" Trent asked.

"He's got a team in Belize, chasing after Hogan," Jesse offered in response.

Trent wanted to spit. The bastard who had paid to have Rylee—Devon's wife—kidnapped had escaped during her rescue. Trent hadn't stayed around for them to resolve that part of the mission. He'd been there to help save Rylee, and when they'd accomplished it, he'd left. "Got a good lead on him?"

Jesse nodded his answer. "The only ones in the states are who you see here."

Cheesy grins from Rob and Joe—two HIS team members—Kate and four of the Hamilton brothers stood before him.

"Tell us about Kelly." Jesse's swift change of subject from Hogan had Trent's eyes shifting to Devon to gauge his reaction. Nothing. It had to be eating Devon up inside that he was here and Rylee was—He glanced around and then narrowed his eyes. "Where's Rylee?" he countered, noticing her absence. Something told him he didn't want to know her location. That churning in his gut was as active as a tornado.

Devon spoke through a clenched jaw, "She's with Brad."

"What?" Trent roared, stopping all chatter in the

room.

Devon stood and grimaced. "She wanted to take Hogan down herself."

"And you all allowed her to get close to that monster again?"

"You forget she can hold her own," Devon said in fierce defense of his wife.

"I'm not saying she can't, but still…." He didn't know what he meant to say. Rylee was tough as nails when she needed to be, but the thought of her near Hogan again sickened him. He knew it was just overprotective instincts that wanted her to remain behind. He had to get a grip if he planned to come back here. Devon was right that she could hold her own. Trust.

Jesse's phone rang, and he walked away answering it.

"Believe me, I'm not happy she went," Devon said, "but you've worked with her, so you understand there's no stopping her. She's part of HIS now. She works missions, and I put my trust in her doing her best."

Working with Rylee in the FBI had been enjoyable. They'd only been assigned to one case together, but she'd been a badass as far as Trent was concerned. But Devon being okay with her going on a mission after a sicko? Trent would never allow Kelly to do that. That stopped everything in his world. Realization slapped him hard across the face. He wasn't thinking of Rylee; he'd been thinking of putting Kelly in danger. He'd gone into super-overprotective drive about her. Her pregnancy turned a key inside him. He'd have to work on it, but right now, he needed to figure out if she was in danger or not.

"Devon, can you run—"

Jesse's roar interrupted Trent's request for information on Brian. "Fuck!"

"What?" Trent asked as his pulse sped up. Nothing good ever came from Jesse's bellows.

Jesse turned to Devon. "We need to get to Belize, now. Get us a plane." Then, he turned to the group. "Rob, Joe and—" He spun around. "—Kate, get suited up."

"I thought you just said that Brad already had a small team there." Trent's observation skills at noticing the new table might suck, but his hearing worked fucking fine.

"He does. Only they landed in jail." Jesse turned to Kate. "I'll let Mrs. Kessler know so she can watch Reagan."

Trent had missed the live-in nanny slash cook slash housekeeper—Mrs. Kessler, or Mrs. K., as the men liked to call her.

Devon jumped up. "I'm going."

"So am I," AJ and Matt piped in.

Jesse shook his head. "No. AJ and Matt, you stay back in case Trent needs you."

"What would I need them for?" Trent asked, but at the same time was thankful to have help should he actually require it.

"Kelly," AJ and Jesse said in unison.

This was beyond bizarre. He hadn't even told them about the break-in.

"If Megan's worried, something rotten might be happening." AJ grinned like he was proud of his wife's ability to sniff out trouble.

Trent would wait and brief AJ and Matt on the

break-in and theft after the team left since getting Brad, Rylee, and the men out of a Belize jail took precedence.

"It'll be a good time for them to get you up to speed." Jesse slammed a locker closed and approached them with a black duffel bag in his hand, and body armor tossed over it.

"On what?"

"On the business—partner." Jesse reached out his empty hand to shake.

Hands up in front of his chest, refusing to take Jesse's hand, Trent countered, "Whoa. I'm not a partner. I'm just one of the guys." While he'd basically grown up with the siblings, he'd never truly felt like he belonged in the family. This change still took some getting used to on his end.

"We'll discuss this when I return. First, I need to bail our men out and kick some fucking ass."

Trent nodded begrudgingly. A talk was inevitable. Right now though, he needed to figure out exactly what was happening with Kelly. Hustling the few steps to the computers where Devon tossed a laptop in a bag, Trent asked, "Devon, can you pull me some information before you go?" He waved his hand to the table. "And maybe show me how to pull that file up?"

Devon grinned. "Finally. Someone who appreciates my toys."

Appreciate, my ass, Trent thought. His information on Kelly was there, so he didn't have a choice.

Chapter Eight

He's back! Kept shooting through Kelly's thoughts, breaking into her frozen mind. Everything about her was frozen. She'd been waiting on the street, shuffling her feet to keep the blood flowing, while waiting for Adrian's ex-wife to depart the woman's home. His ex-wife had refused Kelly's calls, and one thing Kelly didn't like was someone avoiding her. Like Trent had when he'd been hurt.

When she was younger, she'd set down the parameters necessary for a Mr. Right, as she'd dubbed the man of her dreams, to be in her life *if* and *when* the time was right. The list of attributes she'd required was long, but her most important things were that he had to be honest, thoughtful, trustworthy, romantic, and above all, love her just as she was.

Trent McKenzie had always seen her as a friend, sometimes he'd even treated her like a kid sister. It truly sucked because Kelly knew deep inside her heart that he was the man for her—her true Mr. Right. He just didn't know it.

She sighed and turned in circles to check her surroundings again.

Then Trent had left.

Before that even occurred, she'd settled for another man and was having that man's baby, so her chance with Trent had been flushed down the toilet. His horror at her being pregnant said it all. Disapproval. Disgust. Really, he didn't act disgusted, but he might as well have with the way he'd pulled back in conversation. The way he'd pushed to find out more about her being an unwed pregnant woman.

Her stomach rumbled, and she considered giving up her position and going into the office when the townhome's front door opened. A petite, bleached-blonde emerged and said, "Son of a bitch. I thought you'd have left by now."

Kelly smiled before she fell in step with Nikki Copeland. The little woman definitely had a fast stride. "Mrs. Copeland, I'm Kelly Williams with—"

"I know who you are and who you're with, Miss Williams. What I don't know is why you're bothering me. Didn't you get your pound of flesh about Adrian when his case happened?"

A well-deserved jab, but things had changed. She just had to get this woman to understand that. "Well, I'm not entirely certain that Adrian is guilty anymore." There, she'd placed it out there for the woman to digest.

Mrs. Copeland stopped. With wide eyes, she screeched, "What?"

Kelly couldn't tell if it was anger or incredulousness in her tone. Either way, it didn't bode well for Kelly's chances of interviewing the woman.

"I've some new information that casts doubt on your husband's guilt."

"Ex"—she stressed the word—"husband."

"I'm sorry, your ex-husband. I'd like to sit down with you and ask a few questions."

The woman studied her for a moment then shook her head. "No." She turned and walked away.

Just like that? Oh, hell no. She'd chased stories before, and this wouldn't be any different. Kelly double-timed it to catch up to the woman. "Mrs. Copeland, this could mean a guilty person is out there while Adrian is in jail for a crime he didn't commit."

"Fuck Adrian. He certainly fucked me over."

With nothing to say to that, she tried her stance again. "Mrs. Copeland, may I please have a little of your time to discuss this?" Hell, she'd start asking her questions on the street in a few minutes. Only she'd have rather read the transcripts first to know what the woman had said in court.

Mrs. Copeland stopped and turned to her. "Read my lips. I want nothing to do with this. I don't give a shit whether Adrian is innocent or guilty. Leave me alone, or I'll file stalking charges against you."

Stunned, Kelly could only stand there when the woman hurried away. What the hell happened in that marriage that she'd allow him to remain in jail if he was innocent? Good grief.

Kelly quickly hailed a cab to the newsroom. Her thoughts about the couple didn't stop until she reached the warmth inside the building. As the cold washed away, Kelly removed her coat as she approached her seat.

Even after a busy day, Kelly still thought of her interaction with Nikki Copeland. A bitch of the first degree. How could she get her to agree to talk? Kelly had promised to try and help Adrian and that meant speaking with Nikki. There had to be a way. Kelly had to find something that would benefit the woman. That was all there was to it.

"Earth to Kelly." Megan interrupted Kelly's

wayward thoughts.

Shaking herself to awareness, she smiled. "Hey, Megan. You've been out all day. Was it productive?"

Megan dropped into a desk directly across from Kelly's. After dropping her purse into a bottom drawer, Megan nodded and leaned forward on her forearms. "It was good, but we can talk about it later. Trent's home."

That reminded Kelly that Megan had told Trent that she was worried. Wondering if Megan had brought him home, she almost missed the woman's next words.

"The woman he traveled with died."

A lump jumped up her throat and lodged there. Knowing he'd ridden off without a word had been bad enough, but the fact he'd done it with a nurse from the hospital had been a terrible pain in her heart even though she'd already decided to give up hope of him and marry Brian.

So excited to have him home, she'd forgotten about his companion when he'd visited the night before. Anger at and concern for him raged through her veins. "What happened?" she asked, unsure she truly wanted to know.

"Cancer." The one word was the extent of Megan's answer.

The jealousy that had lived within her when he'd left with the woman fled. Although admittedly, a residual amount remained. She couldn't help it.

Picking up her notebook, Kelly set it back down and shifted it on her desk, trying to find the proper angle for it. Grabbing her pen to line it up—just buying time before she needed to respond—the movement of several people to the mounted TV screens caught her attention, but she returned her focus to Megan. "He says you're worried about me. What'd you tell him?"

A blush crept up her friend's neck. She should be embarrassed. Although, it had brought Trent home, so Kelly couldn't be too angry. "I'm worried. I just told him about the car break-in."

Kelly's brow climbed up her forehead. "And?"

Running her fingers through her blonde hair, Megan cleared her throat nervously. "Well, I told him you always looked over your shoulder." Narrowing her eyes at Kelly, she challenged, "You do."

Someone breaking into her apartment and stealing Brian's bag told her that Megan had been right to be concerned. Whoever had done this had probably been watching for when she was gone so they could get in without issue. They'd failed and caught her and Trent. She winced, thinking how she'd tried to help, thought she was swinging at the bad guy when she'd hit Trent. Hard. It had allowed the thief to get away.

Deciding it best not to share this with Megan, she smiled, hoping it was convincing that she wasn't concerned. "I don't do it any more than normal for living in Baltimore."

"Hmph." Obviously deciding to leave the subject alone, Megan asked, "How's Ashley?"

Kelly placed her hand on her stomach and softly stroked the swollen belly. "She's been active." Every day awe still struck her at a life growing inside her body. Wanting to be a mother since she'd reached adulthood, she still couldn't wrap her head around the fact it was actually happening. With the movements in her stomach more baby and not as much gas, her love swelled for the little girl cocooned in her womb. Just to show her worth, Ashley kicked and Kelly jumped, laughing.

Megan chuckled. "I remember those days." Then with a serious tone, she asked, "Have you decided?"

Stilling her hand, Kelly nodded. "Yes, I'm going to visit Brian's family." That decision hadn't been difficult, but it hadn't been easy either. She'd grown up in that small town of less than two hundred people. After the event that claimed Brian's life, her blood pressure had spiked dangerously high, and she'd had a small bleed, which her doctor subsequently placed her on bedrest for two weeks. In her condition, Mike hadn't wanted her to travel for the funeral. He'd demanded she rest and take care of herself and his grandchild.

"What about your family?"

"I don't know."

"Kelly." Megan sighed. "You can't escape them. They won't think less of you."

"Of course they will," she snapped, then quickly apologized. She'd tossed out everything her parents had taught her. Remaining a virgin until she'd married had been ingrained into her. The importance of it. The gift she offered a husband. Even if she'd had sex outside of marriage with someone they loved like a son, she couldn't face them. Yet she knew going to Brian's home would bring her parents and siblings. Brian's dad was eager to meet his granddaughter.

The crowd around the TV grew. Raising a brow to Megan, her colleague nodded, and they rose and followed the group.

Listening to the broadcast, sadness seeped into her. Another murder in Baltimore. It never mattered that she didn't know the person. It was just an untimely death. About to walk away, a name in the scrolling words at the bottom of the screen caught her attention. Her hand flew to her mouth.

Nikki Copeland had been murdered. Kelly had just spoken with her this morning. She'd been one of the three names on Adrian's list.

The urgency with the thought that this was connected to Adrian's case welled inside her—that she couldn't put this on the side burner as her boss had directed. Kelly had to pick up those transcripts and get busy reading and investigating. Moving back to her desk, she reached the back of her chair for her coat. "I have to go," she told Megan as she bundled up and collected her purse.

Her hands shook at the impact of Nikki's death. One less person who could help, or hurt, Adrian's case. To Kelly, this death meant something was fishy with Adrian's conviction, and no one cared—except her and maybe the real culprit.

****

Leaving Esme, a box of the transcripts in her hands, Kelly's mind fluttered to the paperwork of Brian's that had been stolen. There had to have been something there that had led to his death. It just had to. Why hadn't she read through it? *Because it had been none of my business, and I hadn't wanted to acknowledge Brian's death.*

She stepped down the courthouse steps, and relief coursed through her that no ice existed on the sidewalk and road. Ashley kicked again, and Kelly smiled while looking both ways before stepping into the roadway part of the parking lot.

Hopefully, Trent and HIS found out something, and they could find the hit-and-run driver and put him behind bars. Although, according to Jason, the driver was supposedly paid to do it, which meant someone was pulling the strings that they also needed to find.

Mentally shaking her head, she continued across the road. Allowing herself to believe these criminals without any evidence wasn't like her. She strongly wanted a reason behind Brian's senseless death. She couldn't stand it if he was just a meaningless statistic.

Yes, HIS would figure it out. As far as she knew, they always had been successful. Plus, she trusted Trent.

In the meantime, Kelly had a box filled with court transcripts to review. The size of the transcript made her wonder, more than once, whether she was biting off more than she could chew. This had been a well-investigated set of crimes. In the end, only the word of the arsonist had put Adrian behind bars, or so it seemed. She'd see if something else had helped put the nail in Adrian's coffin, so to speak. She had to at least try.

"Kelly!" The masculine cry snapped her head up in time to see a massive body clad in blue jeans and a brown jacket, only a few feet away, rushing at her. With her heart pounding, fear froze her in place, and the world beyond this threat didn't exist. Everything her brothers had ever taught her to protect herself fled her mind faster than the man charged at her. Heart racing, she couldn't believe someone would be so bold as to attack her in this public place in the middle of the day. The man was only a few steps away. *Do something, Kelly!* she demanded of herself. *You know karate, protect yourself.*

No sooner had that thought drifted through her mind, a calm overcame her, and she adjusted her stance to defend herself. An engine revving caught her attention, but that was when she recognized the man running at her—Paul. With Brian's death and the death in her news story, her unexplained fear of him sent a sliver of dread to the base of her spine, coiling in angst.

However, something made her glance back, and her eyes widened. A dark car neared her, picking up speed. The arm she'd raised in greeting was yanked as Paul pulled her toward him. Pain ricocheted through her hip and thigh as she was hauled out of the open part of the parking lot and between two parked cars. A squealing of tires moving away from them filled in the picture for her. Someone had been about to hit her and Paul had saved her.

Panting, Paul held onto her arm a bit too tightly, and concern filled his eyes. "Are you okay?"

Okay? Her heart pounded trying to escape the confines of her chest. Was he fucking kidding? She'd almost been run down by a car. If the raging throb on her hip and thigh were any indication, she'd actually been clipped by it. Good God. Pulse racing, she looked down at her shaking hands, wondering how bad it would've been had Paul not pulled her out of that car's deadly path. "What…?" Her broken voice drifted off before tears escaped her eyes and slid down her face, and she took in a gulp of air. Paul's strong arms wrapped around her, and she found herself crying against his shoulder.

"It's okay. I've got you. You're safe." His comforting voice only allowed her to finally react to the danger she'd be in. Heart pounding, it hit her that her baby could've been killed. She could've been killed. With that realization, wracking sobs continued and

Kelly buried her face deeper so the mortification creeping up her neck and into her face wasn't evident.

Somewhat under control, she pulled back a few moments later and looked in her purse for a tissue. That was when she realized she'd lost the transcript box. Turning frantically, she noticed the box had slid near where she stood. At least it hadn't opened and spread the papers everywhere for her to chase. After blowing her nose, she looked back at Paul who watched her intently. "What are you doing here?" she asked more bluntly than she meant.

"Testifying. I think they clipped you. Are you hurt? Do you need an ambulance?"

The pain in the area where she'd been bumped roared to life, but she knew it wasn't ambulance-worthy. She just needed to sit down, catch her breath, and then maybe cry again. *This can't be happening.* Suddenly, her head snapped up. Holy hell, was that the same person who ran down Brian?

Anger at that possibility radiated through her veins almost singeing her toes and fingers.

What the hell was she supposed to do now? *Thank God, you've come home, Trent McKenzie.*

With the rush of emotion and her brain overloaded with the possibility of what could have been, black spots filled her eyes, and her limbs turned to jelly. "Trent," she whispered before collapsing into darkness.

Chapter Nine

"Dammit, I wanted to have Devon pull everything he could on Kelly's Brian, but he took off before he could finish," Trent groused, thinking that even though he'd come for Kelly's sake, Jamie would be proud of his reuniting, in some semblance, with his...*brothers.* In truth, he knew they were blameless. He did miss the men. They'd had good—and bad—times together. Bonding times. Any one of them would've taken his, or Les's, place in rescuing their niece.

"What'd you expect? Rylee was in jail," Matt stated, as if everyone should understand Devon's reasoning.

Always the peacemaker, Trent thought.

Planting his palms on the high-tech conference table, that he'd somehow locked up, making it unusable except to hold shit, Trent ground out, "I'd have expected him to not let his personal feelings interfere with his job." Anger boiled in him at the entire situation.

The irony washed by him that he was doing the same thing with Kelly.

"Don't worry. When he gets there and sees that she's safe, he'll be back online." Matt took a long drink from a bottle of water, then set it on the table. In bafflement, Trent watched him pick it up and spotting the water ring, stand to grab a napkin off a side table holding the coffee pot and place it under his drink.

Trent shook his head at the absurdity of it all. This goddamn table and its importance…and current uselessness. He needed to get a check on his frustration. He wasn't helping anyone like this.

Matt shrugged. "Devon would have a fit if we messed up his table. As for Belize, we can't fix it, so let's work on what we can. From what you've told us about Kelly, something is wrong, but it doesn't sound as if there's a threat to her."

There was the rub, and it bugged the shit out of him. Nothing had happened directly to her—except the thefts. He only counted the break-in as a theft at the moment since they'd obviously been after something specific. Although he wouldn't forget it, or the face of the man who'd attacked him. Convincing her to go to the police would've been the smart thing to do. With Kelly, though, she could ask him to paint the sky pink, and he'd do his damnedest to make it happen for her.

"I needed that information from Devon. Now I have to wait while he gets settled, and I don't like it."

"I think he's still pissed you skipped out on his wedding in Vegas," AJ said around a mouthful.

He shrugged. "He's a guy. They don't care about that shit. Besides, they were already married."

The two men chuckled, but AJ spoke. "Men don't care, but when their wives do, men do. Rylee's the one who was put out that you didn't stick around."

Trent shook his head and smiled. "I'll kiss and make up with her when she returns."

Pushing the almost empty bowl of popcorn away, AJ shook his head. "Do you have a death wish? You can't keep kissing other men's wives."

"Hey, I kissed Megan before you two were even an item," Trent countered jokingly, knowing that one kiss had been a big mistake, that while he joked about it, he regretted it since the action bothered AJ so much.

"Enough, you two. Trent, what do you want from us?" Matt waved a finger back and forth between himself and AJ, effectively bringing the conversation back to their main reason for meeting.

"Besides fixing this goddamn table so I can look at Kelly's file?" He huffed out a breath. "I don't know yet." And that kept the frustration level high.

After his reluctant admission, Emily Cavanaugh, the Hamilton family's baby sister, strolled into the room. "Trent," she squealed and raced over to him.

He'd barely landed on his feet before she launched herself at him, knocking him back a step and winding him. When her arms around his neck started choking him, he tried to peel her away. Before the accident...before finding out she was his sister...they'd always been close—not close like he and Kelly—but close.

After the accident, when he'd saved her daughter, their friendship became stronger. As one would expect in that situation.

Funny how he'd never balked at her being his sister compared to Jesse, Devon, Brad, Matt, and AJ being his brothers. Sins of the father....

Measured in intensity, Em's embrace beat all the others he'd received from her. Obviously, she'd missed him, and that made him smile. Holding her at arm's length, his grin broadened and he winked. "Doll, you look good."

Slapping him on the arm playfully, she laughed

while redness crept into her face. "You're still the shameless flirt." Surprising him, she kissed him on the cheek. "Amber will be glad to see you. But—" She paused and laughed. "She still says she won't go swimming with you again."

Hearty laughter erupted from the table, and Trent couldn't help but join in. After taking the little girl for a scary plunge into the swimming pool at the Hamilton's Oxford home—to save her life—he was lucky she even wanted anything to do with him. Yet at that age—what was she three or four?—they tended to be pretty smart.

"You missed her birthday."

So, she'd turned four. Holy fuck. Had he really been gone that long? Well, he must have if Amber had a birthday. Jamie had been right; he'd missed so much by taking care of her, but he wouldn't have given up that opportunity for the world. She'd deserved the care, especially after all she'd done to heal him both physically and emotionally.

The laughing had stopped and looking around, Em drew in her brows. "You boys look in desperate need of help. Maybe I can do something."

With a disappointed exhale of breath, Trent shook his head. "I don't need anything financial." Em was their forensic accountant and was damn good at it. "I need this table working and some background. Devon said he'd pull the information when he could." Shrugging, he almost sighed again in despair. He needed to help Kelly, and that wait didn't sit well with him, even though nothing appeared to be urgent in her situation.

Except she was pregnant and husbandless. Not that she needed a husband, but she'd had Brian.

Kelly didn't show it, but she had to be devastated at losing the man so close to their wedding. Jealousy shot through him, and he didn't quite understand why he'd be jealous of a dead man. Still, she was alone and needed someone to take care of her, no matter what she said. *One problem at a time,* he reminded himself.

Locking her fingers together, Em stretched them in front of her body and then released them. "Step aside, boys." Pushing past Trent, she leaned forward and typed on a keyboard that had mysteriously appeared. What the fuck? Devon could've shown him how to bring that up. Maybe he could've salvaged the time he'd wasted just tapping on the damn table everywhere, hoping something worked.

"Okay, here's your file. Now, don't screw it up again," she warned. "I'll get you what background I can. I'm able to acquire basic information easily, but anything deeper requires Devon. He hasn't taught me all that spook stuff he knows." She chuckled at what must've been a joke between her and Devon. "I need some information from you, though."

Still staring at the table, with its picture of Kelly on a file folder, he spouted off from memory, "Brian Platt, lived in Reed Point, Montana. That's about all I have."

"Wow, she's been busy," Matt said in relation to Kelly.

He turned back to his brothers—*wow, that label came off my tongue without thought this time*—and speared Matt with a steely glare. Protectiveness welled inside him like an ugly monster. "Get out of her file." Kelly's personal information was no one's business. After reviewing it, he would decide what to share with everyone.

Hands raised, Matt leaned back in his chair. "Just looking at the stories she's investigated."

Resuming his seat, Trent touched the table and spun the display toward him. With his finger, he flipped through screens, like paging through it on a computer. As long as Devon always had it set up like this, the men on the team wouldn't mind. However, if they had to figure it out—like he had—then the table could end up being kindling. No matter Devon's desire to bring them into the twenty-first century, the men preferred their low-tech, caveman ways. It worked, so why change it? was their philosophy.

"She likes to rock the boat." AJ's voice came from behind him.

Looking up, he found the man leaning over his shoulder. How had he not noticed that?

"Yeah, she does," he conceded. If it stirred controversy, it stirred Kelly into action. He couldn't be prouder of the work she did, but it also twisted his gut.

Em walked to the table with a printout. "I've got something for you to start." She bumped Trent's chair aside a foot. "Here." Reaching out, she pulled up that magical keyboard again and the next thing he knew, a file—similar to the one on Kelly—appeared on the screen with Brian's name on it. "Now," she smiled mischievously, "don't tell Devon, but here's a printed copy also. I figured you'd want to take something with you besides an extra laptop."

He accepted the papers from her, and relief whooshed through him. He stood and kissed her cheek, similar to how she'd welcomed him. "Thanks, Doll."

She smiled. "Anytime for you, big brother." Winking, she walked back to the computer bank.

Warmth spread through him to hear her call him that. When they'd been growing up, he'd felt like her older brother, keeping her out of trouble while her brothers ignored her.

Enough emotions for the day. The frustration close to overwhelmed him and he didn't like being like that. Being back in control of his feelings was what he needed. He'd faced down his brothers and sister and survived. He had stuff to look into for Kelly. Good start.

With everything in printed form, he prepared to leave. Grabbing his jacket, he thanked everyone and collected his helmet before exiting through the house, giving a quick hug and kiss to Mrs. Kessler.

His phone rang, and he considered ignoring it, but curiosity rose up within him, and he checked the phone number on display. *Kelly.* Answering the phone, his gut clenched, knowing something was terribly wrong. Had someone gotten to her? It took him a couple of minutes to understand her through her blubbering tears. She was at the hospital. *The fucking hospital,* his mind screamed. Without hesitation, he started his bike and jammed the accelerator forward.

He never should've left her alone.

Chapter Ten

After being unhooked from a monitor to check the baby and a sonogram, Kelly slipped off the bed and quickly dressed when she'd been left alone. Finished, she sat in the chair beside it meant for a guest because she couldn't make herself get back on the mattress. Her hands shook. Ashley was okay. After what had happened following Brian's death and the risk to her baby, she was nearly ecstatic that things were well. However, her heart still fluttered in fear. She and her baby could've died. If Paul hadn't been there.... She wouldn't allow her mind to go there.

"Here's your paperwork, Miss Williams," the kindly nurse who'd been helping her said, as she reentered the room.

Being thankful they weren't going to choke her arm again with the blood pressure cuff or worse, she sat and listened to the instructions. Her muscles already began to ache, and she wanted to get the prescriptions the doctor promised her were safe for her to take while pregnant.

After being released, Kelly told them she was waiting for a ride, so they allowed her use of the room for a few more moments. As soon as the nurse left, her bladder sent her to the restroom again.

When she'd spoken with him, Trent had not been happy. No way would she tell him that she thought it might be intentional. She had a hard time wrapping her head around that because there was no reason someone would kill her. They had everything of Brian's, except for the baby. No. That was stupid. Maybe it was an accident like it appeared. Just because she liked to find conspiracy theories didn't mean one existed in everyday life.

After taking care of business, she blew her stuffy nose that had clogged with too much crying when she told Trent she needed a ride. Leaning forward, her hands on the edges of the porcelain basin, she took in her puffy eyes and red nose. She'd been so concerned for her baby that she'd turned into a blubbering mess with the doctor first. The man probably thought she'd lost her mind. Then again, he'd seen plenty of pregnant women, and Kelly imagined they'd freak out too if they'd been hit by a car and then passed out. The doctor had described it as a "tap." He wasn't even freaking there, but he'd downplayed her hysteria. *Men.*

A pounding sounded on the door, startling her. Turning around, her hand over her rapidly beating heart, she heard, "Kelly, get out here so I can see you."

Excitement bubbled up. He'd come. She knew he would since she'd pleaded with him about not having a ride, but still, he'd come. She wrenched open the door. "Trent."

"Come here." He stood right outside the bathroom doorway, in her hospital room.

With no shame, she threw herself at him. She wrapped her arms tightly around his waist. Dropping her head to his shoulder, she cried...again. How could she have not cried herself out already? It was plain ridiculous that she'd cried with Trent, yet she couldn't stop the flow of tears. Relief at having the man she loved there for her did wonders for her nerves.

"Shh…it's okay. I've got you." His low voice, the rumbling in his chest, soothed her weary emotional bank.

He kissed her temple, and her pulse rate increased, sending warmth flooding her body.

"You"—she sniffed—"you ca–came." As if by magic, saying the words—mangled as they'd been—began to clear her head and right her emotional purge of tears. Pulling back from him, she sniffed again. "I'm sorry. I'm a mess." Stepping backward, out of his arms, she went into the bathroom to pull some tissues from the dispenser and without embarrassment, blew her nose.

With his arms folded over his chest, Trent eyed her up and down, making her feel like he was doing his own exam. "Are you okay?" he asked softly.

"I'm just bruised. The doctor says I'll be sore on my right thigh and hip for a bit."

"And the baby? Is she okay?"

"She's okay." *Thank God.*

"Are you ready to tell me what happened?"

With a heavily burdened sigh, she asked, "Can we just go home and talk about this later?" She almost felt the juvenile need to cross her fingers behind her back to ensure he'd agree to leave it for now and just take her back to where she felt safe. Although, after the break-in, she truly didn't feel as safe as she had before.

"I've got my bike." With his thumb, he pointed to where she knew the parking lot resided. "Are you up for it? If not, I'll get us some wheels."

Hands firmly on her hips, Kelly narrowed her eyes.

"You will not *get* us some wheels, Trent McKenzie. I'll ride, and if I couldn't, we'd get them legit."

With a look of feigned innocence, Trent put his hands up as if in surrender. "Did you think I'd steal them?"

"I think based on the look in your eyes when you saw me, that you would."

"For you, I'd do anything."

If only that anything meant you loved me like I've always loved you.

Chapter Eleven

Planning to carry her out, Trent had backed off when Kelly got agitated about how they'd leave the hospital. Concern already swam through his system at her being hit—even if it had been just a glancing blow—but he couldn't fix it, and that tore at him. Hell, he'd had a hard time with the hospital not keeping her overnight. She was pregnant for fuck's sake. They couldn't go so lightly on her care.

Bundled up, she had demanded he take her home so she could have a hot bath—which she had. He'd run the damn thing—with all her cherry-scented bubble bath—to ensure she didn't have to do anything that might make her feel any pain or discomfort. He'd even lit candles because he knew women dug that kind of shit when they relaxed. Almost chuckling now, he guessed offering to undress her and place her in the tub might've gone too far.

Considering the fact he wanted to hold and love her, it'd been the right idea, just the wrong time.

While she soaked, he'd opened the file Em had given him. Brian's father owned a huge stretch of land in Montana. Nine thousand six hundred acres worth close to nine million dollars, if he chose to sell.

Kelly had shared that Brian had been in Baltimore on business. At their ranch, they bred horses, which could be why Brian had been in town. They offered a few sportsman vacation packages so he could've been lining up more business. Trent wished he knew. Even though he hated to admit it, Kelly being almost run down, like Brian, firmed in his mind that Brian's death wasn't an accident. Neither was Kelly getting hit accidentally.

He needed to decide what to do about her safety. Figure out what he could do about the situation.

After resting, she'd corralled him into catching a cab with her and going to Babies R Us. She'd wanted to go before she got too stiff and the pain sunk in deeply. He hadn't been keen on her leaving the house at all, but he had to trust her knowing her body. He'd watch out for the threats while they put together her gift registry for an upcoming baby shower the women she worked with planned to throw for her. The concept of wedding registries had reached him, but he had no idea they did this for babies. Probably a smart idea to keep from getting two cribs or some shit like that.

"So," the retail worker told them, handing Kelly a handheld scanner, "it's all set up. You just scan the item you want and scan it again if you want more than one. If it's something you want in abundance, such as ten onesies, just let me know, and I'll fix it for you."

Trent didn't know what the fuck a onesie was or why a baby would need ten, but Kelly smiled and nodded so it must be something normal. If he planned to help Kelly—and he did—he'd best get spun up on this shit.

When the retail assistant left them alone, Kelly turned and winced.

He rushed to her side and touched her arm. "Kelly, are you truly okay?"

With what appeared to be feigned nonchalance, she waved her hand as if that was supposed to indicate everything was okay. It was not fucking okay. She'd almost been run down by someone brave enough to swipe her in a government parking lot. Thank the fuck that corrections officer had been there to grab her.

With a reminder to call security at the courthouse, Trent had to get the security footage to see if they could identify the asshole driver. Without Devon to do the techie stuff, and Jesse to pave the golden way, he wasn't holding his breath on getting to see it without a fight. Maybe if he used his "father." *No. It'll be a cold day in hell before I ask Blake Hamilton for anything.*

"Oh my God," Kelly said. "Look how adorable."

Even his insides did a little flip. He accepted the tiny shoes from her. Was a baby really that tiny? Awe struck him hard. In his mind, he saw Kelly holding an infant this small and looking glorious. He gulped at the warmth flowing through his body.

Breaking into his vision, she scanned the tag on the little white shoes. "Ashley must have a pair of those. Although I know they won't fit her for long," she rambled on, and he still stood holding the tiny footwear. The kid didn't walk anywhere at that age. Why shoes?

Sure he'd never figure out merchandizing, he shrugged, sat them back on the shelf and moved over to little outfits with snaps on them. Looking at the label, he almost laughed. So this was a onesie. Still, why did a kid need ten? He picked up one with pink flowers on it. "Don't you need some of these?" he asked, then jokingly added, "Ten maybe."

With a bright smile, she came to his side and scanned it. "This one is so cute."

Pride swelled in him that she'd approved of his choice. That made him want to dig more. To do more for her and Ashley. This would be the best damn baby shower ever. He'd make sure of it.

After scanning more than ten of those onesie things, they moved on to diaper bags. Who knew they were so large? What kind of crap did a baby need? Boy, he was out of his element on this, and he knew it. But, he'd find his way. For Kelly.

Kelly held up two bags and looked at him quizzically. "What do you think? This one"—she lifted a smaller paisley-looking one—"is the size I'd like. But, this one"—she lifted a large one with pink bottles, rattles, and ribbons on it—"can carry everything."

How the fuck should he know the answer to this question? He should've called Megan to come help with this. She'd just had a baby. She'd know what to get.

"Trent?" Kelly raised her eyebrows expectantly.

"Well," he said, stalling until he found an answer. It seemed obvious she preferred the smaller one but would need the bigger one to carry all the crap she'd just scanned. "Um, why can't you add both? Maybe only one will be bought and your choice is made."

So they went, picking up impossibly small things or things needed by the baby. Didn't she only need food and someone to clean her little butt? He doubted the baby would care what color receiving blanket was used.

After what seemed like forever of Kelly playing with strollers, she called to him, "Come on, Trent. Tell me what you think?"

He touched the stroller and shook his head. "It's good."

"No, push it and tell me what you think?"

She truly expected him to push an empty stroller in a store. The woman had lost her damn mind. Despite that, he stood behind the stroller and pushed it to the end of the aisle to please her. A welcoming pang sounded in his heart at the thought of pushing Ashley around in it. "Like I said, good."

With laughter, she told him, "Okay, I get it. We're almost done. I have a few more things."

Still holding the handles of the stroller, he looked at her. Finally settled, he said what had been prominent in his mind—hoping it wouldn't hurt her feelings. He really needed to know. Some inane need to protect her stirred his blood. And that protection was also from heartache, which he'd failed miserably at by not being here when her fiancé had died. "What are you going to do about the baby?"

She rested her other hand on her belly and rubbed it. "Have it, of course." She chuckled before moving over to car seats.

Following her, he clarified, "No, I mean without her father." In his mind's eye, he saw Kelly walking along with a miniature of her, except the child's hair was auburn-colored, like Kelly's natural color. Yet, in the picture in his head, Kelly's hair was blonde, so he'd come to think of her this way. Maybe it just didn't matter.

"I'll make do. Many single mothers do." She tested several car seats for weight before he continued.

It almost broke his heart to ask, but he had to know. "You loved him that much?"

"What do you mean?" she asked nervously, then handed him a seat. "What about this one?"

Damn, he was hitting a nerve, but there'd never been any barriers between them before, he'd be damned if he'd create them now. He reached for the seat and held it. Like he was supposed to know if it was good or not. Bouncing it up and down a bit like she had, he stated, "I mean that you loved him and that no other man will do."

Accepting the car seat, she settled it back on the shelf and scanned it. "I loved him…enough." Her voice was laced with hesitancy. "We only have cribs left, not that I expect someone at the office to purchase me one."

He really had to know. Something didn't seem right. She'd always searched for her "Mr. Right." Whatever the hell that meant. Wouldn't settle for less. He knew because he'd listened to her with each breakup. "Enough?" he asked, following her from crib to crib while she ran her hands over each one.

She leaned over a white crib, and in a low voice answered him. "Okay, so I wasn't *in* love with him, but I had enough love and respect for Brian that we would've been very happy."

A Mr. Right-Now. Something wasn't right. Had the man lured her to bed and she felt she had to marry him? Being pregnant might do that. "If you weren't in love with him, why? Why not wait for that perfect guy you always hoped for?"

She raised and lowered a side rail on a walnut crib and then sighed heavily. "I got tired of waiting."

His arms resting on top of the raised rail on the opposite side of the crib, he took a moment before responding. "Sometimes it takes longer to find him."

She shook her head and moved to the next crib. The rich mahogany finish caught his attention. He ran his hands lovingly over it. This was the crib for Ashley. He knew it.

"No, I found him all right." The irony in her voice fueled his curiosity.

"And?" he prompted.

"He's not in love with me." Sadness wove its way through her statement, and it hit his heart with the power of a sledgehammer.

"Tell me who it is, and I'll have a talk with him." The man would be a fool to pass up someone as precious as Kelly. She was smart, funny, beautiful, and damn good at her job.

At first, he thought she wouldn't tell him, then she fired, "It's you, Trent," at him, knocking him mentally off-balance. "I got tired of waiting for you to notice me as anything other than a friend."

A sucker punch to the gut would've felt better. What the hell was he to do with her statement? The fact she'd been waiting made him sick to think she'd passed up so many possible good men. *I loved him...enough.* Her voice rang in his mind. "Kelly—" He cleared his throat to start again, even though he had no idea what to say.

Holding up a hand to stop his flow of words, she said, "No. It's okay. I like that you're still my best friend." With that, she scanned the tag on the crib. "We're done."

What the fuck did he do now?

Chapter Twelve

An uncomfortable vibe bled into the remainder of their evening. With the shopping trip ended, they returned to Kelly's apartment. She didn't even balk when he'd said he was sleeping on her couch again.

Lying on the gray cloth-covered piece, with his hands folded together behind his head, he put his mind to work since it refused to allow him to slumber. Keeping her in his sights from here on out would not be easy. Keeping his suspicions from her for long would be difficult. She could read him like no other. That was because—

What in the hell was he supposed to do with her bold statement that she was in love with him? *I love her like my best friend, but I'm not in love with her.* He had no idea what in love meant. Could he actually be? He felt protective of her, wanted to be around her, wanted to take her to bed and love the hell out of her—even pregnant, and he thought of her when he had something to share, and he thought of her every day he'd been gone. *Ah, hell.* He felt something deeper for her than just love. But, in love?

"Trent," Kelly whispered as she quietly entered the living room. "Are you awake?"

Rolling to his side, pushing against the couch so his back was hidden from sight, he propped himself up on an elbow while tugging the sheet to cover his bare chest. Forgetting his overnight bag at his apartment, he hadn't had anything to sleep in, except his underwear. He'd have been damned if he'd have gone home to pick it up only to come back to a possible locked door.

He answered, but only after soaking in the sight of her in flannel pajama pants and a long-sleeved T-shirt. "Yeah, I'm awake." His voice sounded gravelly—like he'd just woken—even to his ears. Clearing his throat, he watched her gingerly sit in a chair across from the couch. "What's up? Are you okay?" Panic suddenly flooded him. Oh God, was she hurt worse than they'd thought? The baby? His stomach plummeted at the thought and rolled into a nasty ball of stress.

"I'm fine. We're fine," she said, putting his mind at ease. At least on that front.

"What's going on?"

"I wanted to talk with you about what I said earlier."

It was difficult, but he held back the groan of frustration that roared within to escape. He still didn't have a response for her. Nor did he think he would since his mind couldn't deal with that type of personal shit when her life might be in danger.

"I'm sorry I threw that out there. It wasn't fair."

No, it fucking wasn't, but she'd done it anyway.

"I understand you don't feel the same, and that's okay." She paused. "It has been for a long time. That's why I was going to marry Brian. I did love him, you know."

Shards of jealousy shot through his veins. He had to stop that. Brian was dead.

"Kelly," he began then stopped. What could he say? He may have been a bit of a ladies' man, but being good with conversations like this had always been AJ's forte. His charm had been his smile.

"It really is okay. I just don't want anything to change between us."

"Marry me," he blurted out, even to his own surprise. *What the hell did I just say?*

Staring at him, with her wide-eyed gaze, Kelly shook her head. "No, Trent."

At that moment, he got it, and his mind went on a roll. "No, listen. It makes sense. You're pregnant and alone. A husband would be good for you and the baby. A baby should have a father growing up." He stopped, and his father came to mind. The man who'd lied all those years to protect him. "Not that she wouldn't know about Brian, but someone to help you raise her." He drew in a deep breath and continued, firm in his decision. "We get along great. It all makes sense. Let me be there to help you."

Tears glistened in her eyes before one slid down her cheek. Christ, his proposal had made her cry. He hadn't planned to propose, and it hadn't been eloquent, but he hadn't wanted to make her cry because of it. Needing to fix it, he quickly scrambled off the couch, donned a T-shirt, moved to her, and dropped to one knee in front of her. "Marry me, Kelly."

"I can't, Trent. You don't love me, and you'll come to regret our marriage. I won't live out my years with you being unhappy."

Reaching up, he wiped away the tears on her cheek with his thumb. "I'd never be unhappy with you, Kelly."

"The answer is still no. If you ever fall in love with me, then I'll change my mind, but until then, let's remain friends."

As she stood, so did he. They were close, and her lips looked so tantalizing in the light spilling in from the streetlamp. With his right hand, he cupped her cheek and leaned in, putting his lips to hers. Barely touching, heat soared up and raged through him.

All the reasons why he shouldn't have kissed her slipped his mind. In fact, his mind went MIA while he suckled on her lower lip until her arms came up to his chest. Even through his shirt, her hands drove him to want more. Her touch excited him more than he'd ever been turned on. One might argue, but deep inside, he knew it had nothing to do with him not having sex in five months. It was Kelly. Dear, wonderful, Kelly.

Needing more, he covered her lips fully and used his tongue to probe until she opened for him. Slipping his tongue inside her mouth, she welcomed it as he tasted her sweetness for the first time and knew he'd never tasted anyone so perfect for him. Her active participation sent him out of control, ramping up his need and eliciting a physical response from his dick.

Lips feasting on hers, he knew he had to stop before she noticed his tenting underwear. Reluctantly, he pulled back. With ragged breathing, she dropped her head to his shoulder, and he stood still. Uncomfortable, but still. What he wanted to do was grab her and take her to her bedroom, remove her clothes and taste her essence, make her come, and please her like she'd never been pleasured before.

"Now will you marry me?" he said hoarsely.

She straightened, and he missed her leaning into him. Missed that feeling of rightness. "No, Trent. That kiss didn't change the fact that you're not in love with me." After separating herself from him, she steered to her bedroom. "Good night."

Standing there like an idiot—one with a semi—he could do nothing but gawk at her retreating body. But his eyes dropped to her luscious ass as it swayed with each step.

You should be happy she said no. You don't really know what you want with your life, and you definitely don't want to get married. She'd have to see you without your shirt and then she'd never have sex with you.

Coming to his senses, he trudged over to the couch and plopped down. He'd really asked her to marry him. Had he taken leave of his senses? Thank goodness she'd had the smarts to say no.

A sudden jab to the heart hit him. What the hell was wrong with him? Besides having half-wood and wanting his best friend who only wanted him if he was in love with her? Almost laughing out loud, he thought about all his other problems and could imagine Jamie just shaking her head at him for this one.

Kelly said no. So no it was.

Unexpectedly, disappointment settled deep in his heart.

Ripping the covers aside, he lay down, and this time, he fell asleep quickly.

Trent woke to the tantalizing scent of coffee and immediately reached to his chest to ensure he was covered. Kelly would probably accept his scars, but he wasn't ready to show anyone, even her. Just like he'd like to see her pussy, but she wasn't apt to show him so he could drive deep inside. *Shit.* He couldn't think like that.

How she would act, after their kiss, was something he'd thought about, but came to no conclusion. Would she act like nothing happened? Be angry at him? Fall all over herself at him? He laughed at the last one and must've caught her attention, because he heard, "About time you rolled out of bed, sleepy head."

After reaching for his watch, he jumped up at seeing the time. *Damn.* Then he went to rip his covers off. *Shit. Morning wood.* Grabbing his jeans, he quickly shoved his legs in and pulled them up, stuffing himself in just in time for her to come into the room with two cups of coffee.

Accepting a mug from her, he thought while he first blew on it, then sipped. Protecting Kelly was important. Critical. Everything. He wanted to stay close to her and had to do it without her realizing why.

"What's your plan for the day?" he asked nonchalantly.

She frowned. "I have to go to work."

Surprised that she'd go back so soon, he blurted out, "But you were almost killed yesterday."

With a shake of her head, she sighed before she sat in a chair. "Don't be so melodramatic. I barely received a scratch."

Grumbling, he sat to put himself at her level. "I at least need to take you to your car." He'd just follow her to work from there. Hoping she'd stay safe at the newsroom, he said, "I'll be by tonight, and we can go to dinner." Meaning that he'd be there when she left work because he didn't want her to be vulnerable.

"Trent, you don't need to do that."

"Why wouldn't I? We've always gone out to eat together on Thursday night." That excuse had popped into his head, and thankfully it had because it didn't allow her to argue without seeming as if she was putting a wedge in their friendship.

His kiss had already placed that divide. Repairing any breach in their relationship was his goal. Kelly belonged in his life, even if she married someone else. He almost doubled over with the pain that lanced through him at the thought. Damn. It'd only been a kiss. A fucking mind-blowing one, but still, just a kiss.

"Okay, but no more proposing," she said firmly.

"No more proposing," he agreed. Something inside him broke, and he knew he had a lot to work through before it could happen, but he had to have her and the baby as his. Under his breath, he added, "For now."

Chapter Thirteen

The next evening, Kelly strolled beside Trent wondering why he'd followed her to and from work. Maybe he thought she wouldn't notice, but his big, noisy Harley stood out. It did to her, but she also looked for him every time she noticed a motorcycle. There was probably a psychological term for that, but she never felt being a bit obsessive about the man she loved was a bad thing.

But his following her, while any other time she'd have been overjoyed, today, she worried. She couldn't decide if he thought she was in danger, which drove her nerves into a frenzy and had made her jumpy, or if it was some possessive thing after the haphazard proposal, that she'd oh-so-wanted to accept. And her reasoning for declining made her the world's biggest hypocrite, and she was damn lucky Trent hadn't called her on it. He probably hadn't realized it at the time, like she hadn't.

She hadn't been in love with Brian and had been willing to marry him, yet, she'd demanded Trent not only love her, but be in love with her before she'd marry him. She wanted to bury her face in her hands at the absurdity of her requirement to wed the man she loved with all her heart.

Why? she wanted to cry out. Why couldn't she have gotten it together and just said yes? It was what she'd wanted for longer than she liked to remember.

Yet, she'd held back with Trent, and he probably held as much love for her as she did for Brian. She just wanted him to be in love with her like she was with him. It was stupid compared to her past decision about marriage, but it was what her mind and heart chose for her reality.

Plus, there was Jamie. Had he rebounded so quickly or was she a poor substitute?

And that kiss….

It didn't matter because he hadn't really meant it. She'd noticed his surprise when he'd asked her. As if it had occurred by accident. It hadn't been a thought-out decision, so she knew he'd regret it when he considered the ramifications of marrying her. Heck, the kiss had probably been a fluke, spur of the moment. He hadn't tried to kiss her again this morning, so it couldn't have been that good for him.

A small sigh escaped past her lips. A life with Trent was her heart's desire. Having little boys and girls that belonged to the two of them filled her romantic fantasies. And saying no to his proposal had squashed that fantasy.

"Are you okay?" Trent slid his gloved hand into hers.

The touch, even through the material of their combined gloves, sent a jolt of electricity through her, leaving behind a tantalizing tingle that awakened her senses.

When she made to pull away, he held tight. "Don't make it awkward, Kelly. I held your hand before the kiss." He squeezed her palm. "Now, I heard that sigh. Are you okay?"

True, they'd walked hand-in-hand before, but that proposal and kiss had changed so much. At least it had with her. He appeared unaffected, almost destroying the hope she'd always carried for them. She couldn't blame him because she was the one who'd crushed all hope by saying no.

He briefly squeezed her hand again, reminding her of his question. As for his asking if she was okay, the question was too open-ended. Okay about what? Being a single mother? Being in love with someone who didn't love her back? Being a hypocrite about marriage? Almost getting run down by a car? Just life in general? Deciding it best to lie instead of getting into a debate on the sidewalk or making things any more tense than they were, she turned to him and smiled. "I'm fine."

After a right turn onto Thames Street, Trent laughed, and joy flooded her. She feared he'd never laugh this heartily again, or at least for a long time, after all he'd gone through—the family thing, the bombing and losing the love of his life to cancer—and how hard he'd taken it. That alone made the sound the most beautiful she'd ever heard. "I know what fine means." Before her temper could rise, he asked, "John Steven's tonight?"

Of course he'd picked her favorite restaurant. "Fine," she answered with purposeful irritation. *He thinks he's such a smarty-pants. Let him figure that fine out.* She almost laughed out loud at the juvenileness of it.

"Touché." He dropped her hand and opened the door to the restaurant. With the crowd, she wondered about their getting a table until she realized he'd made a reservation. What if she'd said no? She almost shook her head. That wouldn't have happened. Damn if he didn't know her too well.

They were seated, and the waiter seemed put out they ordered nonalcoholic drinks. Maybe the man hadn't seen her belly. With his being close to seven feet tall, he probably didn't see past her swollen breasts.

Drinks delivered and food ordered, Kelly decided it best to go on the offensive and keep all talk away from the two of them or of her and Brian. "When are you going to tell me about your being a Hamilton?"

"Don't call me that."

"According to Megan—who told me and not you," she accused, "you are actually Senator Hamilton's son. Odd how that has stayed secret with a growing number of people who know." She chuckled at the absurdity of it. "Including two journalists." Their love and respect for the Hamilton family kept her and Megan from exploiting them. *Sometime soon, though*, she worried, *someone outside this family will.*

"That's what I want splashed across the papers—Trent McKenzie, illegitimate child of Senator Blake Hamilton." Shaking his head, he added, "Being a bastard child in private is bad enough."

"Trent," she whispered, not knowing what to say. He hadn't reacted like she'd thought. Why wouldn't he be happy since he loved that family so much?

"Part of why I left was because my brothers smothered me in welcoming me to the family, but mostly though, it was because of *him*. He wanted to get to know me better. Like I needed a new father just because mine was dead." Anger radiated off him in waves, and she almost had to sit back at the potency of it.

Since the subject of Blake garnered such hostility, she went back to what should be a good thing because they'd been buddies since they were small. "How are things with your brothers?"

He shrugged one shoulder and took a sip of his ginger ale. Setting the glass back on the table, he looked up and smiled. "Okay. At the hospital, I thought I'd strangle them. Since I've returned, they don't act any differently than before we found out. Jamie assured me they wouldn't, but I didn't believe her."

She wanted to scream. Of course Jamie had been the one to soothe him. She'd been the one to obviously capture his heart. The heart Kelly had wanted since she'd first met him. A jealous rage attempted to overtake her. Instead, she took a breath and said, "Tell me what happened," and was surprised with how he'd changed the topic back to Senator Hamilton.

On what sounded to her like a soulful sigh, he spoke, "Blake and his wife were divorcing. I don't know why, but they were split. My mom was Blake's assistant." With a slight tremor, he took a sip of his beverage. He looked back at her after setting the glass down, more with a clunk over his unsteadiness. "I guess she must've been infatuated with him or something."

The waiter interrupted with their soup. Kelly dove into her Maryland crab bisque with gusto. Another thing she found herself craving. Thank goodness she didn't live too far away.

"Yeah, well, as his assistant, she was always around him. Short story is that they had an affair. He got her pregnant, and he went back to his wife."

"Oh, Trent." Reaching across the two-top table, she

pulled his hand from his drink and clasped it tightly.

He surprised her by jerking away. The same thing he'd forbid her to do earlier. Not holding tight enough, his hand slipped from her grasp, and he clasped his hands together in front of him. "Don't. Roger McKenzie was a good father. Plus, I think my parents were in love."

A thought struck her. "Is that why you grew up on the grounds of the Hamilton mansion?"

He nodded. "It makes sense now. At the time, I thought it was just to keep my mom close for whenever Blake wanted something."

"Mrs. Hamilton must've been one heck of a woman," she murmured but guessed Trent heard her when he nodded. "Do you think you'll ever call him Dad or Father?"

"No," he said vehemently.

Their food arrived, saving Kelly from responding. She had no idea what to say anyway. Finding out something like that about her family now would be devastating to her.

While savoring her twin filets, Kelly wondered what she could do to help Trent. He tried to hide it, but she knew him well, and he was hurting on the inside. Heck, they hadn't even talked about the accident that could've claimed his life. Swallowing, she thought, *I'm not sure I can tackle that subject. I almost died inside when I heard.*

Between bites, they chatted about the baby. He seemed genuinely interested. Of course, he'd always appeared genuinely interested in anything she told him.

Forgoing dessert at the restaurant, she dragged Trent with her to get ice cream, something he thought stupid for winter weather in Baltimore. She didn't care what he thought. Little Ashley wanted mint chocolate chip ice cream and she was going to get it. Almost giggling, she enjoyed how she could blame almost anything on the baby, which was allowed.

Since the temperature had dropped, the sidewalk was nearly deserted. "People are smart enough to be inside," Trent had told her.

"It's supposed to snow again." Trent reached for her hand, and she happily allowed it.

"Hmph. The weatherman said that last week." Although, Kelly had a feeling the current forecast would come to pass. Bad weather had been moving their way. She had a strategy this time when she and Trent got into an inevitable snowball fight.

A man stumbled toward them, and Trent's hand tightened, guiding her to drift closer to him. Maneuvering her to the other side of the sidewalk, Trent kept his eye on the man bundled in a torn khaki jacket. When the man weaved in their direction again, Kelly brushed him off as a drunken bum.

Trent reacted differently.

Yanked behind Trent, Kelly felt the impact of the two men connecting while she remained safely an arm's length away. Trent's hand slipped from hers and he dropped to one knee, doubled over a bit, and clutched his stomach with one hand while the other settled on the ground, steadying him.

Fear lanced through her system and set her nerves on edge. With wide eyes, Kelly froze as the man stepped near her. Thankfully, her feet took over, and she began backing away, keeping distance between them. Her heart beat so fast, she worried for the safety of her baby. Hell, she worried anyway. This ugly, menacing man had obviously hurt Trent, or he wouldn't be this close to her.

Her only option was to make a run for it. The man might catch her, but she had to try. After becoming pregnant, Kelly had given up running for walking, but she remembered how, and she used to be pretty fast. Of course, then she hadn't been carrying a small basketball in her stomach.

"Stay still, bitch. I'll make it quick," the man growled.

Unable to stop her shaking with terror, she realized running wouldn't work. His steely, determined glare told her he'd run her down. She'd learned Karate as self-defense, but it wasn't like she'd achieved her black belt or anything. She'd just learned the basics and never against an attacker so large or with a protruding belly of her own. The thought of Ashley had her realizing it had to be enough because running would only prolong the inevitable. So, she needed to stand and fight for her baby and for an obviously injured Trent.

Taking a calming breath to clear her mind and focus, she shifted her body to a ready stance. Then the man's eyes changed, and he stopped, then raised his hands, a knife gleaming in one of them. She could've sworn it had blood on it. Trent's? *Oh no.* That was why he'd doubled over.

Had her change in demeanor been enough to put that fear in his eyes? She'd heard she looked fierce in class, but this surprised the hell out of her.

"Drop it, asshole," Trent demanded, gruffly.

The man's hand opened, and the knife clattered to the sidewalk.

"Kelly, are you all right?" Trent's pain-laced voice reached her from behind the attacker.

Relief surged through her, and she wanted to run around the man and hug him, but she still had no desire to be near the man who'd tried to hurt them. "I'm fine. How about you?"

"No one told me you'd be carrying a gun." The man grunted.

"Who would've?" Trent peeked around the side of the man and winked at her. Her heart soared.

"I ain't saying a word."

"Trent, you didn't answer me." Kelly's stress level increased when he took the time to answer.

"I'll be fine. Call 911."

"Do you need an ambulance?"

"No." He chuckled. "It's just a scratch."

Scratch, my ass, she thought. He would never've taken so long to help her if it had been just a scratch.

"While we're waiting, I want to know who would've told you about us," Trent demanded.

"Fuck you," the man retorted.

Trent tsked. "I hope you enjoy jail. Trying to mug us and stabbing me."

"Stabbing!" Kelly couldn't help but screech. He'd said scratch. She'd known instinctively it was more than a simple scratch, but a stabbing brought to life a gaping wound in him. All the blood rushed from her head, and black spots swam before her eyes. "Trent." Her weak voice must've drawn him to her because before she lost consciousness, Trent had his arms around her, telling her, "I've got you, Kelly. Always."

Chapter Fourteen

With Kelly's condition to consider, Trent had informed her that two rides on the back of his bike had been the extent of risk he'd go with her and the baby. Since his nerves couldn't take another ride, she'd driven her car to headquarters, and the entire trip had him wound up inside, feeling trapped in a metal box. It'd been too long since he'd taken a long trip in a car. Since he thought of one day becoming a family man, he needed to get more comfortable with something on four wheels, and he didn't mean any newfangled bikes on four wheels. Before he'd considered purchasing a truck because riding his bike in shitty weather held no appeal, but with a baby on the way, a car seemed more suitable. They'd at least have Kelly's for a while. That was…once she agreed to marry him.

That revelation blasted him after the incident with the knife. Thinking he could have lost her or the baby had wrung his insides out. It was then that he knew he'd been right to ask her to marry him. *Your back,* his conscience pricked, and he ignored it. Then it whispered, *Les*, and his heart nearly stopped.

Outside Jesse's home, he told Kelly to go ahead of him. With extreme concern in her eyes, she obeyed. That left him pacing in circles outside the residence wondering what the hell he was doing with Kelly. He'd decided it was right and then—How could he grab onto what would surely be extreme happiness? It wouldn't be fair. Jamie's words kept reminding him that he did deserve to live a full life even though Les had lost his. Death was a fucked up possibility of the job. Not a normal occurrence by any means, but a possibility. They should've found another way. But deep inside, he knew that if they'd wanted to save Amber, no other way guaranteed that outcome. If they'd shot the terrorist, the bomb could've exploded, killing them all. If he hadn't done what he'd done to protect his niece, she never would've made it.

When a fine sheen of sweat formed on his skin— out in the fucking cold—he stopped and took those damn breaths Jamie had ordered. They definitely worked, and he wished he'd remember to take them from the beginning of a mental explosion like that.

Having had enough, he slammed the door closed on his problems. He had to take care of Kelly. His shit could wait. Sure, he had a hard time fighting those demons, and they arose when he needed them least, but he had to overcome them.

Finally, when a calm rested inside him, allowing him to focus on Kelly and the trouble she had, not on what he'd lost, he moved toward headquarters, and that step brought him closer to a free life.

The walk beside AJ into the war room reminded Trent of old times after they'd just joined HIS. He'd been a team member and AJ had been a full-fledged partner. *They offered you a partnership.* Of course, they'd only asked him to be one out of pity. Hamilton blood may run through his veins, but he was not a Hamilton, and HIS was a Hamilton family business. That didn't mean he wouldn't exploit what he could to get what he needed for Kelly's safety.

Before, he'd been invited to attend meetings between the brothers to decide which cases to take and plan. After learning of their familial relations, they wanted him to believe himself equal to them. He'd balked and left the entire conversation open when he'd hit the road. Being back and needing them, he'd definitely sit at the big boy table, and they would listen.

Flipping the light switches, he glanced up and noticed the small, wet spot on AJ's shoulder. With the unpleasant odor that floated to his nostrils, he knew the residue had to be Alex's spit up, and a light chuckle escaped him. Picturing AJ as a father a year ago had been an impossible task. They'd been hangout partners at the bars from time to time over the years. If he hadn't seen AJ hold Alex a few moments ago, Trent would still struggle with the image.

Then he thought, *Ashley won't be much younger than Alex*. Only about six months would separate them. Considering how close Megan and Kelly were, the two would grow up together, which meant poor Alex. With the Hamilton men adding wives, there would be a lot of women fussing over him, and if Trent had to guess, one little girl toddling after him. Ashley.

"Thanks for bringing Megan to visit with Kelly while we meet. I didn't want to leave her alone." Still reeling from the prior night's events, Kelly hadn't argued when Trent refused to allow her to remain alone. She'd tried to remain strong, but he'd noticed the trembling as she changed his bandages from the stabbing that morning. Mothering came naturally to her, and he loved the attention. Now that he knew she loved him, he noticed how that love seeped through in everything she did for him.

Em had told him before that Kelly was in love with him, but he'd never believed it. He'd just been friends with her, kind of like with Em, except he and Em shared their growing up years, many with the two of them watching the Hamilton boys from the sidelines or bushes, as Em would be apt to do.

Following behind her, and keeping her out of trouble, had become a job in itself. One day, he'd asked his mom if since she had been an assistant to the senator, would he have to be an assistant to Em since she needed him to keep her out of trouble?

At twelve years old, he'd been completely serious, but it'd only earned him a laugh from his mother. The discussion that had followed, and the push for him to stay away from Em, should've been another indicator that he and Em were siblings. But, what did a twelve-year-old truly understand?

AJ pulled him back from the memory. "Once Kelly called in sick, my wife did the same. She'd already insisted I take her to see Kelly. She was worried it might be the baby and wanted to comfort her however she could."

Pain lanced through his gut and it wasn't from the knife wound. It fucking could've been the baby. Luckily, she'd regained consciousness as the ambulance arrived and all had checked out fine at the hospital. God, another trip to the hospital for her. Him too, but he'd been more worried about her fainting than his injury. All he could think about was that it could've been Kelly with the knife to her pregnant belly.

Matt walked into the room, pulled out his cell phone, then punched in a number—obviously speed dial—before activating the speaker function and setting it on the conference table.

The men huddled around as it rang twice before Jesse answered.

"Is something wrong with my kids?" Extreme concern wove around his words.

Matt cleared his throat. "As far as I know, they're fine."

"Then what the fuck?" Jesse's roar sounded less severe with that just-woke-up raspy voice. "Why are you bothering me at six o'-fucking-clock in the morning? This shit had best be good."

Of course it was good. It involved Kelly's safety. No way would he allow his older brother to get to him. Belize being in Central Time Zone had slipped Trent's mind. *What the fuck?* he also said, just not aloud. Jesse and the men were usually up that early.

"Have you turned into some kind of princess who sleeps the morning away?" AJ teased.

"Fuck you. No, we didn't get them out of jail until a couple of hours ago."

Tied up with thoughts of protecting Kelly, Trent had nearly forgotten the reason Jesse had to travel to Belize. It took them a long time to get the men—and Rylee—out of jail. He wanted to know what the hell had happened, but he needed the focus to remain on Kelly. So, he didn't ask.

"Now, what the fuck do you want?" Squeaking sounded, like the springs of a mattress, as if Jesse, or Kate, moved around. Hopefully, it meant he was getting his ass up.

Before Trent could speak, AJ laughed. "Our new brother"—he gestured to Trent with a finger and a head nod even though Jesse couldn't see it—"decided he hadn't had enough injuries, so he got himself sliced and stitched last night."

"I take it he's okay."

"I'm fine," Trent gritted out. He didn't want this to be about him.

"Hang on, let me get Brad," Jesse said.

Trent scowled at AJ while they waited and waited and waited. Pacing, he heard Kate murmur something before a door clicked closed. After a knock, a door opened. His blood pressure raged at the delay. Didn't they understand how important this was? Kelly was in trouble.

Then the telephone receiver had been covered, or mute enabled because it was too quiet.

He'd been about to say, "fuck it," and hang up and do this without them when Brad's surly voice came across the line. "Trent, you're going down in the world if you go from a bullet wound to bomb blast to piddly-ass knife slice, and then call for our help."

Son of a bitch! If he didn't need these men, he'd flip them the bird and take Kelly far away from it all. His bullet wound—that he'd earned protecting Megan—happened before he'd become a team member with HIS. Thinking back, he'd not been ready to open his own security business. After losing his partner on that protection detail, joining the men he'd grown up with had been a wise career move. The only one at the time since they'd ended up saving Megan while he'd convalesced.

Unable to keep completely silent about the insult, he grumbled, "It wasn't small." It'd been said not as much to argue with Brad, but because Trent didn't want to think about the blast and how it had ruined his back. A meddlesome voice crept into this head and blurted, *Maybe that's why Kelly said no.* He had to believe that she wouldn't be like that.

If only that voice of self-doubt would disappear.

"We're ready," Jesse stated.

With all sides of the conversation quiet, Trent remained still and outlined what had happened the prior evening to include his receiving twelve stitches, since Brad wouldn't let that fucking detail go. Sure it had hurt—still pained him—but not enough to cry to the men about. It didn't prevent him from doing anything, except maybe sex and heavy lifting. But when would he be doing either of those? Not in the near future. Although when he couldn't sleep the night before, he'd been thinking of sex with Kelly. Kissing her from head to toe stood high on his list of things to do.

Jesse broke into his derailed thoughts. "Is Kelly okay?"

Leaning forward, hands on the table, Trent dropped his head in relief. "Yes."

"It's good you were carrying. Did they give you any shit?" Jesse probed.

Of course the Baltimore PD officers did, and Jesse well knew they would've. Sometimes he thought his oldest brother asked questions, just to hear himself speak. "No. I had my license with me." He'd never been more thankful for that little piece of paper because, after the break-in, he'd refused to go unarmed around Kelly. She needed his protection.

"What's going on?" Devon's sleepy voice sounded on the other end of the phone.

Hell, the men in Belize couldn't just pack up and

come back to help him. They had a job to do. Maybe, since Rylee was free, Devon might be on the ball with information gathering.

"How are things there?" Trent thought if they could capture their target fast, they could get back just as fast.

"Your dipshit of a brother royally pissed off the local police," Jesse said in a rather pissed off voice of his own.

Fucking Brad. Wait, he couldn't discount it being Devon considering Rylee was involved. Before he could contemplate that or ask a question, it hit him that none of them calling him brother, or he calling them that in his mind, had affected him. Yet, he still didn't want to be a Hamilton. He wanted to be a McKenzie.

"Let's get back to you," Brad directed. "Are you sure it wasn't just a mugger?"

He shook his head and frowned. "No question in my mind. That fucker was after Kelly." Pushing his hands deep in his pockets, he grimaced. "He just tried to incapacitate me while he went after her."

Pulling out a chair to sit, Matt waved them down to empty chairs. "Do you think he planned to kill her or just hurt her? What if he planned to kidnap her or something?"

AJ poured himself a cup of coffee, then plopped in a chair on Matt's other side.

His pulse ratcheted up at what he'd heard. "The asshole said he'd make it quick. With the thefts and break-in, something is definitely going on. She needs protection. Round the clock."

Matt toyed with his cup "Do you even know what this is all about?"

Frustrated, he finally sat with the men instead of hovering. Matt's unflappable ability to remain calm, in any situation, must've served him well as a Navy SEAL. "I got nothing from the guy last night, so I'm not certain. It could be a story she's written, or writing. She's trying to help a convict who claims to be set up, but—" He paused and sighed. "—my gut tells me it has to do with her dead fiancé."

Yawning, Matt stretched his arms over his head. Dropping his forearms to the table, he pulled his lips in tight. "Seems awfully coincidental. His death and then everything else." He nodded. "I'd have to agree it has something to do with him."

"So do I," Jesse, almost forgotten, said from the phone.

AJ sipped his coffee. "What was he into? I thought he was a rancher."

Trent nodded. "Horse breeder mostly, but they have cattle too." The background Em had pulled had been pretty thorough on the business, which had surprised him. His little sister had her shit together. They'd always underestimated her talents.

"He is," Kelly's voice interjected from the doorway. The men stood, out of respect and ingrained manners, as she, Megan, and Em walked into the room. "But, they also started some type of vacation retreat for sportsmen recently."

"You know, Trent," Devon said, "I did some aerial of Brian's father's ranch. It's not a bad place to hide out until we can get back and help."

"We're not hiding out," Trent ground out. No way would he sit back and let everyone else solve this mystery around Kelly. He almost snorted out loud. Like she'd allow it to happen with her journalistic curiosity. Yet, part of him needed to see her hidden away with him protecting her so nothing could touch her—not even something as simple as worry. It was a goddamn dilemma he didn't relish solving. Now he knew why Jesse, AJ, Jake, and Devon had almost lost their shit protecting their now wives.

"That's exactly what I was going to say. Mike—Brian's father—has been after me to visit since he lost his oldest son." She swallowed hard, and he could've sworn a tear came to her eye.

His gut clenched at her sorrow, and he fought rushing over to hold her in his arms.

"It's time I go. Maybe he'll know something," she finished.

"Trent, spending time talking with Brian's father wouldn't be wasted. You can make it two-fold—investigate and keep her and that baby safe." Damn Jesse. He couldn't help always being the voice of reason.

With no other option but to agree, he grumbled, "Okay." Glancing over at Kelly, he caught her bright smile and knew her mind was on investigating. He'd just allowed her to get involved when he'd thought going to Montana was safe. Now, he'd have to make her understand that her job was to keep Ashley protected and to let him do his job. How the hell to convince her of that was the million-dollar question.

"Kelly," Jesse said, "you've got to let my brothers handle this. I know it's in your nature to dive in, but let them do this. You worry about that baby and know they'll protect you."

Thank the fuck for Jesse. She'd agree quicker with

Jesse than with him. He'd have to buy his brother a beer, or hell, even a case if she listens, for that one.

She sighed heavily. "Okay." Not looking okay with it, Trent almost smirked. He knew his girl. This could get interesting.

Jesse spoke again. "Matt, you've got the lead on this. Let us know if things get too hot for just the three of you. Jake and his team can't get there. They're bare-bones as it is."

"We'll make do," Matt said with confidence. "Devon, I need everything you have on this, ASAP." He turned to his sister. "Em, care to share what you've found?"

How did he lose control so damn fast? This was not happening. Not with Kelly's life.

"I'm taking point on this one," he said loudly enough to stop all side conversations on both ends of the phone call. His heart pounded loudly as he waited for the rebuttal that would surely come. He'd fight for this right. Although he didn't want it, he'd take the damn partnership if that was what it took to remain in the lead. Anything for Kelly and Ashley.

"All right," Jesse said.

Then all eyes in the room shifted to him, full of expectation. His mind reacted in fear until he pulled himself together to discuss how they'd protect Kelly.

Chapter Fifteen

Did Trent really think it was his idea to go to Montana? As she'd told Megan, Kelly had already decided she would be going. The trip would've been with or without him. She'd be safe at Brian's home. With Mike and the few ranch hands, she'd rarely find herself alone, if at all.

In Trent's infinite wisdom, he'd agreed with Devon that the place would be a good hideout while also finding out more about what Brian was involved in from his father. She'd rolled her eyes when he'd said that. Men were sometimes clueless.

After agreeing to let them do the investigating, a bitter taste still rested on her tongue. Well, she wouldn't push it, but she'd learn everything. One way or another. Truth be told, she didn't think Trent would keep anything from her. So, she'd put her trust in him.

Unlike her, who felt the many people on the ranch would be enough to watch over them, Trent corralled AJ and Matt into accompanying them. She'd guiltily smiled at Megan as they'd finished up the meeting for taking her husband away for an indefinite period. Well, the meeting the women were allowed to participate in. The men met again, on the sly. They thought they were so smart. They had no idea women were smarter.

With his brothers there, any privacy between the two of them went out the window. Not that she'd expected another kiss or anything, but the chances were going to be slim.

She'd wanted to be involved in the planning in any way she could so he'd allowed her to make the hotel reservations. Hoping for something bigger, she'd settled for that task anyway as she had to do something, plus it was her hometown.

When she hit a roadblock, she called Brian's father. "Hello, Mike. It's Kelly."

"Kelly, it's so good to hear from you. How's that grandbaby of mine doing?"

Chuckling, she answered, "She's as active as ever."

"She?"

"Yes." She placed her hand on her belly. "I'm naming her Ashley."

A moment of silence ensued. "After my late wife." Mike's choked-up voice brought a mist to Kelly's eyes. That had been Brian's wish, and she couldn't back out of it. It'd meant too much to him. And by the emotion in Mike's voice, it meant that much to him also.

"Yes," she said softly.

"She would've loved that."

Clearing her throat to dispel the sadness welling within, Kelly said, "Mike, I'm coming to visit and am trying to book accommodations, but I can't find a working number of the historic hotel downtown?"

"It closed, but you don't need a hotel. You can stay here."

"Well—" She swallowed nervously. "I'm bringing a few…friends."

Pause. "I see. And will these friends need their own rooms?"

Had she been that transparent that he'd realized at

least one was a he? "Yes."

"Then, you'll stay here."

After a bit more discussion, Kelly ended the call, a bit exhausted by her worry about what Mike would think when she brought the Hamiltons with her. She'd promised not to mention why they were visiting and that ate at her. Trent said he'd tell Mike when they arrived, but she'd wanted Brian's father to be prepared.

Mike had pushed her to contact her folks, but she still didn't know how to explain, even though she knew she'd have to. What would she say to them? She'd be a disappointment to them. Plain and simple.

Even if she stayed at Mike's ranch, someone would talk about her visit. Inevitably, her family would find out. The town was too small for her to slip in and out without their hearing about it. So, she'd need to figure out what she'd say to them before that happened.

Trent approached her desk in her apartment. "Are you okay?"

Smiling, she nodded. He didn't need to know her family problem. With problems of his own, he didn't need more of hers. "I'm fine."

Hands on hips, his sweatpants hanging low, he made a handsome picture. "It's getting late, and we've got an early flight. Are you finished packing?"

"Yes, except for my stuff in the morning." She stood and, with her hands at the small of her back, stretched. The baby was becoming more and more uncomfortable. She caught Trent staring at her belly and blanched. What did he really think of her being a single mother? *Well, he thinks you need to marry. That's what he thinks.* "I'll turn in now."

Leaving him on the couch, she made her way to her

bedroom. While changing and preparing for bed, the vision of Trent standing before her at the desk made her libido come alive. Geez, she became horny at the worst times. She'd ignore it like always. Well, sometimes she took care of it, but not with Trent in the other room. *Maybe he'd.... No, he wouldn't.*

After slipping into bed, everything began crashing together in her mind, and she started to tremble. What if whoever had almost hit her followed them? What if it was the same person who killed Brian? What if the guy with the knife came to Montana? They might or might not be the same person.

The thought of finding Brian's killer sent adrenaline slipping through her system, but the fact it might not have been an accident sent fear sliding right behind it. People killed to keep things secret. *Remember the arsonist in Adrian's case?* That brought her up short. How would she handle Adrian's investigation if she was out of town? He'd just have to wait unless she could figure something out for him. Someone needed to be on his side.

Crossing her arms over her chest and pulling her knees up, Kelly hugged herself as best as she could. Things had to go right in Reed Point. They just had to. Tossing and turning, unable to calm and comfort herself, she gave up and left the bed for the living room.

She meant to ask Trent to hold her until her fears subsided like in the old days. Instead, she whispered, "Make love to me."

****

Shocked beyond measure, Trent found himself speechless. Part of him wanted to jump up and carry her to bed, but part of him worried about what she'd say when she saw his back. He couldn't handle pity or revulsion from Kelly. Sure, his mind kept returning to the fact that she wouldn't do that, but somewhere in his mind, he doubted.

Clearing his throat to find his voice, he observed her in her flannel pajamas, which looked sexy as hell on her shapely body. The baby bump caught his attention, and his mind halted. "We shouldn't."

She shrugged. "Then if not, please come hold me like you used to. All of this is getting to me, and I'm a little scared."

Hold her? In the past, he'd curled up, holding her in a spoon fashion, but his growing erection could be a serious problem. But, at least in that position, she wouldn't see or feel his back. "Is it that bad?"

A tear glistened in the moonlight as it rolled down her cheek. "I keep thinking how someone came at me with a knife to hurt me, maybe even kill me, and I can't shake the fear. I just need comfort, Trent."

With the knowledge that he could do nothing else, he nodded. "Give me a minute, and I'll be in."

She hesitated. "Thank you." Then she slipped back into the hallway.

Chastising himself for being every kind of fool, he checked to make sure his dick wasn't tenting his sweatpants and put on his T-shirt and made his way to her bedroom. He could sleep beside her and not make love to her. He'd done it plenty of times before. *But, before, you weren't falling in love with her.*

He stopped in his tracks and grimaced. Sure, he wanted to fall in love with her, but he didn't think it was actually happening. The strange mix of feelings he had, had to be because danger targeted her, and he wanted to be the one to protect her from it all. That was all.

While standing at Kelly's bedroom door, he took a deep breath and then entered. Although dark, enough moonlight spilled into the room for him to find his spot on her bed. *His spot?* Maybe he'd done this too many times.

After crawling into the bed under the covers, he rolled to Kelly, who faced away from him. They slid toward each other—front to back—and she rested her head on his left arm. A sigh escaped her as she wiggled to get closer.

Trent gritted his teeth as her butt slid back and forth over his crotch. "Enough," he ground out.

She turned her head toward him. "Thanks for being here." She turned back away, and her body relaxed into him.

Wrapping his right arm around her, his hand rested on her belly. He almost snatched it back, feeling like that privilege should be private to the baby's parents, but then he felt a slight movement and his heart leaped as intrigue filled him.

"She's active tonight," Kelly informed him. Her hand covered his, and she moved them across her stomach.

The thump hit his hand hard, and he jerked back in surprise. How could Kelly endure that?

Kelly giggled. "That's nothing."

He lifted his head to see her better. "Does it...hurt?" How could it not? The kid was trying to kick its way free.

"Hmm. I wouldn't call it hurt, but uncomfortable fits nicely."

Fascinated, he asked, "How much bigger will she get?"

"Oh, hopefully not much bigger. I'm already quite round for the end of my second trimester."

Having no idea what that word meant but realizing it had to do with her pregnancy, he had to know more. "How many of these trimester things do you have?"

With laughing eyes, Kelly turned to him. "Are you kidding me? It's a trimester. Tri? Three?" She giggled.

"Of course, I know what tri means," he grumbled. Hell, he wasn't stupid. There was trifecta in horse racing, triple play in baseball, and triangle defense in football. Her being close to his body, and his growing hard-on had sucked his IQ points away.

She yawned, using their joined hands to cover it.

He'd go to the ends of the earth for this woman, but covering her yawns—His thoughts broke off when she resettled his hand on her breast. Her rather plump breast. His pulse raced and fire zipped through him.

"Good night," she whispered. Her breathing shallowed and quickly evened.

Un-freaking-believable. The woman had put his hand on her tit and then fallen fast asleep. He didn't know whether to be offended or relieved. Knowing the latter was the best option, he slipped his hand free and moved it around, trying to find where to properly rest it before deciding upon her hip. Then he lay his head down to sleep. Although that action did not come easily or as quickly as it had for her. Maybe he knew better than to rest his hand on her breast, but his dick didn't. Hard as a rock, he slid his hips back from her bottom so if she woke, she wouldn't realize.

Then again, she had asked him to make love to her.

143

Confusion about what to do with their relationship roared inside him. That kiss had changed everything for him. It'd made him realize what an idiot he'd been all the years he and Kelly had been only friends. Had he pulled his head from his ass, he'd have noticed what a perfect woman she was, and maybe, just maybe, that'd have been his baby growing inside her.

Frustrated, he wiped all thoughts from his mind and finally fell asleep.

In the middle of the night, Trent woke to soft kisses being placed on his throat and a hand covering an ass cheek. Automatically, he reached out and pulled the woman closer until his hard cock rested at her juncture. He felt the baby bump and froze.

"Make love to me, Trent." Kelly rubbed herself against his painful erection.

"I-We—" Hell, what was he trying to say? The area where he'd had stitches burned, but no way in hell would he allow it to prevent him from this, no matter what activities the doctor said to avoid. There were ways to have sex without it being super strenuous.

"We can." She tipped her head back and leaned in to kiss him.

A groan began low inside him and worked its way out his mouth as his resistance snapped. As heat surged through him, he took over the kiss, dominating, letting her feel his built-up desire. He wanted this woman, and she wanted him. There was no reason to hold back any longer.

His tongue inside her mouth, his lips tight over hers, Trent reached up and cupped a breast, finally feeling, kneading the softness. Tweaking the taut nipple elicited a moan from her that had a deep-seated need shooting through him.

"Now, Trent," she whispered her demand against his lips.

Wanting more time to prepare her since that'd been the shortest amount of foreplay he'd had since he was a teenager, he stood and slid her pajama pants down her legs while she removed her shirt. Rolling on her back, he caught a perfect view of her trimmed mound. His mouth watered, wanting to taste her, but he had other things on his mind first.

After removing only his sweatpants, he crawled back up on the bed. "Turn back on your side."

She opened her mouth to say something, but obviously decided against it as she did as told.

With his hand on her hip, he slid her back to him. Reaching around, he probed her entrance with a finger and found it slick and warm. If possible, he'd just hardened to stone. "Damn, Kelly." So much for needing to prep her for him.

"I want you, Trent." She turned her head toward him, and he leaned over and kissed her hard. The angle made it awkward, but their tongues still found each other and danced together. Damn, she tasted sweet.

"I don't have a fucking condom," he bit out in frustration. Of all the things not to pack when to stay over at her place.

She chuckled. "You don't need it. I'm already pregnant."

True, but that wasn't the only reason to wear them. "I'm clean. I swear it, Kelly." Fuck, he had to get inside her, but thinking of a condom had been automatic for him. He'd never had sex without one. Until now....

That settled, slowly, he picked up her leg and

pulled it back over his, then slid even closer. Anticipation licked through his system. He guided his rigid cock to her entrance and slid inside her velvety heat. The deeper he sank, the more he fought coming with how good…how perfect it felt to be inside her. Damn, he'd been a fool not to fuck her before now.

Wanting to ensure she enjoyed it as much as he was, he gritted his teeth and reached around to rub her clit. Savoring the feel of being inside her, he moved his pelvis slowly, slipping deep in and then almost pulling out completely. The pulsing of his cock told him that even that wasn't working at holding back his orgasm. He wouldn't last long.

He made circles on her nub, kissed her neck and back, and smiled at the mewling sounds she made. When her body tensed and her breathing came in heavy pants, he knew she was close and focused his efforts on bringing her to climax.

"I'm gonna come," she rasped. Her breathing hitched. Then she made the sexiest sounds as she splintered in his arms.

Moving his hand back to her hip, he pumped into her a few more times before enjoying his own release. An off-the-charts climax that had him almost seeing stars.

Both spent, they lay connected until Kelly jumped up and raced to the bathroom with, "I've got to pee," following in her wake.

Chuckling, he stood and found his sweatpants, grateful Kelly hadn't said anything about him removing his shirt. Checking his stitches, which pained the fuck out of him after that activity, he found them thankfully dry but a little red probably from the irritation of his movement. He was lucky as fuck he hadn't ripped any, but he and Kelly's sex had been tame in that position.

Dressed, he straightened the covers for her return. For all he knew, she could ask him to sleep on the couch now. He'd tempt fate and stay. Holding her for the rest of the night seemed right. Plus, he found he really wanted to do so. He missed those nights of holding her. At least this time, it would be in the throes of sated bliss versus her needing only comfort.

Reality hit him with the strength of a two-by-four to the forehead. He'd had sex with his best friend. How did he handle things now? He wanted to be the man for her, but she wanted him to be in love. He wanted to be free of his demons.

Sighing, he slid onto the bed since he didn't have the answers. Nobody said this shit would be easy.

Kelly reentered and slid back into bed, naked.

His dick twitched at the temptation. *Already? Christ.*

She gave him a quick kiss on the lips, then turned on her side and scooted into him. She fit so perfectly. "Thank you." She dropped off to sleep again.

What the fuck? Wasn't it the guy who fell asleep right away? The question he really needed to be asking was if they would feel awkward come morning? He knew their making love changed things between them. But how exactly?

Chapter Sixteen

There'd been no time for awkwardness when Trent and Kelly awoke to the pounding of workers outside. Once he'd finally drifted off to sleep, cuddled next to her, it'd been the most peaceful night's sleep he'd had since the bomb blast. No nightmares. No waking in a cold sweat. Not wanting it to end, he pulled her closer and groaned, attempting to tune out the unwelcome sound.

When he realized the noise was actually on the front door, he rolled away from Kelly and dropped his feet on the floor when realization dawned that they'd overslept and their ride had arrived.

He checked the peephole before answering and stared at one pissed off Matt Hamilton. "Get the fuck up! Do you know how much it costs to keep a plane waiting?"

Rubbing his hand over his face, Trent frowned at his brother's unexpected, harsh tone. "We're up. Give us five"—he glanced back to the bedroom, thinking she might need longer—"no, fifteen." He closed the door behind Matt. He hoped Kelly could get ready that fast. Then again, the faster he pushed her, the less she would want to talk about last night and with someone driving them, there'd be no possibility of it on the way to the private airport.

He returned to the bedroom, ready to roll her out of

bed and pull a football coach approach if needed to hustle her up. Instead, he found the bed empty but smiled when Kelly popped her head out of the bathroom with a toothbrush in her mouth. Around the suds starting to dribble down her chin, she said, "Give me ten minutes."

Fighting the urge to walk over and wipe her chin for her, he nodded and returned to the living room and his overnight bag to change. Since Kelly had sworn off caffeine during her pregnancy, he didn't even attempt to make coffee and drink it in front of her.

After changing, brushing his teeth in her other bathroom, and loading his bag in Matt's car, Trent sat on the couch with his brother in silence and wondered how long she'd actually take. To avoid unnecessary conversation, he kept himself occupied by playing around on the Internet on his phone. He checked a Facebook page he'd started long ago but didn't maintain. A few women he'd dated—he used that term loosely—had been trying to locate him while he'd been out of town. He noted how most were blonde, like Kelly had changed her hair. Funny how now that he had Kelly in his life—however he had her—he didn't care about the other women. Not that he'd cared that much before. They'd been a means to an end. Unafraid to admit it, it used to be, he lived for a piece of ass and a good time.

Never in his wildest dreams did he think deciding the one person to spend the rest of one's life with would be so confusing and difficult. No wonder they wrote so many country songs about the heartache of finding love. There was that word again. Love. If he wasn't in love with her, was he feeling sorry for her being alone and that was why he wanted to marry her? Although he still feared she'd turn him away because of his scars, he also knew no other woman would accept him as he was. So, did that mean he was settling?

And, why the fuck did he have all these crazy feelings? He was a guy for Christ's sake. Eat, fuck, and sleep. That was all that was needed in life and not necessarily in that order.

"Ready." Kelly, dressed in light blue pants with a blue-and-white striped top, tugged a wheeled suitcase into the living room.

Popping up, Trent approached her and reached for the suitcase, picking it up. His shoulder muscles immediately struggled. "Good God. What have you got in here?" He made a show of walking to the kitchen and peeking into the room.

"What are you looking for?"

"Just seeing if you had the kitchen sink in here."

Laughing, she walked past him to the door. "Don't be silly. It's just what I need." She turned to his brother who held the door open. "Hello, Matt."

A smile raced across his brother's previously grim face. "Morning."

"It's enough to move a small family," Trent muttered under his breath, still on his conversation, not hers and Matt's. Was he truly jealous of the attention she showed his brother? He shook his head at the insanity. Having sex with her had definitely screwed with his head.

While Matt drove, he and Kelly sat in the back even though Matt grumbled about not being a fucking chauffeur. Trent tried to keep the conversation off anything that would make them think of the night before. His mind went through and discarded topics. Knowing they'd never resolved this one before they'd agreed to the trip, he broached it. He turned to her. "Are you going to go see your parents while you're there?"

"I don't know." Her gaze slipped to the side, looking out the window.

"We've discussed this. They'll want to see you. They love you and won't care that you're not married." At least he hoped they didn't. With as close a family as she'd always described, Trent couldn't imagine anything but them embracing her. Although they might convince her to move home, and that wouldn't do for his purposes.

She turned to him. "If I go, will you go with me?"

Happiness slipped through his veins, and his heart leaped at her wanting him to meet her parents, even though it was just for support. Her choice of letting them know he was the one she leaned upon when she needed it gave him hope for her to change her mind about the two of them. "Of course."

They arrived at the plane in forty minutes to a frowning pilot who'd been hired last minute to get his ass up early for the flight he and Kelly had delayed.

With a smiling and chatty AJ waiting, Trent didn't have a chance to speak with Kelly again before takeoff. Not long after they were in the air, sitting across from each other, she dozed and Trent watched her. What to do now? She hadn't said anything this morning, nor acted any differently. Although what had he expected since they hadn't been alone? Maybe she'd have tried to avoid him or been all touchy-feely close. She'd been the same. As if it hadn't happened. That made him feel a bit cheap.

"You know, it's funny," AJ said, sliding into the seat next to him, "pregnant women can get horny as hell."

Bristling, he growled at his brother. "What the fuck's that supposed to mean?" Had he been just a fuck for Kelly instead of anything special? Something to scratch her pregnant itch? No, she said she loved him. Was in love with him. He groaned at allowing AJ to get into his head. "What do you want?"

"What are you doing?"

He turned and pulled his eyebrows low in confusion. "Thinking of our trip."

With a sigh, AJ shook his head. "No, with Kelly."

A sudden panic filled him. Could AJ tell they'd slept together? No. That was ridiculous. He had to be fishing, nothing more. "Protecting her."

"You're wrapped up in her, different than I've seen you with her before."

Sighing, he decided if there was anyone he could talk about this with, it was AJ. They'd been as close as brothers for a long time before they'd found out they were actual brothers. Funny how that worked out. He sighed and hoped AJ didn't laugh at him. "I asked her to marry me."

Shock flashed on his brother's face. "You— Wow." AJ shifted in his seat, crossed one leg over the other thigh and bounced it. "What'd she say?"

Trent gave him a look of disbelief. "She said no."

"Oh."

"Yeah. She said I wasn't in love with her."

"Are you?"

"Well, no." He had something deeper than just love for her, and sleeping with her had only reinforced it.

But in love? He still didn't believe that. "At least I don't think so."

"I see."

"What do you mean you see?" Trent asked testily.

"It's just that you must have some pretty strong feelings for her to offer to marry her and raise someone else's child from an infant."

"What's wrong with raising someone else's child?" Irritation spiked through him. Roger McKenzie had done it and had done a great job at it. At least Ashley wouldn't find out her father had abandoned her on purpose for his own political career.

AJ held up his hands to ward off an argument. "That didn't come out right. Nothing is wrong with it."

"Men do it all the time."

AJ gave a single head bob. "You mean like your father?"

Trent nodded in response. "Yeah, like my father."

"Did they love each other?" AJ paused. "Your parents, I mean."

"Yes, I believe they did."

"Then you see why Kelly wants someone who loves her enough to make a life together."

"When did you get all knowledgeable with shit like this?"

AJ smirked and his face brightened. "When I got a wife and child of my own."

Megan was a great woman, but not the woman he'd want to spend the rest of his life with. He looked again at Kelly, her head lolling to one side while she slept. Standing, he moved to her and pulled the blanket up to cover her better. In his heart, he knew that the woman for the rest of his days was Kelly. To win her, he needed to have her accept his scars, accept that he could have that life, and solve the mystery around the threat to her.

Oh, and fall in love. Piece of cake.

Chapter Seventeen

Nervousness and foreboding struck Kelly as she exited the airplane in Billings, Montana. She and Trent had not had time to talk about what had happened between them. Maybe she'd been wrong allowing her hormones to take over and convince him to make love to her. He obviously hadn't wanted to at first, but then he'd been turned on so, of course, he wouldn't turn away a willing woman. And she'd been more than willing.

The sex had been amazing, and her imagination drove her wild in her dreams thinking about how it would be if they took their time and loved each other's bodies first. That'd mean he'd have to take off his shirt. No, she hadn't missed that he'd left it on. They hadn't talked about his accident or what she knew had to be extensive scarring.

At one time, she'd thought them the best of friends, but his keeping all of that from her was a burden she hated resting on his heart. Surely he'd shared it all with Jamie, who'd been the one to care for him both in and out of the hospital.

It was wrong of her to be jealous of a dead woman, but she couldn't stop her heart from feeling the pain. When she'd found out she, along with everyone else, had been barred from Trent's hospital room, she'd almost gone into mourning over the hurt and pain it had caused. But Brian had been there to pick her up.

Thinking of Brian, she had one hour to prepare herself for seeing his father again. She didn't know what kept her from visiting, but knowing her baby needed a family kept her tied to Brian and his father.

When they'd crossed the tarmac, it had been cleared, but she could see in the rental car parking lot, there had recently been snow. With the overcast sky that greeted them, they might be in for more snow soon. Shoving her gloved hands into her coat pocket, she cradled the sides of her belly. Although the doctor said she was fine, in her mind, she appeared big for six months.

Something hit her square between her shoulder blades and she froze, then smiled. Ducking down as best as she could, she removed her hands from her pockets, wrapped them around a big pile of snow pulled up between the cars and made it into a ball. The three men, carrying luggage, acted as if nothing had happened. The corner of Trent's mouth ticked up and she had him. Standing, she launched her snowball and hit him squarely in the chest before he could react.

Since he sought a somewhat dry place to place the luggage before playing, she had enough time to make another snowball and launched it as he squatted down, nailing him on the forehead. With exceptionally fast snowball-making skills, he launched them at her one after another, beating her two to one, hitting her almost everywhere but the belly. She gingerly moved from spot to spot, hoping to throw him off, giggling the entire way.

Breathing hard, she had to call a halt because her side hurt from so much laughing and running. Then,

Trent threw her off by grabbing her up and spinning her around until he winced at what she suspected was a twinge in his stitches. Her breath caught when he gave her a quick peck on the lips before setting her down.

Without a word, he returned to collect their luggage while she fought for control of her breathing and her heart. The man didn't realize what he did to her.

Settled in the backseat of the rental beside Trent, she folded her hands in her lap and stared straight ahead, unsure how to act.

The hour went by quietly with a strange tension in the vehicle. When they reached Reed Point, AJ laughed at the sign that said, "Sheep drive capital of the world." Kelly perked up at it. Driving down the main street—the only real street with businesses—she pointed out the interests.

She directed their attention out her side window. "That's the Waterhole's Saloon. Best lunch around. Next to it is the old hotel and lounge." She frowned. "Like many businesses, they've closed their doors."

"What about getting basic supplies? Do you have a Walmart or Target here?" Trent asked.

Almost hopping in her seat, she said, "No, we have better. It's almost like an old general store." Giving them directions, they found a newer part of town with a few businesses lining one side of the street.

"Pull in, would you?" Kelly asked. "I want to get something."

Matt caught Trent's eye in the rearview mirror and pulled over at Trent's slight nod.

When Kelly entered the store, an older man, graying and slightly stooped smiled broadly and greeted her by name. She rushed into his arms and kissed him on the cheek when they parted.

"Look at you, young 'un," Marvin Sinclair said.

With her hand resting on her belly, she laughed nervously. Now her parents would know as word would spread. "I'm hoping you might have pickled bologna." When the man's brows drew down, she rushed to add, "It's a craving I haven't been able to satisfy."

Nodding, Marvin walked down one of the aisles, looked around, examined a jar and then handed it to Kelly. "It's the last one, and I had to check the date I've had it so long."

She hugged the jar to her chest. One might not be enough. Ashley had been asking for strange things, things she'd never have eaten otherwise. Glancing to Trent, she almost burst out laughing at his disgusted look. She'd probably be the same way if it hadn't been for the craving.

After settling the bill, they returned to the car for the final drive out to Mike's ranch. Closing her eyes, a peace fell over her with the mountains to one side and Yellowstone River to the other. If it hadn't been for her wanting to be a big-time reporter, she'd never have left Reed Point. She'd also never have met Trent, so there had been a good trade-off.

When she opened her eyes, the open range spread before them. They arrived much faster than she was prepared for.

Stepping out of the car, she inhaled the scent of the woods not far away and the crisp, mountain air. *Home,* her heart said.

Mike Platt, a man of about fifty years of age, stood on the front porch of a two-story wooden home that

Kelly remembered running around as a child. Even young, she and Brian had been paired by their parents.

The dog at his side barked once but quieted when Mike placed a hand on the dog's head.

Kelly shook away the memories and focused on the home. The white paint had seen better days, but the wood appeared in good repair. She wasn't sure why she'd assumed Mike had let everything go when he'd heard of Brian. Yet, it'd only been a short time and he still had Luke. Then again, according to Brian, there was no telling where Luke was at the moment. Once Mike had apparently laid down the law with him, Luke had lit out like there'd been no tomorrow. Maybe she could help reunite the two. Somehow.

Mike opened his arms wide and almost croaked out her name. "Kelly."

Falling into his embrace, tears streamed down her cheeks, and she couldn't speak. Her heart hoped he didn't hold Brian's death against her. When she felt a drop she suspected was a tear from above, she pulled back and wiped her face with the back of her gloved hands. "I'm so sorry, Mike."

Using his coat sleeve to wipe his face, Mike said, "There's nothing to be sorry about. Now, introduce me to your friends and then we can get inside, and you can tell me what this is all about."

Perceptive man. Then again, why else would she bring three men with her?

It took a while to handle introductions and get everyone settled. The men wanted to scope out the place right away, but she pulled Trent aside and explained that Mike needed to know something before they went off and did their jobs. Having them stroll the grounds without a word would not only be rude but add to the concern the man must already feel.

She had to threaten to go back on her word and get involved if he didn't do this first. Not that she would've, but he obviously didn't look forward to doing it, and a kick in the pants had been needed.

Sitting in the living room, Kelly squished between Trent and AJ on the couch. She glanced between Matt and Mike, looking comfortable in the chairs.

"So, how do you all know Kelly?"

Kelly spoke up before the men could. "They're one of my good friend's brothers-in-law." Trent stiffened beside her. Maybe he'd planned to keep his association with the Hamiltons secret. It wouldn't be possible because from what Megan had said, once the senator spoke with Trent, he wanted to publicly announce it.

AJ smiled and nodded. "I'm Megan's husband. She works with Kelly. We've kind of adopted Kelly into our family."

"I'm glad to hear it. We didn't like her being alone in the big city."

"We didn't like it either," Trent added.

Straightening in his chair, Mike cleared his throat. "I'm awfully glad you brought Kelly back, but I know you aren't here just to escort her."

Trent shook his head and frowned. "No, sir, we're not."

"Then, son, you'd best tell me what this is all about."

"Well, we think it's possible Brian's death wasn't an accident," Trent informed him more bluntly than Kelly would've liked. "And, someone is after Kelly."

Quite unexpectedly, Mike grabbed his chest and doubled over.

Chapter Eighteen

Mike stopped them from calling an ambulance after taking a tablet for his heart condition. Then, he took a nap to rest. It took him a while to recover, and Kelly informed Trent, AJ, and Matt that Brian had told her that his father's health was failing. Trent swore. She could've told him before he'd been so blunt about the death of the man's son. Then again, he hadn't expected such a physical reaction.

While Kelly napped and the men scoped out the place, Trent took advantage and settled down with a recovered Mike to find out everything he could. With a bottle of water in his hand, he joined the man in his office. The first time he'd seen the room, he'd had a tough time believing it was an office because it was so damn neat and organized. Not what he'd expect the men of this ranch to be, yet he'd never met Brian, so what did he truly know?

Sitting across from Mike in a worn but comfy leather armchair, he considered how to broach the subject without causing distress.

"I'm fine. Just spit it out."

Trent nodded respectfully. "Okay. We don't know for sure, but after your son died, his suitcase and then papers were stolen from Kelly. That's why she didn't have his stuff for you."

Mike didn't speak but nodded.

"Since then, there have been…incidents that make me think someone might be after Kelly." That was an understatement after the knife attack, but Brian had had enough tough news to take.

The man's hands slammed on the desk. "You have to protect her! She's carrying my grandchild."

"That's why we're with her." That and he didn't want to let her out of his sight for longer than necessary.

"Are there enough of you? I have a lot of land."

Taking a slow drink of his water, Trent remembered how he'd thought the same thing, but Jesse and Devon had disagreed. "A lot of it is open range, so we can see for miles. If we think we need more men, we'll address it then."

"Okay." Mike nodded once. "How can I help?"

"We need to nail down the why. Have you had anything happen here, or to you personally?"

Mike appeared thoughtful before he spoke, "I've had a few livestock found dead. It can happen, but we suspected poisoning."

Wheels spinning, he asked thoughtfully, "How easy is it to do that?"

"It's not, which is why the cause of their deaths is questionable. Someone would've led the cattle off and fed and watered them separately. It is possible though."

"Anything else?"

He shrugged. "I did have two men quit on me, about that same time. I didn't think anything of it as they are all about the money so bigger money can tempt them away."

"What are their names?"

"River Montgomery and Tim Warren."

Trent put the names into his memory. If bigger money would draw them away, it'd also draw them to do something like separate a few heads and poison them. Not having Devon do the thorough background checks frustrated him. His brother had to teach Em his tricks.

It sounded like scare tactics, but why kill Brian and not Mike? It didn't make sense to him. He reminded himself that he'd just started collecting information. "Is there anything else?"

"I've also had two people who have been persistent in their offers to buy the property."

That caught Trent's attention. Scaring someone off their property made sense if it was valuable. Nine million was a lot of money, but ranches weren't always that prosperous. Not willing to ask the man if he was making money, he settled for a different tact. "Are you planning to sell?"

Mike shook his head. "No interest whatsoever. One offer is repetitive, but one came out of the blue."

"Tell me about them." While the two cowhands might have dirtied their hands, it had to be for someone else, someone with money, someone who might want the land for themselves. Yet again, he reminded himself they killed Brian not Mike. Maybe Mike was in danger also.

"Christian Kent of Kent Oil has offered about once a year for the past ten years. This year, he's upped his offer and been more hands-on, trying to open negotiations personally. I guess he thinks this'll be the next big strike for his company, as if they aren't rich enough sucking up the land," Mike scoffed and shook his head in disgust.

Pulling his brows down low, Trent contemplated this. "Is there any reason to suspect you're sitting on a goldmine in oil?"

"No. Although we haven't surveyed or probed for it either."

"But this year is different?" Christian Kent obviously knew something they didn't.

"Yeah. Just the amount and him trying to talk to me directly instead of going through lawyers."

"Have you spoken to him?"

Mike nodded. "Only to tell him no and to call my lawyer if he didn't understand my answer." The man chuckled.

Smiling, Trent decided he liked Mike Platt, and he wanted to settle this for his son. "You said two offers. What's the other?"

"Young, rich kid named Reggie Brightmore who stayed when Brian experimented at making this a sportsman vacation spot. Reggie loved it so much, he wants to move here permanently." The man laughed then coughed as he caught his breath.

"He loved it enough to buy a fully functioning ranch?" Trent wondered how a small herd of cattle and breeding horses could draw such attention. "Does he have ranching experience?"

With a brisk shake of his head, Mike answered, "No. He's a city slicker—full up greenhorn. No telling what he'd do with the place. Probably just have his rich friends out to kill off all the wildlife, then move on to a new place." Mike's mouth tightened into a tight line, and his jaw clenched.

Unfortunately, Trent could foresee that happening also if the proper management and oversight weren't put into place. The idea of managing a ranch like this tickled something inside him. "From what I can tell from Kelly, your son was pleased with the results of the vacation getaways he'd hosted and was going to approach you with expanding the number of outbuildings to include some cabins and renting them out regularly for the sportsman and fisherman vacations."

The raspy sound of Mike's hand rubbing over his nearly gray-bearded chin broke into the air as the man appeared to consider the idea. "I believe it has merits and saw the enjoyment of the vacationers. As for expanding it, I wouldn't have been opposed to the idea. Heck, even one of the hands mentioned offering trail rides. But it would have to be managed well enough not to deplete our resources."

Trent leaned forward in the seat, resting his forearms on his thighs and thought for a moment. Something just wasn't right. "Was Brian your heir?"

A heavy sigh released from Mike. "He was. Now it's my grandchild."

Bristling at the lack of name being used, Trent added, "Ashley."

Mike nodded. "Yeah, Ashley," he said softly. "After Brian's mom."

That was new information to him, but it didn't matter. "What about your other son?"

A scowl appeared on the man's face. "I wrote Luke out of my will regarding the property when he took off. I didn't trust him not to sell it without thinking about what would happen to it," Mike spat out. "He just wants the money."

Trent kept to himself that he'd been told Mike

made him leave. Two sides to every story, he guessed. "Does he know he's out of the will? Even with Brian gone?"

Mike nodded, then stopped his head's movement midway. "He knew when I wrote him out and gave it all to Brian. He may not know about Ashley."

While considering this, Trent took a long drink of his water as he stared at Mike's red flannel shirt. It wasn't unheard of for greed to go too far in a family. "Where's Luke now?"

"I don't know." The heavy sorrow in the man's voice told Trent he still cared deeply for his son, no matter the reason for the estrangement. "Do you think someone's trying to kill my heirs?"

Looking Mike in the eyes, he pushed confidence in his voice. "I don't know. It appears that way, but it doesn't make sense. I'm missing something."

Mike leaned forward with an elbow on the desk and placed his chin on a fist. "Do you think Luke is in danger?"

At the unexpected question, Trent raised his eyebrows, hating what he'd have to say, but answering honestly, "I don't know." Seeing the concern cross the man's face, he decided to return to the topic. "How many times have the two men made official offers on the property or pushed you to sell in the past year?"

Seeming happy with a question that could be answered, Mike pondered, "Let's see, Kent Oil has offered three times, and Reggie has offered four times in the past year."

"That seems excessive if you told them no." Trent drew his eyebrows down in thought. "If you don't mind me asking, did they increase their offer each time?"

Mike nodded. "They did. But I still said no. The place isn't for sale. It's for my family." A heavily burdened sigh escaped the man, and he seemed to fold up on himself.

Trent swallowed hard thinking about little Ashley potentially growing up here. Away from him. "What are you going to do now?"

"Me? I'm going to watch my grandbaby grow up while you make it safe for my family."

That was exactly what he planned to do, but their family would soon overlap.

Chapter Nineteen

Not stocked for company, Mike's pantry didn't have enough food to serve up the men in the style Mike had wanted, so they rode into town to the Waterhole. Entering through the old-timey saloon doors, Kelly didn't balk, but knew the more she was spotted in town, the sooner her parents would know she'd arrived. In her heart, she knew Trent was right, and they'd love her no matter what, but the embarrassment of it all kept her away. And the disappointment that surely would come already had her insides in turmoil.

Seated at wooden benches and long tables with sawdust at their feet, the men kept up a lively conversation with Mike about his ranch and the area. AJ seemed keenly interested in the annual sheep drive. Kelly doubted Megan would want to come to Montana just for that, but she did love her husband enough she'd do almost anything.

Love made people do strange things—like make love to a man because you were so damn horny for him you couldn't stand it, even though he didn't feel the same way about you. Not sure how to act around Trent, she'd tried to avoid him as much as possible, but that hadn't been easy when he tried to remain close to her. She could only take so many naps.

After a meal where the men had eaten practically half a cow, Whiskey Straight, a country band, began to set up on a makeshift stage on the side corner of the saloon. Memories flooded back. She'd first danced when she and her father had attended a daddy-daughter night here. She'd been eight then, and her momma had dressed her in her prettiest blue dress and tied a ribbon in her hair. Her vision misted. Around and around her father had spun her until she'd almost lost her breath from giggling so hard.

"May I have this dance?"

It took Kelly a moment to realize the words had been spoken to her. Turning, she saw Trent standing with his hand outstretched to her. Glancing nervously at Mike for a moment, not wanting to offend his son's memory, she shook her head at Trent. It wouldn't do to show her desire for this man while she'd agreed to marry another. It was too soon.

"Go on, Kelly," Mike said loud enough for her to hear over the music that had started playing.

The twang of the guitar sounded, and the male singer began a song of unrequited love. How appropriate.

"It'll be good for the baby," Mike added.

She couldn't see how that would be the case, but with Mike's blessing, she stood and met Trent. With his hand resting on the small of her back and sending erotic tingling sensations throughout her body, she didn't know how she'd handle the dance. Had she paid more attention to the music and noticed it was a two-step before, she'd definitely have said no. The last thing she needed was his hands on her, burning memories into her skin.

"Do you know how to two-step?" she asked Trent, hopeful he didn't so she could gracefully back out of the dance.

Smiling, he held out his arms for her to step into for proper positioning. "I wouldn't have asked if I didn't."

Taking the leap—so to speak—she slid one hand in his and put her other hand on his shoulder as he guided her closer. Too close for public display as far as she was concerned. But, she didn't say anything.

They stepped off in time with the music. Trent winked, and longing shot to her core. "Relax, Kelly. It's just a dance."

Just a dance? Was he out of his ever-loving mind? Intimacy would be a more appropriate term. Then it hit her, he didn't see it that way, just like he didn't always want her like she wanted him. Her dinner turned in her stomach.

"Are you going to see your parents soon?" he asked as he slid her along the dance floor with his steps.

"Are you going to show me your back soon?" she countered, then immediately felt contrite when his expression fell into what appeared to be pain and hurt. What the hell was wrong with her snapping at him like that over something so serious? It'd been his question about her parents, but still...he hadn't deserved that. He would've if he'd wanted to talk to her about it. She had to remember that Jamie still existed in his heart. That woman had known...had seen...had been there with him. "I'm sorry."

His gaze left her face and moved over her shoulder. "Don't be."

No. Enough of his hiding. She wanted their full relationship back, and then some. "You used to share everything with me." He turned her in time with the music. "At least I thought you did. But you didn't with being hurt." Sighing, she continued, "I wanted to be there for you." *Not Jamie*, she wanted to say aloud. "But I understand you fell in love and had someone else to share with."

Trent stopped them on the dance floor, and another couple bumped into them, pushing her closer to him and her belly bounced off his. After he gave the couple a nasty glare, they moved around her and Trent.

"What are you talking about?" he demanded, his hand tightening on hers. The gentleness of the touch had disappeared. She didn't think he meant to hurt her, but she'd definitely struck a nerve.

Oh shit. Another thing he hadn't wanted to share with her. His being in love with someone else. When had things gone so off-kilter for them? *When Jamie had come along. That's when.* She couldn't begrudge Trent falling in love; she only wished it'd been with her. Realizing they were garnering too much attention standing as they were, she said, "Trent, we need to move or get off the dance floor."

As if just realizing where they were, Trent began to two-step with her again, scooting her backward into the small throng. "Now, what are you talking about?" he said as if they hadn't just created a small traffic jam on the dance floor.

"You—" She swallowed hard past the lump in her throat. Confronting this had to happen, even though she hadn't expected it to be in the middle of a bunch of strangers. "You fell in love with the nurse, Jamie, and took her with you." She paused. "I'm so sorry for your loss."

Kelly counted the steps before Trent spoke—they

were in double digits—because she didn't know what else to say at this point. What follow up was there to that type of statement? She figured asking if he could find himself falling in love with her also in poor taste, so she bit her tongue to keep quiet until he was ready to speak.

His Adam's apple bobbed before he spoke. "I wasn't in love with Jamie."

Needing to focus on keeping her feet moving, elation washed through Kelly's system. "Oh," was all she could muster even though she wanted to dance a jig. That meant Trent's heart was free. Maybe she could make it hers one day. Just maybe.

"What gave you such an idea?" He guided her in a turn.

"Oh," she said again, almost unsure how to phrase the words even though they'd been on her mind for months now. "Well, you took her with you when you wouldn't share with anyone else. I just assumed…."

"Kelly," he said, looking deeply into her eyes and somehow avoiding a collision from a possibly drunken patron, "I had a lot of shit to deal with and Jamie was dying. It wasn't planned. There was no love. We just took off together to lick our wounds." Glancing back up at the dance floor, then back to her, he said, "I thought of you every day."

Her heart expanded in her chest, and she thought it'd burst from joy. "But—"

"I couldn't offload those problems on you. I still can't—"

"Yes, you can," she rushed out before he could finish speaking.

Laughing, he lifted her hand and twirled her like a

ballerina on the song's last notes. "Maybe one day," she heard him say softly.

Back at the table, she'd forgotten Mike and what he might think, and guilt slipped through her at how close she'd allowed Trent to hold her. However, the man's smile confused her. Maybe he didn't notice and his happiness was because she was there with his granddaughter.

Before she had time to figure it out, AJ stood. "Teach me how, Kelly?"

Shocked, she imagined the surprise brightened her face. "You want me to teach you to two-step?"

Nodding and grinning, AJ said, "Yep."

With a laugh, she accepted his hand and wished she'd worn boots to protect her feet. Megan had told her once that AJ, while graceful in what he did for a living, had two left feet on the dance floor.

As AJ tortured her feet learning to two-step, all Kelly kept thinking of was that Trent's heart wasn't taken.

I still have a chance.

Chapter Twenty

Time to pony up. Odd expression, but Trent had heard Mike use it and he liked it. After Kelly's almost plea for him to share while they'd danced, he decided it was time to start. She couldn't run from him here, so if his back disgusted her, he could work to help her deal with it. Or, he could live his life with a broken heart and spirit if she, of all people, turned him away.

As a friend, she'd never do that to him. She'd stand by him no matter what. But, as a lover, she might not want to be near him, and that had his mind in a tailspin. If it grossed her out too much to touch him, to be with him, that would crush him.

Part of him still couldn't believe he'd never noticed he felt so deeply for her until this obstacle stood in their paths. Of course, there was still the "in love" thing. That was secondary to this because if she couldn't overcome his grotesqueness, then he wouldn't have his heart ripped to shreds.

And what of Mike? Trent shouldn't worry about the man, but when Kelly had been teaching AJ to dance—no, how to injure her feet—Mike had slid down close to him and confided that Kelly liked him much closer than as a friend.

When Matt scoffed, it became apparent he'd been eavesdropping as their voices had risen to normal levels. Even the music in the background hadn't hampered his hearing. Damn former SEAL.

Mike didn't know it, but Trent loved Kelly and could love her enough for a lifetime. And if they married, surely he'd fall in love with her along the way and then she'd be happy. How did he convince her of that, though? A woman's mind was tough enough to figure out; add in a pregnancy and he was more than stumped.

Jolted out of his thoughts, he bounced around in the back seat of the truck he, Matt, AJ, and Kelly had taken to scope out the land. He yelled at Matt, "Slow the fuck down! Kelly's pregnant, remember?" Looking over at her, sitting beside him, with her death grip on the oh-shit handle, his gut clenched for her safety.

Slowing, Matt said, "Sorry, Kelly, that hole was deeper than I thought."

"It's okay," she said, seemingly unbothered by the jostling of the truck.

They continued along the road made from years of vehicles using the route, amidst some of the most beautiful scenery he'd experienced. The snow-capped mountains, lakes, and forests were brilliant enough to take his breath away.

To their right, a buck—at least a ten-point—stepped from the thin woods with a doe and two fawns behind it. Ignoring them driving by, the adult deer made tracks in the slushy mud left over from the last snow while the fawns played around, jumping at each other, one sliding until it regained its balance.

Passing a few of the ranch hands—which Em had been checking out for them with some assistance from Devon, who was splitting his focus—the men tipped their cowboy hats at them as they drove by the few cattle they'd been wrangling.

It'd been intriguing to learn how much work went into this ranch. Mike had said it was small compared to so many others. The horse breeding was Mike's pride and joy, and Kelly seemed to favor it also. Mike had been shrinking his cattle herd the past couple of years, which might be why Brian thought they needed to bring in more business. He sighed. They'd never know.

"What are those caves?" AJ pointed up to the right.

"Nothing," Kelly answered. "We played there as kids pretending to find hidden pirate treasure or Big Foot." She laughed, and he loved the sound and the idea of her childhood playing in such a place.

Trent turned to her. "And did you?"

"Find Big Foot? No. But we always found something cool in the caves." She pouted then laughed. "No pirate treasure, though."

"Do you think these were mines back in the day?" Matt asked her.

Shrugging, she bit her lip in thought. "I couldn't tell you. I'm sure Mike would know."

They'd been riding for a couple of hours, and with the lay of the land, they could be out several more and still not see it all. Trent touched Matt on the shoulder. "I think we've seen more than enough. We can turn around."

"Looks like Devon was right. Except for this—at two hours away—there's nothing close to the house for any threats to hide behind unless they get close enough to the outbuildings. Someone should see them before then," AJ informed them.

"I wonder if anyone would even follow me," Kelly said.

With brows knitted together in a low V, Trent looked at her. "What do you mean?"

"Well, if they think I knew something—something that was in the paperwork—and hadn't wanted me to tell Mike, then it's too late as far as they know. I mean, they don't know that I didn't read anything."

"That's assuming it was something in the paperwork that was the problem," Trent countered, even though he'd bet his life that was the case.

"Oh, you know it was as well as I do. Otherwise, they wouldn't have taken such care to steal it."

Trent sighed, knowing they'd never get anything by her. From what he'd learned, AJ had the same problem with Megan. "We figured that it has to do with the ranch, if that was what Brian's business was in B-More. We just don't know what his business happened to be."

"He didn't tell Mike?" Kelly asked.

Trent shook his head. "No."

"Oh, I was convinced Mike would have the answers." Disappointment laced her voice, and it struck him how vulnerable she must be in all of this. But, you'd never know it with the strength she exuded. Knowing someone might be trying to kill him would definitely fuck up his equilibrium on sanity. It already had with her being a possible target.

A *ting, ting, ting* sounded—metal ricocheting and piercing metal—and Matt yelled, "Get down!" while gunning the engine.

Fuck! Someone had shot at them.

Heart pounding with adrenaline, he slid over, grabbed Kelly around the waist, and pulled her down on the seat, as far as her belly would allow, then covered her. "Get us the fuck out of here!" he bellowed. They had to get Kelly to safety.

"Like you have to fucking tell me to do that," Matt yelled back.

The truck swerved, and Trent held on tight. This time he didn't complain about the bumpiness of their ride. If it got to be too much, Kelly would say something. She'd never allow her baby to be hurt. Yet, that was what he'd just done—given someone an opportunity to hurt her or the baby.

Expecting a threat this far away from the house hadn't occurred to them. With it being more than two hours away, he'd like to say it was an opportunity shooting, but since it happened on Platt land, the incident took it to a whole new level. Kelly might not have been the target, but he wouldn't wait around to find out any different.

"Are you okay?" he whispered in her ear.

"I need to pee," she replied, and he bit back a smile. With this pregnancy, she always needed to pee.

"Can you wait?" He hoped she could because they weren't planning to stop right then so she could drop her drawers and squat.

She sighed. "Yes, if I must."

Despite the situation, a laugh burst out at the way she'd said her resigned words.

"Keep it up, Trent McKenzie," she said, "and I'll show you crazy pregnant lady."

"Bring it on, sweetheart." He smiled and gave her a quick kiss on the cheek. "Bring it on."

"You can probably sit up now," AJ said. "We're a good way away, and no one followed us."

Leaning back in his seat, Trent nodded, then

reached for Kelly before she scooted away. Taking her hand in his, he laced his fingers in hers and set it in the narrow space between them, thinking only of not being able to be parted from her yet. Her touch and nearness were necessary. "Thanks," he said to his brothers. "Did you see anything?"

AJ shook his head. "Nope. They were in the tree line, and I didn't want to shoot without a target just in case there were innocents or wildlife nearby."

Nodding, Trent agreed with that. He'd have done the same even though the bastards could've hit Kelly. "I'm pretty sure Mike won't be happy about his truck."

"I'm just glad he didn't put us on horses like he'd wanted," Matt added with the mood lightening at pushing the topic off the shooting itself in a silent agreement to wait until Kelly wasn't with them.

Trent raised their joined hands and kissed the back of hers. "We have Kelly to thank for that. We might've been on horseback if she hadn't wanted to go with us. Although, we also might not have been this far away."

"What do you think they were doing there? Seems an odd place to wait just in case someone came along?" Kelly asked, bringing them back to the hot topic.

He needed to give her something, to make her feel safe enough. "Oh, I don't think they were waiting in case someone came along. I think they were prepared in case someone came along." Trent squeezed her hand. "I think it's time someone spoke with our oil guy and made sure no one is testing the soil here without Mike's knowledge."

Chapter Twenty-One

It'd taken the remainder of the afternoon for Trent's heart to stop pounding with worry over Kelly's safety. The men had agreed that while it could possibly be connected, none believed the man who'd shot at them waited on the off-chance that Kelly traveled two hours away from the ranch. It hadn't mattered. Kelly had been in danger, and there'd been nothing he could do about it but rely on his brothers to get her safely away.

Devon, thank the fuck, made himself available to check into the buyers and former employees for them. Trent just prayed nothing else happened with Rylee that would take his focus away. It could be a serious problem in the future since Rylee had joined HIS as a team member. From what he'd learned from Matt and AJ, Devon's level-headedness flew out the window at signs of trouble with her even though everyone— including Devon—knew she could hold her own. He'd have to get his head on straight, like Jesse had with Kate, and trust his woman to do her job so he could do his.

Then again, Trent had a feeling he'd be the same if the roles were reversed. Whether she could hold her own or not, he didn't want Kelly in a dangerous situation without him protecting her. Call it caveman or whatever, it was what it was. He didn't see himself changing so he'd give Devon leeway for a while.

He owed Kelly an explanation of what had happened after the explosion that had put him into a tailspin, but there hadn't been a good time to speak with her about it. He'd finally share, but fully admitted he was still a bit chickenshit in many ways about discussing his back. Shutting her out at the onset had been born out of his desire to just die instead of live, and he hadn't been able to face her. He'd failed miserably. Sure, he'd saved Amber, but he hadn't saved Les. Then, when he'd realized that no matter his wish that he had survived, it had turned into his not wanting her to turn away in disgust at his disfigurement. He'd never wanted to lose Kelly. That should have told him something a long time ago.

With his weapon beside the T-shirt on the nightstand, he slid under the sheet and pulled it and the heavy blankets up his chest. Clasping his hands behind his head, he stared at the ceiling but didn't really see it. Emptiness filled him, and he felt alone without Kelly by his side. Many times he'd held her at night, generally after a bad breakup or sad news from home, but none had meant the same as when he'd made love to her. While it'd been brief, it was something he knew he wanted—no, needed—to do again. Being inside her had been what he expected heaven to be like. Holding her all night made him feel complete…satisfied, and as if he'd found his way home.

Sure, in the past, he'd wanted to make love to her. Wanted to fuck her until she screamed his name. But he'd never made that move over the line because of her virginity. *Brian.* The name whispered to him. She'd given her virginity to the man. In love with him or not, she'd allowed him to have what somewhere in the back of his mind, he'd always hoped would be his.

The weight slammed into his chest at the realization. How could he have thought that when he'd been chasing skirts while she'd been looking for her proverbial "Mr. Right?" Only to find out he'd been the man she sought. His brain hurt at how much he'd confused things with them. Had he pushed her to Brian by shoving her away after the incident? No. She'd already been pregnant then. But, she hadn't spoken of her wedding before then, when she would've known she'd been pregnant. Why had she hidden it from him? *Asshole, maybe the same reasons you hid from her. You didn't want to see what could possibly flash in the other's eyes. Any pulling back wouldn't have been bearable.*

The door opened a fraction, and Trent reached for his weapon. Light from the hallway illuminated Kelly slipping inside his room. He released the weapon and reached for his T-shirt. He couldn't do anything about not having on underwear. That thought hadn't occurred to him if he'd had to leave the bed in a rush.

Picking up his T-shirt, her voice stopped him. "Don't put on a shirt."

Motionless, Trent hesitated before slowly dropping the cotton material and reaching to turn on the bedside lamp instead.

She closed the door and approached the bed.

Propping up both pillows against the headboard, he slid up and back, keeping the covers on his lap. He nodded. The time had arrived to show her.

Kelly sat on the edge of his bed and bit her lip. "I couldn't sleep. All I keep remembering is how you'd hold me when I was frightened or sad, and your presence comforted me until I drifted off."

Had she known he'd been thinking the same thing? No. Not possible. Just coincidence. He cleared his throat. "Kelly—" What could he say that would deter her even though he wanted her with every fiber of his being? "I don't think that's a good idea. This is Mike's house." Since he'd come to like the man, he didn't wish to disrespect him in his own home by sleeping with his dead son's fiancée.

Looking around the room, she spotted his underwear sitting on top of his jeans, turned to him and raised a brow.

Although it shouldn't have, heat crept up his neck. "Yeah, I'm naked." He also had a hard-on in the works from looking at Kelly in her thigh-length nightgown that while it lay loose over her belly, remained snug over her plump breasts. The chill in the air had her nipples puckering, and his length hardened even more.

"You can put your underwear on, and I can still crawl in bed with you," she said.

"Yeah, and look what happened the last time we were in bed together." His voice may have been more cynical than he'd meant, but he couldn't take it back. It'd been said.

On her beautiful face scrubbed clean of makeup, she blushed, and the pink tinge to her cheeks made her all the more adorable in his eyes. *She should be cherished.*

"I'll be okay if it happens again."

Trent choked. Had she really just said that? "Kelly—"

"No"—she waved her hand—"it's okay. I really

just wanted to talk with you. Are you ready to discuss what happened?"

It was the perfect time, yet weariness and uncertainty of her reaction crept in, weighing heavily on his chest. How could he be such a pussy when he should be strong? "There's not much to tell. I got injured and now I'm scarred." His response sounded almost flippant, and he inwardly cringed at how he'd spoken to her.

"Hmm. Something tells me there's more to it than that."

"Don't try and go all investigative journalist, Kelly. There's nothing more." Liar. *There's the fact you were the only survivor of the two HIS men. You could've chosen the bomber instead of saving Amber.*

"Let me see your back," she requested softly but with steel in her voice and her arms crossed over her magnificent chest.

"Kelly…," he said, stalling, "I've had second and third-degree burns across the back of me. The third-degree ones were limited to my back, but still, my entire backside is scarred. They had a tough time finding skin for grafts. The insides of my thighs took the biggest hit." Swallowing hard against the lump that had crawled up his throat, he added, "I'm hideous." That simple fact should've stopped things, but not with his Kelly.

Instead of pity, sadness enveloped her eyes. Sadness and a bit of love. Although she always had the last part there. How could he not have noticed it? *Selfish bastard.* Yet, if she'd been his when he'd been injured, would she have stood by him or run? Would he have wanted to live for her? He'd never know, but now he could find out if she'd be by him from this point forward.

He could do this. She'd understand the burden he carried about his burns and scars from shrapnel.

"I bet it was pretty painful." Her eyes misted, and he wanted to pull her to him and assure her he'd been all right. But, it'd be a lie because he hadn't.

Nodding, he reached for one of her hands in her lap and toyed with her fingers. Awareness surged through him. "It sucked. I didn't want the pain meds but had to have them to get through the day or night. Some of the third-degree burns went down to the sensory nerves so I didn't even feel it when they were treated."

"But that wasn't all, though? Was it?"

"No," he said. "I felt the rest, every time they reapplied a salve or bandaged me. It took a ton of pain medicine for me to attend Jake and Em's wedding."

With a slight turn of her body, she clasped his hand and slid her knee on the bed. "I was always jealous of the relationship you had with Emily."

He chuckled. "I could see that. Now," he added. "We've been like brother and sister since we were small." Squeezing her hand, he smiled. "Not close like you and I, though."

"I want to see your back. Please," she pleaded.

Hesitantly, he shifted to a sitting position and scooted forward enough to give her room behind him. Releasing her hand, his insides churned at finally showing his disfigurement to Kelly. Waiting while she stood and moved positions on the bed, he put his trust in her love for him to keep her from getting sick or showing distaste for him.

Looking back over his shoulder, he saw the look of

astonishment flood her face. Whatever she'd been prepared for, it hadn't been what she'd seen.

Her hand came up and covered her mouth. "Oh, Trent. It must've hurt terribly." A myriad of emotions lanced across her expression and when pity flashed, he almost bolted back around, but her words stopped him. "You just don't like to do things halfway, do you?" She caught his eye and flashed him a sheepish grin.

Taking that as acceptance, every muscle in his body relaxed, and he smiled back. *Why in the hell am I not in love with this exceptional woman?* Something niggled inside him and said in a faraway voice, *Maybe you are.*

****

Kelly wanted to be sick. Not at the sight of Trent's scars, but at what he must've gone through in his infirmary. Seeing the extent of his wounds sent pain slicing through her heart. Oh, how she'd have wanted to be there with him while he recovered. "Thank you for the sacrifice to save Amber."

Trent grunted and turned back away from her. "Someone had to do it."

His tortured voice beat at her soul. Something else ate at him, but she'd be patient and wait for it. She just hoped it didn't involve Jamie. He might not have loved her, but he cared for her enough to share this pain with her instead of Kelly.

In an effort to show him that she didn't find him repulsive, she asked, "Can I touch your back?" Her heart broke a bit when he stiffened. This might be too much for him, all at once. "That's okay. I don't have to," she said, even though every muscle in her body screamed for her to reach out and feel him, touch the injured part of him as if she could repair the pain and discomfort he'd once suffered.

He nodded but didn't speak.

Taking that as permission, she reached up with a shaky hand and lightly touched his right shoulder near where the scarring began. He appeared to have about two inches on each side of his back that had either not been touched by the bomb blast or had healed nearly clean. The middle of his back, though. didn't look nearly as bad as she'd expected, considering his phobia of showing her. The surgeons had done a decent job in attempting to make his back look normal.

But, it didn't look normal. Her hand glided toward the center of his back. Nor did it feel that way. The smoothness didn't feel like normal skin. Some of it was a bit leathery and some almost cold to the touch. But none of it disgusted her. While she wished he hadn't been injured, being alive was more important.

Scooting closer, she slid her arms around his waist and tightened her grip. With her head resting on his shoulder, she fought the mistiness of her eyes as she whispered, "I wish I'd been there for you."

He clasped both of her hands in his and leaned back when she looked up at him. "I'm sorry." A tear slid down her cheek as Trent turned his body to her, but he couldn't reach around, considering their positions on the bed. "Come here."

With more tears sliding down her face, Kelly stood and moved in front of him. Trent slipped her onto his lap, where she could've sworn his arousal poked her. His hand almost palmed the side of her face with his fingers in her hair and his thumb on her jawline before it wiped away the stray tears she couldn't stop from falling. "Oh, Kelly. My angel."

She didn't have the time to react to the endearment because he leaned forward and touched his lips to hers, ever so softly. The brief contact lit a need for him inside her that threatened to erupt. "Kiss me again," she whispered.

With a smile, he leaned close again. "Gladly."

Adding his second hand to rest on the other side of her face, he pulled her to him and took her lips in a deep, soul-searing kiss. Their mouths open, their tongues making love to each other, shot fire to her core. Not that she'd need a kiss to want to make love to Trent McKenzie, but the kiss surely enhanced the excitement. The difference this time and the last time was that he wouldn't be hiding from her. She'd have every part of him, scars and all.

She lost herself as their lips moved over each other, and whatever part of her mind had thought not having sex again with Trent was the right thing to do, fled. The part that said she'd take him to her bed any way she could get him danced inside her stomach as it fluttered with desire.

Moving her head, he changed the direction of their kiss as his tongue mimicked what she hoped he planned to do to her. And by the growing arousal beneath her lap, she believed the kiss alluded to an erotic evening.

A moan slipped from within her chest and escaped through her mouth as he broke their kiss and sucked on her lower lip with tantalizing nips.

"You taste so damn good. I can't wait to taste all of you," he warned her.

The thought of him going down on her almost made her cream her panties in delight. If she was wearing any. She'd wait. She might suck at patience most of the time, but with Trent, she had it in abundance. Hell, she'd waited so long for him to notice her as an attractive woman.

Tiny electrical shocks jolted through her as his thumb caressed her bottom lip, and he stared at it as if engrossed in its meaning.

"Did you know you have perfect lips? Not too thin and not too plump?"

How the hell was he talking right now? Not only did she find catching her breath hard, but all she wanted to do was rip off her nightgown and get down and dirty. "Oh," she managed to say.

"I think I'll have to have more." Closing the short distance again, his lips covered hers, gently, lovingly. When she opened to him, his tongue moved in languid strokes within her mouth, like he had all night to do this. She'd only ever been with Brian who didn't believe foreplay should last longer than it took for him to get hard. Trent obviously believed differently.

And she loved it.

A lot.

Shutting down her wandering mind, she reveled in the kiss, the warmth of his mouth on hers, the tenderness yet yearning in his lips. If she hadn't already lost her head over this man, one of his kisses would do that.

The kiss changed to hot and heavy, and she had to break it off to catch her breath. With their foreheads resting against each other, they each took gulps of air. "Wow," she whispered.

He nodded, sliding their foreheads against each other. "Wow." After a pause, he added, "I think you need to lose that nightgown.

She couldn't agree more.

Standing, she slipped her nightgown over her head and smiled when he realized she wasn't wearing panties...again. She held no self-consciousness of her pregnant body. Not with Trent.

He slid his hand up to her baby bump and held it there. "Are you sure we won't hurt the baby?"

Almost snorting at the absurdity of asking this time and not before, she forged a smile instead. "It's fine." Wanting the focus off the baby and on her burning need for him, she guided his hand to her breast. Excitement ricocheted through her at his massaging touch. When his fingers tweaked her hard nipple, she almost came unglued.

She'd heard sex hormones could be strong while pregnant, but she knew it was all about Trent. The man she loved.

Before kneeling on the bed, she moved the covers, displaying the rest of his sculpted body. Kelly let her gaze rake over him slowly. Boy was he ready for her. His magnificent cock stood at attention, and she wanted to reach out and grab it, pump and bring him satisfaction. Instead, she leaned in to kiss him while maneuvering herself down beside him. She planned to be on top during sex, but exploring this position would be a great start.

Taking over the kiss, his lips devoured hers, and little firecrackers of pleasure rocketed through her, focusing their energy on her core and her burning need.

Reaching a hand up to cup her head, Trent shifted her and deepened the kiss. His tongue probed and stroked and loved every inch of her mouth. While delicious shivers skittered down her spine, she reached out a hand and stroked his chest, feeling the firm muscle beneath. During recovery, he might not have been able to work out like he had in the past, but his body still remained a work of art with toned muscles.

He moaned in her mouth when her hand dived lower toward his erection. When her fingers encircled him, he stiffened and pulled back from the kiss. "What are you trying to do to me, angel?"

Smiling, she licked her lips seductively. "I'm just getting started."

With a low growl, he pressed kisses along the column of her throat, eliciting tiny, erotic bubbles to float inside her. As his palm covered her breast, she tossed her head back and moaned in delight before she remembered her mission of pleasing him.

When she leaned down to kiss his chest, his hand left her breast and she almost cried mournfully at the loss of his touch. The enjoyment of her lips on his body added to the pressure building within her core. Sliding down, she leveled herself between his legs. Looking up, she almost lost herself in his gaze as he watched her make love to him.

With a smile, she licked his erection from base to tip before slipping it into her mouth. Lost in pleasure, he closed his eyes and groaned. Moving her mouth over the tip, she swirled her tongue around it. Trent twisted his hands in the sheets on each side of him. Joy at the success of driving him wild surged through her.

She glided her mouth back down, then licked and sucked until his hands fisted in her hair. "Enough," he rasped.

Grinning, she slid up, straddled him, and

positioned his erection at her wet folds.

"Are you ready?" He reached a finger out to check her wetness. "Damn," he said when he found her more than ready. He pulled his finger back and licked it.

She couldn't help it if bringing him gratification turned her on something fierce. "Yeah, damn." Slipping him inside, she slowly slid down until fully sheathed. "Hmm."

Her love for this man exploded with him deep inside her. Life felt right with them together. He may only be offering her passion at the moment, but she'd grab hold and take it wherever it'd go.

Both of his hands raised and rested on her breasts, each mimicking the motions of the other as he massaged them in his strong hands.

Placing her hands on his chest, she began to rise and fall so he could slip enough from her to tease them both before plunging back in deep. Her plan had been to torture him until he was ready to come apart, but the more she tried to drive him crazy, the closer her orgasm drew.

After teasing her nipples, he raised a hand and cupped the back of her head, pulling her down to him, her belly between them. "I'm so damn close," he said in a whisper before he took her mouth in a searing kiss, lips crashing together, his tongue intruding in her mouth, trying to coax hers to play.

Caught by surprise at the intensity of the kiss, she relaxed and allowed instinct to take over, knowing where Trent was concerned, she'd never fail.

She broke the kiss. "Me, too."

Grasping her ass cheeks, he said, "Well, let's get there."

With his hands guiding her, he shifted their movements just enough to ratchet up the urgency building inside her. She needed more and needed it now. "Trent," she begged.

"Let it go, angel."

Passion surged, climbing higher until starlights flashed before her eyes as a blinding wave of red-hot pleasure sought its way through her body, lighting every nerve ending while leaving her limp and sated.

Trent moved her a few more times before claiming his own release, calling out her name on his groan of satisfaction.

She couldn't say how long they lay like that. If Trent hadn't said something about getting them cleaned up, she might've fallen asleep on top of him, probably crushing him with her extra weight.

Rolling on her side, Kelly could only nod when he said he'd be right back. When he returned with a washcloth, she allowed him to clean her before he cleaned himself on his walk back to the connected bathroom.

He slid back under the covers, pulled her close to him, and kissed her on the top of her head. Curled up next to him, she relaxed and her breathing finally evened out.

"I don't deserve you," Trent whispered.

She couldn't bring herself to ask him why he felt that way. One thing was for certain, she had to learn what was truly happening in his mind in order to open his heart and make room for her and Ashley.

Chapter Twenty-Two

He couldn't believe his ears. How could those stupid fuckers not choose to hide instead of shooting at someone? The men had been left to keep an eye out in case that bitch told Mike about the silver, and he investigated his newfound wealth. They weren't supposed to engage anyone, only report what they'd observed so he would know what he'd be walking into when he stepped back on the ranch.

Being the boss of idiots had about run its course. Holding his thumb and forefinger to the bridge of his nose, he sighed in frustration. "Let me get this straight, they were just driving by and you just shot at them. They hadn't slowed or looked like they were stopping at the cave."

"Well, no," the man on the other end of the phone line said hesitantly.

Fucking hell. "Then, why did you attract attention to yourselves by shooting? Now, they'll be all over that area with the police." If the old man didn't know he was loaded down with silver, he would soon enough.

"It was that woman, and we knew you wanted her dead, so we thought we could help."

"Fuck! Get the hell off the land, you asshole." His patience had worn thin with the people he'd had to hire to help him. If that silver mine didn't mean so much to him and his future wealth, then he'd give up his quest for the land. "But stay in the area. Out of sight."

"Gotcha, boss."

This should've been so damn easy, but Brian had been bullheaded, and Mike hadn't done as expected once Brian died. This had become almost too convoluted to handle. But handle he would.

"Did anyone check out the cave before they drove by?" he asked as an afterthought.

"Nope. Not even a stray cow."

Good. Maybe they wouldn't figure there was a silver vein in the cave. He could only hope at this point.

"What do you want us to do about the woman?"

No longer could he trust this to anyone else. Too much was at stake. "I'm coming to town in a few days. We'll take care of it all then. Once the old man and the woman are dead, the land will be as good as mine."

Chapter Twenty-Three

Waking alone in a strange house sucked, the space beside her already cold. It made it worse that she wasn't in the room she should've been in. Anxious, Kelly hoped she'd get back to her room without being seen. The last thing she wanted was for Mike to find her sneaking around.

Trent had made a breakthrough last night, and joy floated inside her. She'd known his back had been a problem for him, causing him angst. His cutting her out when he'd been injured had hurt her like nothing ever had. But she'd kept her secret from him about how she and Brian were going to marry. Heck, she'd just learned she was pregnant the morning of his incident.

Maybe it'd been best at the time, but she'd have liked to have been there for Trent. The two had cheered each other up so many times before. Well, mostly he'd cheered her up. More than once she'd wanted to tell him that he was her Mr. Right, but she'd always chickened out.

Hopefully, his reserve would show signs of cracking, and she'd have a way into his heart. Yet, there was something still bothering him. Something she feared held him back. Jamie probably knew.

At that unpleasant thought, she flipped the covers off, left the bed and dressed. Peeking out the door, she made sure the hallway was clear before she slipped from Trent's room to hers.

Finally arriving downstairs after a quick shower and change of clothes, she followed the scent of breakfast to the kitchen. Her heart sank to her stomach when she didn't find Trent. In lieu of the man she loved, AJ smiled when she entered the big country kitchen with its bright white cabinets and blue countertop. Sitting on a stool, pulled up at the island bar, he said, "Good morning, sleepy head," then shoved a forkful of pancakes in his mouth.

Going to the cabinet that held glasses, she pulled one down and went to the refrigerator for orange juice. "Where is everyone?" *Where is the man who had amazing sex with me last night and left my bed—okay, his bed—without a word?* Again she'd pushed him to sex and once again afterward, he'd acted as if it was nothing. God, she could be so stupid. More than anything, she wanted him to fall in love with her, and she was failing miserably at it.

"Trent and Mike went into town."

She stopped pouring the juice midstream. Trent had left her alone, as in left the house? He promised he would stay by her side through this. She'd figured he'd be outside at the barn again, asking a ton of ranching questions, or with Mike in his office, again asking a ton of ranching questions.

Something about this ranch intrigued him more than she'd ever noticed his interest before. That pleased her.

As if reading her mind, AJ added, "Oh, Trent didn't want to go, but Mike pushed."

Although they shouldn't, butterflies fluttered in her

stomach at the fact that he hadn't wanted to leave her alone. "Oh," she squeaked and finished filling her glass. Moving to the table, she surveyed the spread of breakfast food—pancakes, sausage, and scrambled eggs.

"It's the best I could do."

Surprised, she raised her eyebrows at AJ. "You did this?" Not the cook for the cowboys as had been the case since they'd been there?

Sheepishly, he shrugged. "I needed to do something while you slept."

"Where's Matt?"

"Sleeping. He had watch last night."

Right, they were taking turns providing what protection they could. Her mind went on alert. *The shooting.* Her heart rate accelerated. "What about the man who shot at us?"

AJ shrugged. "The local police are handling it."

"The local police?" she asked incredulously.

"Yeah, Trent and Mike were going by there, but they didn't expect to find anything. We don't have the resources to investigate it and stay close to the house, so we'll let the police handle that one while we stay here." She noticed he left off "with you."

Picking up a plate, she loaded it and sat next to AJ. "Thanks for cooking."

He smiled brightly. "You're welcome. I remember Megan was starving in the mornings when she was pregnant—after the morning sickness had passed. Hey, do you want a separate plate for your pancakes so the syrup doesn't mix?"

She smiled. "No, I think everything in syrup sounds good this morning."

Shaking his head, AJ laughed. "Pregnant women."

After taking a few bites of her breakfast, Kelly had convinced herself it was okay to pry. "AJ," she said hesitantly, "do you know what's going on with Trent?"

Coffee cup to his lips, he halted the progress. "What do you mean?" He took a sip and set his cup down.

"What's eating at him? I mean, I know about his back and letting people see it has been bothering him, but there's more."

"I don't know what you're talking about."

Waving her fork with pieces of pancake on it, she almost growled. "Don't play that male bullshit with me. I know you two were always close, so you wouldn't just let him be like he is without knowing or interfering. So what's eating at him?"

AJ heaved a heavy sigh. "Did he tell you about Jamie?"

Son of a bitch. Had he lied about being in love with the woman? Just her freaking luck. But why would he lie? To spare her heart?

A sickening feeling leveled itself in her stomach, turning the food over and making her nauseous. She wouldn't give up. She'd still fight for his heart, even if it was only part of one to begin with. "Yes, he told me a little about her."

"Well, what he didn't know is that she kept in touch with us while the two of them went gallivanting around the countryside."

Her hand flew to her mouth. Not wanting to believe her ears, she asked, "You spied on him?"

AJ winced. "We just made sure he was okay."

"Put it how you want, you had that woman spy on

him and report back to you when he must not have wanted you to know where or how he was." She took a deep breath, and continued, "Which would've sucked, but still, AJ."

"Look, I found out a man I respected was my brother. Then he almost died. Before he could fully recover, he left without a word. Sure we'd do anything we could to keep up with his progress."

Who was she kidding? If she could've planted someone to watch over Trent, she'd have done the same thing. "Did you have her do it?"

"No. That's where it got interesting. After they'd been on the road for a while, she contacted us. Thought we'd be worried and wanted to let us know he was okay."

"But, he wasn't okay. Was he?"

He shook his head. "No. He has several things happening with him. It was a lot all at one time."

Needing to know what burdens Trent carried, she pushed, "And? They are?"

Picking up his cup, he sipped more coffee. "I'm not sure it's my place to tell you, Kelly."

A heavy discomfort settled in her chest. It wasn't his place, but she'd take it however she could get it. "He showed me his back. That's one thing. You said there were several. What else?"

"I won't tell you everything, Kelly, but this one should be obvious: He needs to settle things with our father."

She wanted to rage at his not sharing whatever laid most heavily on Trent's mind because she knew this wasn't it. Something almost too heavy to bear rested in his heart.

Settling things with his father could happen after they finished what was happening now because she wouldn't even recommend he go to D.C. and speak with Senator Hamilton now.

Fist clenched around her heart, she asked, "AJ, was he…in love with Jamie?"

He scrutinized her face before shaking his head. "Not as far as I know."

Relief soared through her. He hadn't lied. Once she cleansed his heart of whatever held it captive, she could win it, and they'd be a family. Resting her hand on her belly, while Ashley wasn't his, she knew he'd love her with everything he had.

Chapter Twenty-Four

Looking over the area of the shooting, Mike confirmed to Trent that someone had been digging around. When it appeared to be localized near the cave Kelly had told him about, Trent went exploring, and it hadn't taken long for him to notice a shiny pebble on the ground. Holding it up in front of the flashlight, he shook his head, then scanned the walls.

Trent exited the cave to a waiting Mike and handed the man his find. "Did you know you have silver in here?" He gestured to where he'd been searching.

"Silver?" Mike looked at the small nugget of silver in his palm. "No."

"Depending on how much is in there, that makes your land worth a shitload more than it already is. That'd make someone want it pretty badly."

The man staggered back a bit, no doubt realizing someone might've killed his son for the wealth. "Please God," he whispered, "don't let it be Luke."

Not able to assure the man it wasn't, since Mike had told him Luke was all about the money, Trent tried another tact. "Let's keep the silver quiet for now. Let our men do their thing. We'll solve this, and then you can decide what to do about this."

Shoving the nugget in his pocket, Mike nodded. "We need to get some groceries for the house."

On the ride to town, they had a cordial conversation. Then Mike confused Trent with his words. "I guess you'll have to stick around and teach Ashley all she needs to learn."

Shock ignited his system. "Me?"

"Sure. I can size someone up real quick. Aren't you going to take care of Kelly and that little one? I mean, why else would you be here? Sure you say protection, but I see how you look at her and she looks at you. Plus, I'd hate to think I would be handing over management to someone who wasn't staying."

This seemed to be a totally inappropriate conversation to have with Mike, considering who the man was to Kelly and the baby. And turning over ranch management....

Trent knew nothing of ranching except what he'd learned since they'd been there, and it wasn't a whole hell of a lot. Not to mention, they'd just met. The man had lost his damn mind. This had gone too far. "Whoa. Wait a minute. First, Kelly and I aren't an item. She loved your son. She won't jump ship like that just because you want it."

The man scoffed. "It's you," was all he said in response.

Of course, Trent couldn't leave it at that. There had to be something he'd missed. Had he truly allowed his emotions to show for the world to see? He couldn't have that. Not in this stranger's house. "Why me? You don't even know me?"

"Because Kelly is a good judge of character, and it's obvious she loves you."

Another person to tell him that. Christ, he'd been the only one not to realize. "Still, that's Brian's daughter she's carrying."

"Yep, and he'd want her happy and his little girl taken care of. You strike me as the man who could do that. Plus, it's plain as day you love her too."

But Kelly hadn't agreed to marry him. Sleep with him, yes. Marry him, no. And even if she did, he didn't see her staying away from her big city and her career. "But wanting me to manage this for you, that's the stupidest thing I've ever heard since I can barely stay in a saddle as it is."

A sharp pain lanced through his system. Les had taught him to ride as best he could. He'd taken the men on trail rides when they'd visited the Hamilton home in Mississippi.

Les. How could Trent forget so easily?

Being with Kelly did that, but it didn't seem completely right that he should forget. It was downright wrong for him to allow it to slip his mind as he had while thinking he could have a fulfilling life with Kelly. Bile formed in his gut. What kind of friend had he become where he'd allowed his own selfishness to override his loyalty to a friend…even a deceased one?

Laughing, Mike recaptured his attention and assured him, "You'll learn. I've got a few more good years before my maker takes me. I'll teach you everything you need to learn so you can teach my grandbaby because I know she'll want to run this ranch when she grows up."

Not seeing the humor in the situation, Trent crossed his arms over his chest and leaned back in the seat. "I'm pretty sure Kelly will have something to say about this, and I don't want to be within earshot when she says it. The woman scares the crap out of me with those pregnancy hormones." Except for the ones that brought her back to his bed last night. Those he'd keep in a heartbeat.

"Wait until it's your flesh and blood baby in her belly."

That didn't sound nearly as scary as he thought it would.

Before he could respond, Mike parked in front of a place called The General Store. The same one he'd entered with Kelly when they'd arrived in Reed Point. Its old-timey wood façade meshed with the adjoining buildings, so the town appeared to be from times gone by. This town, and its historic look and feel, called to him. Maybe Mike was right, and he could live here. Maybe it was where he belonged. Lord knew that even growing up with the Hamiltons, he'd always been the outsider who didn't belong in their world.

He shook his head to put the interesting conversation aside. of the only good thing about it was that he realized that he didn't have to hide his feelings for Kelly from Mike.

That lightened his heart and soul. Having to suppress how he felt about Kelly outside of the bedroom wouldn't let her know how he really felt. *And that was?* his mind screamed. If he knew exactly what it was supposed to feel like, he just might be in love with her. He wanted to be with her night and day, body and soul, and being parted from her was misery, even for the short trip like now. Might would be a good term to describe where he expected he was with that "in love" thing she wanted.

"Nate," Mike said to a big, beefy man standing behind a wood counter in the store wearing, of all things, an apron, "meet Trent McKenzie. You're gonna see a whole lot of this boy, so be nice to him."

Trent, who'd thought he had big hands, watched his get swallowed in Nate's.

"Heard about you and your friends. You came in with Kelly."

Heard? This wasn't the man who'd met them. How fast did news travel in this town? "Yes."

"Anything I can do for you?"

Trent almost shook his head but stopped. "Nate, do you have any more pickled bologna?" He wanted to wipe the words off his tongue. How could she eat that? Something that foul—he guessed that by name only since he'd never been stupid enough to try it—had to be bad for the baby.

"I did, but according to my dad, Kelly bought the last jar."

Trent figured that meant Marvin was Nate's dad. He stored that away knowing he'd best learn the families if he'd have any hope of a successful life here. Wow. Was he really considering it? If Kelly wanted it for Ashley....

Shaking off those thoughts, he returned to the task at hand. "Would you find a way to order a case of it? I'll pay for the entire thing."

"A case? What the hell would you want that much of that junk for?"

Trent had a feeling the man knew he wanted it for Kelly, but Nate wanted him to say it for some reason. So, he laid it out. "I know the stuff is shit, but my woman has a serious craving for it, and I don't want to be driving into Billings every time she wants some. I've got three more months to go." He might've taken off with Mike this morning—nearly against his will, but he'd be damned if he'd drive over to Billings to get her something to eat. Especially something like pickled bologna. His stomach turned over.

"Your woman, huh? I thought she was Brian's?"

His eyes sprang wide. Had he really just said that in public? Realizing that he'd never said Kelly, his expression had given him away. At Mike's, he'd planned to let everyone know she was his, but the town to know? Too late. His slip of the tongue would be the gossip of the day. He and Kelly had to meet with her parents before they found out she was pregnant by one man and another had claimed her.

Mike slapped him on the back, and he almost stumbled forward. "Way to go."

Unable to tell if that had been a rebuff or congratulations, Trent nodded and moved into the store to help complete their list so he could go home. Crap. Damn Mike and making him think of the place as home. Even if Kelly agreed to marry him, he didn't think she'd want to stay.

Then again, with her family here, maybe she would.

He needed to slap himself. They had lives and jobs in Baltimore. This trip had been to protect Kelly. Although, they might've brought her right into trouble. A sudden need to be back to her, be by her side, flooded him.

His phone rang, and a foreboding settled over him. "Yeah."

"It's Devon. I've got some information for you."

"Can it wait about half an hour so I can get back to the ranch?"

"You left her?"

"AJ and Matt are with her," he said defensively. He'd not wanted to leave her, but Mike had been so insistent, and someone needed to go with him, according to him anyway. After their conversation, Trent realized Mike wouldn't have settled for anyone else to ride with him.

"Although I want to, I'm not going to give you shit about it. As for the information, sure, it can wait a few minutes."

He caught himself before he ended the call. "Oh, Devon."

"Yeah."

Peering around to make sure no one was eavesdropping, he walked toward an empty corner of the store and dropped his voice before continuing, "Near where those guys shot at us, we found silver in one of Mike's caves. I'm not sure how much there is."

Devon whistled. "Call me back when you're with the boys."

Ending the call, Trent wished he'd asked Devon if he'd found out who might be behind it all. Then maybe his mind would rest on the trip.

"Come here and get yourself a real cowboy hat," Mike called.

Cowboy hat. *Les. Les and his cowboy hat.* Dammit, there he went again imagining a life when he shouldn't have one to begin with. Jamie assured him he could get through this when the time came, but was he just grasping at straws?

Chapter Twenty-Five

When Trent had assembled AJ and Matt, they'd called only to find Devon and the team unavailable. Trent wanted to kick himself for putting off the information when Devon had called, but he knew if it had been urgent, his brother would've pushed. So he puttered around the ranch, grinding his teeth, waiting for that chance to speak with Devon or Jesse.

Stepping out on the front porch, Trent inhaled the freezing air, and while his lungs burned at the effort, he wondered at himself for making the call to his brother outside instead of comfy and cozy in Mike's office or his room. *Because Kelly might come to your room before you finish the call.*

He shook off the thought, finding it funny how this was the first time he noticed how dark it truly got out in the middle of nowhere. So unlike the city with its million lights. Here, the lights were like billions of stars, but they didn't light the area like the city lights. No, they left a blackness that Trent was growing comfortable with. In fact, he found himself growing comfortable with the entire life here. He'd never felt more like he belonged.

With the phone to his ear, he prepared himself for whatever news HIS had for him. Not wanting to piss off Devon since he was working a mission, Trent decided not to bitch about no one being available.

Devon cleared his throat when he answered. "Sorry, I don't have much to help yet."

What the fuck? Why had he called that morning if he didn't have much?

"Since we want the three of you to remain on the ranch, we're releasing Danny and Steve from here to do the interviews and investigation. We can swing it with the crew we have."

That would be a great help. "Thanks," he grumbled. He wanted the men to solve the problem facing him and Kelly, but he didn't want them to miss catching that bastard Hogan. "Don't shortchange yourselves, though."

"Nah," Devon said gruffly, "we'll be fine as long as we can keep Brad from telling off the police again."

Laughing, Trent imagined that scene in his mind. "Maybe you should send him to do the interviews."

"Believe me, I tried." A sigh reached Trent's ears. "He's even more determined now that Hogan tricked them into getting arrested."

Trent could understand that emotion. He'd be on the warpath, but he couldn't get involved in it. There were more important things at hand for him. "What do you have for me?"

"Not much at the moment. That's why I need boots on the ground there. Well, boots not protecting Kelly. Anyway, Luke—the other son—is living it up in Vegas. It appears that he's latched onto a wealthy benefactor."

"Then he shouldn't want the money here."

"I don't know about that. Having someone able to bankroll the death of his brother puts the ranch within his reach. And growing up, he probably knew about the silver mine."

"Maybe. Maybe not. Mike didn't know about it, and Kelly said she'd never heard about it from Brian growing up."

"I think he needs to be interviewed at least. Mike isn't telling you everything about Luke. I think he left for more than one reason, whether Mike knows or not. Luke's benefactor—the wealthy playboy—is also his lover."

Trent whistled. "No, he hasn't alluded to that fact. I'm sure it doesn't matter in the scheme of things, except for their relationship." Old-fashioned values ran through Mike's veins. He'd probably have a problem with his son's sexual orientation even though Trent couldn't give a shit one way or the other.

Jesse's voice came over the phone. "Don't be naïve. That could've been the reason he wrote Luke out of the will, not because Mike feared he'd just sell it. Whether he knows about the mine or not, if he becomes Mike's only child with no grandchildren on the way, Luke could expect the property to pass to him. All he'd have to do is eliminate his competition, wait for the old man to change his will, then kill off the dad."

Shaking his head in disbelief, Trent didn't know what to think. "Do you think he's really like that?"

"Don't know," Jesse answered. "While you two were talking, we got clearance for two of our jailbirds to leave Belize, so Danny and Steve will question him first."

"Yeah, now," Devon said, "Kent Oil is buying up land like crazy in Montana and Wyoming. I can only see what they've bought, not what properties they've made offers on, and it's odd. It's almost like they're just buying with a crapshoot of whether there will be oil there."

"I wonder if those men who shot at us work for him. Maybe he found out about the silver mine while prospecting." Trent rubbed a hand over his face. Damn, he needed to shave again. Kelly hadn't complained yet, but he imagined not having red marks from his scruff would be nice.

"It's possible," Jesse said. "Although as a business professional, I can't imagine he'd go onto someone's land without seeking permission."

"Can't trust every employee you have to follow the rules though." Trent sighed at the thought of trying to check out every employee who worked for Kent Oil. It wasn't a large operation, but still, that took more time, meaning Kelly would remain in danger. Someone wanted her and the baby dead. Trent had no doubt of that, even though the shooting may have been a crime of opportunity.

He could almost hear Jesse's neck snap up and a glare come through the phone. "I'd damn well best be able to."

The laugh bubbled out before he could stop it. "Of course you can trust me."

"Don't you go and do some stupid shit, Trent McKenzie," Jesse demanded.

"I'm sure he won't," Devon said to pacify his brother.

"Don't worry." Trent didn't want to think about how Devon had come to his defense so quickly. "Tell me about the other guy—Brightmore."

"Ah," Devon said, "Reggie Brightmore. I don't have much on him at all. He's a spoiled rich kid who owns a bit of property here and there, but I haven't figured out a rhyme or reason to it. Yet. As to why he'd want the ranch there, I don't know."

"Maybe he found out about the silver mine." Trent knew he was grasping at straws, but his gut told him this revolved around the silver in that cave because even though the ranch was prosperous, it wasn't enough to kill for. Unless maybe you thought it was your birthright, but it had been snatched away.

"Possible. You'd have to find out what all he did while there. It's also possible, he just wants a playground to call his. He has an almost endless pot of money coming from his billionaire father, so making more doesn't seem like what he'd want. But we'll check him also."

Shoving his freezing hand into his pants pocket, Trent said, "I'm convinced the silver is the link. Whoever shot at us was there checking it out for themselves or someone else."

"Unfortunately," Jesse said, "someone else could have just discovered it by accident. It could be completely separate."

"Fuck!" He wanted to throw the phone in frustration. With the exception that he'd have help interviewing their suspects, which was at least something, they'd gotten nowhere.

"I'll keep digging into Kent Oil and Brightmore while the boys interview the other son. They'll report directly to you."

They wrapped up the call, and Trent put his phone in his pocket and leaned against the porch railings, looking out as far as he could see. That damn silver. Mike didn't want to bring anyone in to look at it, and

Trent couldn't push him to see the extent of this treasure on his land. Amazing the boys never discovered it growing up. Then again, Luke came to mind, maybe one of them had.

Nodding when he saw Matt walking the perimeter, his worry eased a bit. The men hadn't left him alone to solve this. To protect Kelly. But this was taking too damn long. He wanted her safe.

He slammed his open palm down in frustration, turned and went back into the house and sought out Kelly. She and Mike were in the family room, or den as Mike called it, watching a comedy on TV. Without thought, he leaned down and kissed her briefly on the lips before sitting beside her. When he took her hand, he noticed her rigid posture. She tried to pull her hand from his, but he refused. He figured she was trying to hide from Mike.

Leaning close to her, he whispered in her ear, "It's okay. He knows you're mine." And she was.

When that didn't seem to relax her, he could only squeeze her hand, hoping to impart his calm to her.

"Is everything okay?" Mike asked, not looking away from the TV screen.

"Nothing helpful except some men will do the interviews for us."

This time, Mike turned to him. "Will they interview Luke?"

Trent took a moment to consider how to answer. He didn't want to hurt the man's feelings but decided to opt for honesty. He nodded. "Yes."

"You have them tell him to get his ass back here. He and I need to talk."

That was all Trent wanted—a potential suspect

under the same roof with almost unlimited access to his Kelly. "Will do," he said, unsure if he'd actually follow through.

Chapter Twenty-Six

"I'm not sure I'm ready for this," Kelly said as they pulled into her parents' driveway. The sprawling, two-story home had snow on its roof. Growing up with so many brothers and a sister, Kelly had always appreciated the size of the house. Early on, her father, a cattle man, had done well for himself. They'd never been wealthy, but she couldn't remember ever doing without.

Putting Mike's truck into Park beside her father's well-worn truck, Trent reached over and took her hand before she shoved it back into a glove. "Yes, you are. I'm here with you, Kelly." Leaning over, he kissed her briefly on the lips.

She jumped back and squeaked, and he laughed. Her parents couldn't see that.

"Okay, I'll back off while we're here. You can tell them that you belong to me in your own time."

She belonged to him? Since when? Sure he'd begun to show his attraction for her outside the bedroom, which had surprised the hell out of her and made her uncomfortable around Mike, but he still wasn't in love with her.

Donning their gloves and hats, they exited the truck and trudged to the front door, Kelly's feet feeling as if she dragged stone blocks behind her. What would her family say? Her heart hurt knowing she'd disappoint them. Her mother had instilled virtue as such an important thing.

At the blue front door, Trent raised his fist to knock, but the door sprung open, and her father snatched her up into his arms and held her tight. "My Kelly."

His Brut aftershave gave her a sense of warmth and homecoming. She'd always felt safe in her father's embrace. He let her go, and she found herself engulfed in her mother's arms and heard the sniffling that could only be from tears.

"Kelly," her mother whispered.

Behind her, she heard her father greet Trent as he entered and the door closed. Her mother still held her. Pulling back, she kissed her mother's damp cheek. "Hi, Momma."

Neither of her parents had made a negative comment about her pregnancy, and they both had to have felt it when they held her.

"Honey," her father said to her mother, "this is Trent McKenzie. He's with our Kelly."

"I'm Barbara." She held out her hand to Trent while Kelly used her knuckles to wipe away a few tears she hadn't realized had escaped her own eyes.

Gripping her mother's hand, Trent said, "Nice to meet you, Barbara."

"Come on in. I just put on a pot of coffee to beat the cold. Now, Kelly, I'm sure you aren't drinking caffeine, so what can I get for you?"

That was it? That was all that would be said about her being pregnant? She knew they would've already found out, but still. "Um, orange juice if you have it."

"Take your coats off and get comfortable. I'll be

back in a jiffy."

Shedding their outerwear and placing it on the pegs by the door, Kelly worried over what she'd say.

"Relax," Trent whispered to her, "I told you, they love you."

Being in his arms topped the list of what she'd rather be doing right now, but since that couldn't happen, she took his soothing words to heart. Oh, she still fretted, but she'd let things progress as they did.

Kelly led Trent into the family room, and they sat beside each other on the couch, her father already occupying his recliner. She estimated it to be nearly twenty years old unless they'd replaced it on the sly over the years. No one sat in it, except her father. He never told anyone they couldn't, but it'd been a respect thing for him to have that one luxury to himself.

"Kelly, baby, we're glad you're home. You could've stayed here, you know," her father, Frank Williams said.

"I know, Daddy, but, well…." She took a moment to collect her words. "I thought since Brian had died, Mike might like to be near me since I'm carrying his granddaughter."

"It's a girl?" he asked, not questioning anything else.

Un-freakin'-believable. She'd worried like crazy, yet truly received no angst from her father. Maybe it'd come from her mother. She had been the one to push the need to remain a virgin.

Resting her hand on her stomach, she smiled. "Yes. Ashley."

"And her middle name?" Barbara asked, entering the room carrying a small tray with a coffee carafe, mugs, and a glass of juice.

"Lynn."

Kelly's mother stopped in her tracks. "My middle name," she said softly.

Nodding, Kelly smiled tentatively. "Yes."

Getting herself together, Barbara set the tray down on the cherry wood coffee table and served everyone.

Beverages in hand, the conversation stilted until Barbara said, "I'm sorry to hear about Brian."

"We were getting married, Momma. I swear it."

Her mother set her coffee on the table beside her plaid armchair. "First, don't swear. Second, it doesn't matter if you were or not."

"But-But, you said I shouldn't...you know, until I was married. And I did." She placed her face in her hands as the tears flowed. Her heart ached. "I'm so sorry, Momma." She'd failed her family. The people who had been there for her entire life. The only people who'd truly loved her. And she'd thrown that trust out the window. She hadn't been the good girl her mother had taught her to be.

A weight lifted from beside her and new movement settled on each side of her. Arms wrapped around her shoulders from each side.

"Kelly, baby," her father said from where Trent had been seated, "you didn't do anything wrong."

She shook her head and refused to face her parents because she instinctively knew her mother had to be on the other side. It was how they'd consoled her when she'd thought her heart was broken after her first failed test in high school when she couldn't figure out how to drive a stick shift, and when Brian wouldn't move to Baltimore with her.

"Shh, sweetie," her mother said. "It's okay."

Kelly imagined she might've cried for her own stupidity in thinking anything other than that her parents would love her no matter what. But whether it was that or hormones, she had a tough time stopping the tears. Yet all through it, her parents held her, one on each side.

Once she'd controlled herself enough to lift her head, she blew her nose on the tissue that had been placed in her hand by her mother.

"Sweetie," her mother said over her shoulders, "why don't you show Trent around."

"Uh, sure." Frank stood. "Come on, Trent, let's get those coats back on. Let me show you my ranch. At least what's close." He chuckled. Leaning down, he kissed Kelly on the forehead. "I love you."

"I love you, too, Daddy."

After the men had departed, Barbara stood and claimed her cup of coffee before sitting back down by her daughter. "So, have you thought about what you plan to do?"

Combining a slow shrug and a shake of her head, Kelly waffled. "I don't know." Then stronger, she said, "I haven't decided. I have my job in Baltimore that I can go back to. But Mike offered to let me stay there. He's made Ashley his heir and wants to see her grow up there."

"Damn Luke for breaking his father's heart. Well, you know you can always stay here. We've got plenty of room now that all of you have moved out."

"Thank you, Momma. I'll let you know when I figure it out."

"Now, what are you going to do about that hunk of

a man that came here with you?"

Eyes wide, she half laughed. "Momma." Never had she heard her mother call a man a hunk.

"Don't act all coy with me. I saw how he worried for you when you were bawling your eyes out. I figure he must mean something to you if you were willing to allow him to see you like that."

"But Brian—"

"Pish posh. I know you were never in love with Brian. Otherwise, you'd never have moved away from here to begin with or at least, you wouldn't have waited so long to get back with him."

Kelly bit her lip. Should she? Her mother had already surprised her. Maybe she would again. She blurted out, "I'm in love with him."

"And he's in love with you."

"No. That's the problem. He's not."

"Are you sure about that?"

Chapter Twenty-Seven

With a Stetson on his head, Trent mounted the brown gelding named Rocky that Mike had provided for him and sent his thanks to Les for teaching him how to do it. He'd expected a nearly lame mare to tote his greenhorn ass around, but with Mike working as a horse breeder, no such thing existed on the ranch. So, he'd bundled up and trusted AJ to look after Kelly while she slept, and Mike took him wherever it was he'd planned, hoping it wasn't the two miles to the cave. His ass might not be able to handle that all at once.

With Kelly lying down to rest again, he'd worried since she did it so often, but Mike had waved it off as a pregnancy thing. Even though Mike wasn't a doctor, Trent accepted that, but it didn't stop his concern.

They cantered past two of the men working with the horses. He saw them long enough to see one sit a horse and get his ass thrown over the front of it. A small pang of panic set in. Patting the horse he rode, he muttered, "Nice horsey."

Mike let out a snort.

Glancing around, Trent watched the second ranch hand try to corral the horse while the one on the ground picked himself up like it was nothing to get thrown every day, and maybe it was in their world. When he didn't see the other men, that panic became full-blown. "Where are the rest of your men?" They'd been cleared for the most part, but in his mind, everyone was suspected of wanting to hurt Kelly.

Mike turned to him. "They're with the cattle. Ready to pick it up a bit? I'll show you."

Not really wanting to trot but wanting to lay his eyes on the workers, he nodded, and giving Rocky a bit more rein, he used his knees to direct the horse like he'd been shown.

Close to one mile from the ranch, Trent's skin began to itch leaving Kelly alone for so long. Mike led them along the fence line of a pasture, and the specks he'd seen were taking shape as cattle and men.

"They're moving them up to graze on some fresher grass."

Finding fresh grass in this frozen area surprised the hell out of him, but he guessed the cows would eat any grass—dead or alive. He'd heard how the men broke up the ice for the cattle and horses to have water. Thankfully, he was used to cold in Baltimore, or he'd hate it here. Then again, it was February already.

Shit. Valentine's Day was tomorrow. He and Kelly weren't officially out as a couple, but he knew the importance of remembering that holiday that made grown men groan.

They slowed as he continued pondering what he'd do for her. It probably wasn't too late to order flowers, although her noticing they came express mail would show he hadn't planned.

Halting beside Mike, Trent tossed his hands across his pummel like the other man. The area was amazingly green for winter. The snow on the mountains created a beautiful backdrop for the wide open space.

"I want to know why you move close, then pull

back."

Unsure of the direction of this conversation—as there could be plenty with that opening line—Trent pleaded ignorant. "What do you mean?"

"I watch you. It's obvious you love her. Yet one minute you show it, then the next you pull back, and a faraway lost look appears in your eyes."

Les.

He took a deep breath and almost screamed at how cold it burned down his chest. Could he dump all his feelings out to this man? Could he explain in a way that would make it all better? That would never happen. Even Jamie said it'd never go away completely. He'd just learn to deal with it. But, how?

"The boy—AJ—told me a bit about what happened to you."

A smile slid on his face at AJ being called a boy. He was only a year younger than Trent. He bet AJ loved that title. Then the smile dropped when he recalled the current conversation. "What did he tell you?"

Rubbing his hand around his chin, Mike drew his brows in thought. "Well, you saved a girl and were injured." He dropped his hand to his jean-clad thigh. "Badly."

Trent snorted. Badly was saying it nicely. "Yeah, I was injured pretty bad. Second and third-degree burns on most of my back, ass, and upper thighs. And, they had to remove shrapnel that left holes in my back. It was fucking painful." Heat crept into his face. "Sorry, for the language." Why did he feel that way around Mike and Frank? Maybe because they were like father figures in the way they carried themselves. A way that demanded respect.

Mike waved his thought off with a flick of the wrist. "Don't sweat it. You'll hear that and worse from me when we begin to brand new cows."

Branding cows. Wow. That'd be exciting and, if he truly had to be honest with himself, fucking terrifying at the same time.

"So you were hurt. It looks like you recovered, though."

Nodding to agree to the partial lie, he heaved a sigh. "I look like a monster."

"Hmph. What does Kelly think about it?"

"Um," he said nervously, "Kelly—My back—" He knew he'd revealed too much with his inability to have a simple response.

Shaking his head, Mike frowned but somehow released a chuckle. "Don't think something goes on in my house without me knowing. That little gal has slipped into your bed every night you've been here."

Fuck. And they thought they'd been quiet about it. Kelly would not like this little revelation. She wanted Mike to think the best of her, which was why she pulled back from him when they were around him. Trent adjusted his hat and hung his head. "She's fine with it. Or, so she says."

"She wouldn't say it if she didn't mean it."

True. Kelly was honest to a fault. He loved that about her. He loved everything about her. He'd also realized that he was in love with her and wanted to marry her. But—

"What is it then?"

"What do you mean?" He knew what the man was talking about but still stalled.

"That look you get in your eye before you act like you shouldn't be enjoying yourself?"

Defeated, he let out a weathered breath. "There are times when I don't think I should be. After the accident, I felt like that all the time."

The creaking of Mike's saddle warned him the man had turned more of his body toward him. "Why?"

Trent rubbed a hand down his face before speaking. "A friend of mine, Les, died during that accident AJ told you about." *The man I'm imitating now on horseback with a damn cowboy hat. God, I'm such a lousy friend to the man.*

Nodding, Mike frowned. "He told me. What's that got to do with you being happy?"

"If I hadn't joined into the situation, he might've found a way out. He might've survived." The hoarse croak in his voice surprised him.

"Do you really believe that? It sounded to me like if you hadn't come along, they probably wouldn't have been able to save that little girl."

Trent shook his head. "He'd have found a way."

"If that's true, why did you join them?"

"Amber was squirming, and the woman kept threatening to kill her." His heart plummeted to his stomach and rolled around to churn a sick feeling. That event flashed before his mind—the woman with the bomb vest holding the hand of Amber and telling Les she'd kill her unless Jake could be brought to her. Little did they know at the time, she'd planned to kill Amber anyway. After he'd inserted himself to help settle his niece, they'd kept everything calm until the cavalry had arrived. Only the cavalry couldn't do anything because of the kill switch in the woman's hand. So after much discussion between the crew in their earpieces, nods, and hand signals from him and Les, a plan had been formed. A plan that only gave Les a ten percent chance of survival.

Trent shook his head, trying to clear the melancholy that so quickly slipped into him.

"And, what happened?"

Sliding back to that day, his heart rate accelerated as he described the event. "Once it had been decided no other option was available, I had to look my friend in the eye, knowing he might not survive and I couldn't do a thing about it. If maybe I'd come to stand in a different spot, then we could've changed places. But as it was, Amber stood between the terrorist and me. I was her only hope."

Trent's eyes watered, and he reined back his emotions to keep tears from slipping down his cheek.

Mike didn't speak, just waited for him to compose himself.

"When the time came, we surprised the terrorist. I snatched Amber, turned, and cradled her to me as quickly as possible, then dove into the pool behind us, hoping it would protect her from any blast. Les—Les grabbed at the bomber's hand and the kill switch in hopes of removing it before she could detonate it." He swallowed hard against the lump that had climbed up in his throat, lodging itself almost painfully. "He failed."

After a long pause, Mike sat up straight and folded his arms over his chest. "I see."

Anger raged through him. He wanted to jump to his feet, but his ass'd fall off the horse, and that was a pretty big fall. "No, you don't see," he ranted, and his horse sidestepped. The bit of panic he'd felt must've alerted the horse. He just pictured the thing bolting and him holding on for dear life.

"Calm down and the horse will settle. He's acting off your emotions."

Baffled that a horse could do that, he tabled learning more until after they finished this conversation. "It's my fault. He should've survived. How can I have a good life when he'll never have the chance? It's unfair, and it's worse when I forget and allow myself to be happy."

"Relax, you're choking that saddle horn."

With adrenaline racing through him, Trent almost fought the man's dictate but knew the tight grip did nothing to quell his emotional outburst. Mike didn't deserve his ire. With Kelly at his side, Trent had bottled it up, and he should've known it'd rear its ugly head the first moment it could. The thing was, he was the object of his anger.

"I want you to listen to me, and listen good, boy. You ain't the only one who has lost someone in the line of duty."

Trent narrowed his eyes at the man, ready to take off his head again. He didn't need patronizing.

"I was in Desert Storm."

The man could've knocked him over with a sledgehammer, and he wouldn't have been more surprised. Mike was a country boy, no, a cowboy, through and through.

"Don't look at me so funny. I wasn't always a rancher, and I ain't as old as you think."

"You were in the military?" Disbelief clouded Trent's words.

Mike nodded. "Damn sure was. Lost a lot of

friends in Desert Storm and the aftermath. Some right in front of my eyes. It sucks and it haunts you, but this is where I want you to clean that wax out of your ears. You can't let it dictate your life."

Dropping his head, he exhaled slowly. "That's what Jamie kept telling me."

"Jamie sounds like a really smart person. Why didn't you listen to him?"

A slight chuckle escaped. He'd told her that her name could be construed as a man's, and she'd refused to agree. *Oh, Jamie, I want to do this, but I'm still not sure I'm ready.* "She," he said softly. Then, he added, "It still doesn't seem fair for me to live the American dream and Les be gone. I don't know that I can reconcile that."

And, he couldn't.

"You probably never will completely."

"Jamie said that also."

"Why the hell didn't you listen to her?"

"Because I'm a jackass."

Mike laughed and looked out over his herd. "Well, that remains to be seen." He turned back to Trent. "Someone asked me a question once when I was in your shoes after seeing my buddies die before my eyes."

Trent's gut clenched. *Buddies?* He couldn't imagine living that nightmare over and over and having more people speak to you. To blame you.

"If the roles were reversed and you had died and looked over your friend while he survived, would you want him to have a full life and be happy or not take what was sitting there for him and reliving that nightmare thinking he was at fault?"

That one question struck him in his chest harder than any previously thrown at him by the counselors at the hospital or Jamie. It was like Mike saw to the core of his pain. Of course he did. He'd lived through it too and look at him now. A prosperous ranch owner with a living child and a grandchild on the way.

No, he'd fucking want Les to enjoy himself and not fret over him. In that scenario, he was dead, and there was nothing anyone could do for him. Nothing would ever rid him of the guilt, but things were as they were. He had the option to grab on with both hands instead of one and fully enjoy his life without allowing this to pull him away. Les would have his ass if he knew that Trent wasn't doing just that.

Christ, he'd been a fool. A fool who was damn lucky his woman loved him and was patient while he figured his shit out. No, she hadn't known he had this issue, but Kelly surely knew something kept him from being his old self.

Now he had to figure out, seriously this time, not only how to propose to her but how to support her and the baby. They each had a small apartment in Baltimore, and he had a job that could be deadly, and she had a penchant for getting into trouble with her investigative reporting. Maybe it was time to start giving Mike's offer some serious thought.

"I see you've answered the question for yourself," Mike said, interrupting his thoughts.

"I'm sorry. He'd want me to live." He paused, taking a moment to resolve all his head and heart felt. With conviction, he said, "And that's what I plan to do."

A broad smile swept across Mike's face. "Good.

My offer still stands if you plan to marry that gal." He gestured to the herd and then wider to encompass the area. "I could use help with all of this and know I've prepared someone to take my place."

Grinning, Trent responded, "Oh, I plan to marry her, if she'll have me. As for the offer, I'd have to see where she wants to live." Instinct told him he'd finally found what he'd always been seeking. Without a doubt, he and Kelly living out their days on this ranch was his destiny.

Who'd have thought the city boy would take to the country so easily? Granted, he hadn't spent a day doing the chores, but it beat carrying a weapon any day.

"I think she's ready to come home. I'll talk with her."

"Mike, I can't replace Brian." He pulled his lips in tight. "Or Luke," he added hesitantly.

"I'm not asking you to. Brian's gone, and I'll figure something out for Luke. I'm asking you to take care of my granddaughter and that wonderful mother of hers."

Excitement rode him, and he leaned back in the saddle. "You'll teach me everything and be patient when I screw up?"

Mike shook his head. "It's not that hard, just hard work. You'll catch on quick."

This was the chance he'd been thinking about when he'd assessed their situation in Baltimore. He didn't begrudge Jesse, AJ, or Jake for raising their children there; he just wasn't raising his daughter there. *Daughter.* Calling Ashley that had come about so easily for him.

He'd miss the men at HIS, but his family came

first. While enjoying growing up on the Hamilton estate, it'd never felt like home to him. Something had always been missing. Sure it'd been opulent with all the amenities of a large hotel, but his family had only been tenants.

Here he'd be a tenant of sorts since Mike planned to will the property to Ashley, but this house and this property, hell, even the small town called to him in a way he'd never imagined. And he'd seen the change in Kelly once she'd landed on Montana soil. She'd relaxed and let her guard down.

Knowing there'd be reminders all around of Brian did pull at him. He didn't want Kelly mooning after the man, but he'd have to trust she wasn't in love with him. Since he'd promised Ashley would know her father, they'd need something of Brian anyway, so he'd have to get used to it, for his daughter's sake if nothing else.

Decision made, Trent reached out a hand, and Mike shook it, each with a firm grip. "I'll be glad to stay if she agrees to stay with me."

"Oh, she'll stay with you all right. You'd best do the proposal up right, though. Women like that kind of thing."

After thinking for a long moment about what he could do, what he hoped would be a brilliant thought came to mind. While not original, he'd heard someone's friend of a friend had done it; he liked it for Kelly. Trent smiled. "Mind if I add to the headcount here?"

"What do you have in mind?"

Trent told him and Mike slapped him on the back in approval.

When he arrived back at the barn, after learning to

put away his horse and brush him down, he snuck into a corner and made a call. He dialed Jesse's number, knowing Jesse and Kate were still gone. "Mrs. K., I need a favor."

Chapter Twenty-Eight

In nothing but his underwear, Trent surprised Kelly when she snuck into his room by meeting her at the door and pulling her into his arms. Clasping his hands on her butt, he pulled her close and covered her lips with his in a demanding and needy kiss. Exactly how he felt about his need to make love to her.

Turning her head, she fell into the kiss and gave as good as he did. Their tongues fought for domination, battling for control over the other. They were definitely made for each other.

Reaching down, he grabbed the hem of her nightgown and pulled it over her head. Without warning, he scooped her into his arms, balancing himself with her extra pregnancy weight. Not that he cared. He loved all of her, just as she was.

With great care, he lay her on the bed where he'd already pulled down the covers. Her hair spread across the pillow, and her luscious body splayed for his viewing pleasure. As his erection strained against his underwear, he stood there and gazed at the beautiful woman who was his.

Soon she'd know it for truth.

Christ, he loved she wasn't wearing panties…again. He'd have to keep her that way. Before joining her, he slid his underwear off. His cock jutted out, ready to take her. Telling himself that while it might be a bit painful to wait, he had work to do to pleasure her. Tasting her essence was paramount. The little tantalizing lick he'd had before hadn't been enough to satisfy him.

On his side, he leaned in and kissed her, but only briefly. He immediately began a trek down her throat, placing kisses along the way.

"Did you have fun with Mike today?" she all but whispered.

He lifted his head to look at her. To evaluate her reaction. "I enjoyed myself. I like it here."

Closing her eyes, she smiled and arched her neck again.

It took him a moment to realize, but Kelly was rubbing his back like any lover would, without cringing or pulling away. That innocent act had his love for her soaring.

He dropped his head and drew one of her nipples between his lips and laved it with his tongue. Her throaty moan fired his already burning need for her.

While he explored her breasts with his mouth and tongue, he moved his hand slowly down her stomach, over the sexy baby bump, to slide his fingers through the curls covering her mound. Finding what he considered a slice of heaven, he split her folds and sank a finger into her heat. He groaned at the shot of urgency that went to his stiff cock. In no way would he ever tire of this woman in his bed.

"I have to have more. The one small taste of you only intensified my need to be between your thighs."

With a burst of throaty laughter, she said, "I'm not stopping you."

Shifting himself down, he climbed over her and

then slid down between her thighs so his eyes were level with her sweet core. When she tried to move, he lay a hand on her thigh.

"Just lie still, angel. My turn to pleasure you. I've been waiting for this since the first time we made love."

With his first lick at her center, he felt precum on the tip of his erection. *Ambrosia.* That word best described her taste. He'd never tasted better. And since she'd be the only woman he was with his remaining days, he'd never taste better.

After a couple of strokes, he took her hard nub between his lips, sucked and tugged.

On a long, sensual moan, Kelly arched her back off the bed.

To add to her pleasure, he slipped a finger inside her.

In response, she threaded her fingers through his hair, pulling his head closer to her core. Her reaction drove him harder.

Mimicking the movements he planned to do with her shortly, he slid his finger in and out of her, adding a second one along the way. His mouth continued to torture her clit with pleasure.

"Let go, angel," he breathed against her core.

In a few short minutes, Kelly came apart on his mouth. The erotic noise and movement she made had his balls drawing up. He had to be inside her. Now.

Kissing her belly, he continued his movement upward until he rested his cock at her slick entrance. Their lips locked, he slid inside in one swift stroke. Stopping to keep from coming, he pulled back from the kiss and rested his forehead on hers. "Good God, Kelly, you drive me crazy."

She moved erotically beneath him, and he snapped, unable to stay still a moment longer. They made love, hot and frenzied, and when pressure built at the base of his spine, he knew he had to rush things along. Shifting his movements, he barely held back until she came once more in his arms.

Before her cry of pleasure ceased, an orgasm ripped through him, and as he spilled himself into her, he understood when people said they saw stars when they came.

Exhausted and sated, he remembered to roll to the side instead of collapsing on top of her. Breathing heavily, he ran a hand over her body, then kissed her slow and sensually. God, he loved this woman.

"That was the best," Kelly said as her hand played mindlessly in his hair.

"It was."

"You're just saying that. I can't compete with all the women you've had."

"Hush. First of all, I wasn't just saying that. That was the best sex I've ever had. Second, there is no competition. You are, without a doubt, the best."

Her quietness worried him, but he couldn't have this discussion now. He had a plan and if he talked too much mushy crap, he might ask her without waiting for it. That couldn't happen.

Groaning, he lifted himself and stepped to the bathroom to get a cloth to clean up. Coming back to bed, he caught himself whistling. He couldn't remember the last time he'd whistled without thinking. Happiness. It was within his grasp.

Both clean and back in bed, Trent pulled her close, relieved their lovemaking hadn't bothered his incision.

"Mike knows you've been sneaking in here."

Her head snapped up from his chest to look at him with frightful eyes. "Oh no."

"It's okay. I told you before he knew about us. Didn't you notice him smile when I held your hand or kissed you?"

She blew a strand of blonde hair from her face. "Honestly, no. I was too uptight at you for doing it. It's got to bother him. I mean, not long ago I was to marry his son."

"Maybe you should talk to him about it. Put your mind at ease. He's given me the green light to pursue you. Says Brian would be happy."

Her eyes widened. "Really?"

Nodding, he smiled, then touched his forefinger to the tip of her nose. "Yes, angel."

She snuggled back onto his chest and hummed. "I like it when you call me that."

Trent tested the waters. He didn't get a read on her earlier when he'd told her he liked it here. Hell, he really hadn't been thinking of anything but getting his dick deep inside her. "Are you enjoying yourself here in Montana?"

Her hair rubbed his chest as she nodded. "Especially since things are good with my parents."

So maybe she'd like to stay. That possibility had him wanting to leap for joy. Okay, not that exactly, but it poured hope and excitement into his veins. The thought of running this ranch with Mike sounded more and more appealing each time he turned it over in his mind.

Running a ranch had been Les's dream. Nope. He slammed that thought shut. He would not go there.

Instead, he talked to Les, *Buddy, this will be the last time. It's not that I won't forget you, I must move my life forward. Mike made me realize you'd want that. I've asked many times why you put yourself so close to the bomber urging me to remain close to Amber. I've tried to complicate the answer, but I guess it's as simple as that's where we ended up when the need arose.*

Kelly's even breathing told him she'd fallen asleep. He smiled at her curled up next to him, her leg and arm tossed across him and her belly poking him in the hip.

Les, she's special to me, and we're going to be a family. I have to let go of the guilt for her and the baby she's carrying. I know you'd approve. Tomorrow I'm asking her to marry me, and this time, she'll say yes.

Chapter Twenty-Nine

Settled in the glider chair Mike had assured her was perfect for helping a baby go to sleep, Kelly rested her hand on her belly. It was probably more like Nate had convinced him since he hadn't had a little one in the house when gliders became more popular than rocking chairs. Either way, Mike was thinking ahead and would make an excellent grandfather. Looking around the den with its warm, rustic look, Kelly didn't regret her decision to stay in Montana and raise Ashley here. Having a big family around would mean the world to a child growing up. It'd mean the world to her also.

A trip to Baltimore would be necessary to wrap up things with her job and home, plus she owed Adrian and needed to see what she could do for him. He deserved that much from her. And she needed to do it right away before it was too late to fly. She didn't know the cutoff date, but it had to be done, and she wouldn't drive two thousand miles to get there.

Thank goodness Paul had noticed where the box of transcripts that had flown from her arms landed and had collected it for her. Reading them gave her something to do while she pretended to take frequent naps. She wasn't sure how Trent would handle her investigating on her own after she'd promised to stay out of it. Granted, she was only reading and searching for clues, not running the streets trying to collect them. Maybe something was there—

On the small table beside her chair, her cell phone rang. A Baltimore number. She answered it with a curious, "Hello," that sounded more like a question.

"Kelly, it's Paul Lintz. I meant to call you, but time kept slipping away. I thought you might want to know that Jason Brock died the other day."

"How did he die?" Kelly queried, unease settling in her stomach. The man had spilled his guts and then died.

"Apparent suicide."

Shit. "How?"

A heavy sigh reached her from the other end of the line. "Kelly, you know I can't go into all of this until it's released."

"Just tell me one thing, Paul. Why did you say apparent since by now it's been determined?"

Paul groaned. "Dammit. Okay, but it best not end up in print or our friendship is over. It appears he put up a small fight, but that could've been from something earlier that we haven't determined. I gotta go. Your buddy Adrian has asked for you."

"Tell him that I haven't forgotten him." Admittedly, she had from time to time lived in her little dream world. She had to get serious. No, he needed to hire an investigator. He needed HIS. They'd work with him financially for her since she couldn't do anything from here.

"Paul, tell Adrian that I said I want him to call Hamilton Investigation & Security. They'll understand his financial situation and work something out with him since once he's free, he'll have his money restored by the insurance companies. Tell them I referred him.

They won't turn him down." At least she hoped. She'd best speak with Trent fast about it.

"All right. Are you coming home soon?"

She was home. "I'll see you soon. Make sure to tell him, Paul."

"Okay, Kelly. My wife says hi and to stop in and see her when you return."

"Bye."

"Bye."

She made a mental note to discuss it with Trent. Surely HIS would do the work on a commission basis. She'd been wrong when the fires had first happened, and she no longer thought Adrian had been to blame. With two deaths in the mix, something really fishy was going on, and it went beyond what she wanted to deal with now that she had Ashley to consider. Before her baby, she'd have been all over it. That told her the decision to move here and give up her job was the right one.

Rubbing the spot where Ashley kicked, she smiled with excitement. Then she winced in discomfort. "Well, my baby girl, it's just us. We do have your father's family and my family, thank goodness. I don't think I could do this alone." Yet, she still felt alone, even with Mike and her parents and siblings. If only Trent stayed with her, all would be right in her world.

It sucked to realize on St. Valentine's Day, of all days, she'd failed and she'd be alone. How could she have expected him to suddenly fall in love with her enough to marry her? Sex was a pleasant pastime with him, and she'd fallen right into it. Amazing, mind-blowing sex, so she couldn't complain. It explained why women chased him once he'd left them. She wouldn't be one of them. Couldn't be one. She was to be a mother and even though she wished differently with all she had, this wasn't Trent's child. The two of them weren't his responsibility.

Besides, he probably wouldn't want to live out here. He'd been a bit saddle sore yesterday, and Mike had only taken him on a short ride. Besides, what would he do? It'd be too inconvenient and expensive to fly to Baltimore every time HIS had a mission, not that she'd want him in such a dangerous job. Sure, he blew off the danger, but he carried a gun when he worked, so that made it dangerous in her mind.

Maybe he'd learn to ranch.

She raised her brow in surprise when a small Dalmatian puppy with a cute pink collar stumbled over its large feet in a rush toward her. With a whine, she—Kelly assumed it was a girl with the collar color—lifted its front paws on the chair with something one could call a jump to get into Kelly's lap. Laughing at the too-cute-to-ignore animal, Kelly picked the spotted puppy up into her arms and settled it over her belly as best she could, allowing it to frantically lick her face while its tail wagged like it was trying to generate wind power.

Her face thoroughly wet, Kelly pulled the puppy back and cooed to it. "You are such a sweet one." Where had she come from? There weren't any Dalmatians hanging around the ranch. A herding dog and a couple of mutts made up the brood here. Barn cats, on the other hand, were plentiful.

Trent walked into the room, smiling. Joy surged through her at the sight of him. Something in that smile sent warmth radiating from her belly outward to her limbs, leaving her fingers and toes tingling in delight. "I had her flown in from B-More. She's one of Dottie's new litter." Nodding to the puppy, he added, "I think her name is on the collar."

Instead of asking why he'd done this, because even though it was a simple question, she was too afraid to ask, she swallowed and asked, "She's yours?"

He shook his head. "She's yours. Happy Valentine's Day."

Her heart soared. "Oh, Trent." Her eyes watered. Damn pregnancy hormones. "That was so sweet." He'd said she'd needed a pet, but she'd expected to claim one of the next litter of kittens. This was much better. "What's her name?" Did Kate name them before sending them off? Probably not, then again, Kate just might with an expectation her dog's pups were handled properly.

"Check her tag."

Still a bit stunned that he'd remembered Valentine's Day while they'd been holed away and somehow ordered her this cute pup, she sniffed and with shaking fingers she reached around the collar in search of a tag. When her hand snagged something that wasn't a dog tag, her movement froze. Holding her breath, Kelly fingered the object to make sure it was what she thought.

In answer to her silent questions, Trent settled down on one knee, and her heart swelled to monumental proportions. "Kelly, you've always been perfect for me. It just took me a while to figure that out. Will you do me the honor of marrying me?"

Her fingers held tight around the engagement ring on the puppy's collar. Her life had been her dream since she'd met Trent. She'd told him not to propose unless he was in love with her so her heart soared with hope that it had happened even though she wasn't turning him down.

But.... "Trent, are you sure?" At the devastated look on his face, she hurried to explain, "I mean, I'm having another man's baby. I was supposed to marry him not too long ago."

"And she'll know about her father. I'll love her as if she were mine. In fact, in my mind, she is mine."

A lone tear slid down her face at his words. Could this man be more perfect for her?

His Adam's apple bobbed as he swallowed. "Do you still love me?"

"Of course I do."

"Good. Now, I can't guarantee we'll always be happy. Marriage can sometimes be a trial. But I am in love with you, Kelly Williams. Heart and soul. Now, will you marry me?"

The puppy resumed the face licking, and Kelly moved her onto what remained of her lap. Her heart pounded. "You're-You're in love with me?"

Nodding, his smile grew, and his face lit up in delight. Even Ashley bumped her in glee. "Yes, I'll marry you." Tears rolled down her face.

Trent reached for the puppy. "Hand her to me."

She did, and Trent fumbled with the puppy's collar before retrieving the engagement ring he'd stashed there. Such a cute idea, it'd be a great story to tell their children. Their children. She liked the sound of that.

"Give me your left hand."

Clasping it, he pulled it to his lips and kissed it before sliding the ring on her third finger. The ring fit a bit loosely. He looked into her face, pleading with her to understand. "Your dad suggested getting it a bit loose because your fingers would continue to swell. Then get it sized down after you have the baby. Are you okay with that?"

Kelly laughed. "If anyone would know, it'd be Dad since Mom had seven of us. I heard him joke one day that he'd had three sizes of her wedding ring made so she could always wear his ring."

"Your dad sounds like a smart man. I'll enjoy getting to know him."

Her hand flew to her mouth. She'd best tell him now about her plans. It could be a deal breaker for them. "Trent, I want to stay here and raise Ashley. I really want to be near family now. The big city no longer appeals to me now that I have a baby to raise."

"Well, that's a good thing, because I took Mike up on his offer to teach me to run this ranch for him so Ashley will have someone to teach her when she's old enough to take over."

"What about Luke?"

"I don't know. He talked about sharing the mineral rights with him, hoping the silver mine would bring his son around. I don't quite understand that logic if Luke only wants money, but I think it's to keep him away from going after the ranch itself."

"Do you think we'll be safe?"

"We won't rest until you and Ashley are safe."

The puppy whined, making her presence known, and Kelly leaned her face to the little one. "What's her real name?"

"That's up to you."

"Hmm. I think I'll call her…Mollie."

Raising one eyebrow, Trent shrugged a shoulder.

"Mollie it is. The first of many children for us."

"I like that, and I love you."

"I love you, too."

Chapter Thirty

Finally, they'd have some answers. Waiting to line up all the team members necessary for the phone call drove him nuts. When it came to Kelly's safety, Trent quickly learned he had no patience.

How could he have any patience? They really had nothing concrete that led them to a person who wished her and their baby harm. They had possibilities, but they could be a stretch. Heck, he could write off everything as a coincidence except for the man who went after her with a knife. There was no way that had been a crime of opportunity.

Assuming Brian's death hadn't been an accident, then it all led back to the land and who would inherit. That was the only way Kelly tied into it all. If Mike hadn't made it public knowledge that he'd left the ranch to the baby—he smiled at the thought of baby Ashley and then frowned at his other thoughts—then Kelly might've been left alone.

Locked in Mike's office, AJ and Matt lounged in chairs on one side of the desk while Trent sat in Mike's chair with a trio of large windows behind him. With his cell phone on speaker sitting on the desk, they spoke with Jesse and Devon, who were conferencing with Danny.

"I hear congratulations are in order," Jesse said.

Glancing sideways at AJ, Trent muttered, "Word

travels fast." He'd only asked her the previous afternoon. He should've guessed AJ or Matt would've told their brother. Jesse always knew everything that happened with the family. Devon's marriage came to mind, and Trent's lip quirked at that one slipping by their eldest brother.

"We like Kelly and are glad she's joining the family," Devon added.

Trent closed his eyes in dismay. The Hamiltons and HIS. He had to speak with Jesse today about it since he'd promised them an answer about the partnership long before now. A partnership he hadn't earned and didn't deserve.

"While we're waiting for Danny," Devon said, "I can give you this. Brian having business in Baltimore seemed odd, so I did some digging. It took some work, but I found that he did several things, but this one stood out. He met with a firm that conducts mineral testing."

Trent's mind went into a whirlwind. "The test results were probably in the stolen papers."

"Probably. I checked it out and it was testing for silver," Devon added.

AJ stood and walked around the desk to look out the window. "Which could mean they thought she'd seen the results. so they went after her. At least, before Mike announced the future change in ownership."

Trent nodded. "Someone didn't want Mike to find out that he had silver on his property, which would've made the price skyrocket if he changed his mind and decided to sell."

"But," Matt said, "he wouldn't sell it. Maybe whoever it is thought that if Mike ran out of heirs, he'd sell."

"Or," Trent thought out loud, "Luke could've made sure his father only had him left as an option, so he'd have to leave it to him."

"Hold on to that thought, Trent," Jesse said. "Let's hear what the boys have first. Danny is on the line. Go ahead, Danny."

"Steve and I were able to meet with Luke and Christian Kent."

"Not Brightmore?" A tingle started at the base of Trent's spine, warning him something bad was on the horizon.

"Couldn't nail down where Brightmore was. The kid travels a lot. But we do need to speak with him."

"Why's that?" Jesse asked.

"Because I didn't really get anything from the other two. Luke doesn't seem to be the type to steal the ranch, nor does his current lover. He doesn't begrudge the ranch not being left to him."

"Bullshit," AJ interjected and returned to his seat. "Who doesn't get mad when your birthright is taken from you?"

Danny chuckled. "Oh, I didn't say he wasn't mad about it—at first, but when I asked if he thought his brother's accident might've been on purpose to get their dad to sell the land, he went ballistic at the thought. He tried to hire me to find out the truth."

Frustration welled within Trent, and he stood and paced behind Mike's desk. Growing up without any siblings and without a home the family-owned, Trent didn't know how he'd react in that scenario. His parents had only left him money and lies. *And love. They loved me.*

"Well," Jesse said, "that still doesn't clear him."

"No, but the more he and I talked, the less my gut told me he was involved. I don't think he's our man."

"Okay." Trent stopped his pacing and turned to the phone. "What about Kent?"

Danny cleared his throat. "Christian Kent is buying land in abundance, and he sees the resources around the Platt ranch as a bonus. He isn't focusing only on their land, and, as far as Steve and I could find, nothing is happening with other places he's trying to buy. So he's not strong-arming others to get what he wants."

"But there's silver here. Maybe he found out." Trent knew the silver mine had to be the crux of it all.

"He didn't seem too heartbroken about not getting the ranch. He said he'd keep trying just like he would for other ranches in the area." Danny sighed. "I don't think he knows about the mine. He was too easy to let it ride like he has in the past."

"Shit! This is too damn frustrating." Trent's pulse rate spiked in disappointment. He guessed it'd been too much to ask for one of them to just flat-out admit to doing it all. That'd be too fucking easy and stupid on the criminal's part.

"I did find one interesting nugget, though. Not from Kent, but from Luke."

Danny's statement perked Trent up. "What's that?"

"Someone approached Luke about buying his family's ranch should it fall to him. He thought it odd how it had been worded, but at the time he'd been drinking, so he didn't think too hard on it. He only saw dollar signs. After sobering up, he worried about it."

"But did he do anything about it?" Matt asked.

"No," Danny said. "And worse, he doesn't remember who it was, and the description could be

Brightmore or Kent, but it could also be millions of other men."

"Hang on," Devon interjected. "I've just found something that's interesting. I started that research for Kelly's friend in jail."

Trent growled. "He's not her friend. He's just a story, and I don't really care about it right now." What the fuck did that have to do with the here and now? They had Kelly's safety to worry about. Copeland could stay in jail until they had ample time to deal with his plea for help.

"You might be, brother. The Platt case made me wonder if someone had been trying to buy up Copeland Enterprises and had framed Adrian to make it easier to buy. It was as good a reason as any I could think of at the time."

Trent grumbled, "Don't make me wait in suspense, Dev, what've you got?"

"The same someone trying to buy the Platt ranch also tried to buy Copeland Enterprises."

"What? Who?" Trent slammed his fists on the table in frustration. Why couldn't Devon just spit it out all at once? His need to tease them and keep them in suspense wasn't even in the least funny since it involved Kelly's safety.

"Reggie Brightmore."

"Fuck. Think he hired the arsonist?" Matt questioned.

"It's possible since Adrian didn't want to sell," Devon answered. "When I spoke with Adrian, he did mention the offer and then the fires, but we didn't automatically connect the two."

Anger boiled inside Trent. This little shit of a rich

man's son had tried to kill his fiancée. The man didn't deserve to live. "Wait, you already knew Brightmore was involved?"

"No. Brightmore used an attorney to make the offer. It took some—" He cleared his throat. "—*digging* to find out who the client was."

But, of course, Devon found out. Pissed at his brother for spending time on their other case and not his, Trent fought for control because the fact that he had may have been the break they needed. Or, at least gave them someone to focus their efforts upon. *Deep breath out*, he reminded himself, trying to bring calm back into his sphere. Okay, he could deal with Devon's split focus, but he'd be damned if he'd thank Devon for taking his eye off solving Kelly's situation.

The sound of keystrokes told him someone—most likely Devon—was typing. Hopefully to find Brightmore's location. Danny and Steve not finding the man bothered Trent. Those two men could usually find anyone, especially with Devon's help.

"Unless there's an unknown variable we haven't found, it has to be Brightmore." Trent's gut went with Reggie.

"You could be right, but the two cases aren't connected. However," Jesse said before anyone could interrupt, "Copeland not selling out and having issues does make your situations similar enough to put the man front and center."

Trent sighed. "I doubt we'll get a confession from him. Hell, if we don't even know where he's at—"

"Trent," Devon interrupted, "you'd best gear up, ASAP." His directive was backed by the sound of keyboard clicks.

Adrenaline on overload, Trent clenched his fists at his side. "What's going on?"

"Reggie is on a flight to Montana."

"Fuck!"

"We'll get there as soon as we can," Jesse assured.

Christ, he needed them here now. If Brightmore was their man, his coming here couldn't be good. Maybe he was just making an offer again, but maybe he was coming to take care of Kelly personally. *Fuck!*

They spoke for a few minutes about tactics and set plans because they expected Brightmore to arrive and speak with Mike again. Not tipping their hand in case he was innocent would probably kill Trent. Anger at the man raged through him.

Before they disconnected, he asked, "Jesse, can I talk to you a minute? In private?"

"Sure."

Trent picked up his phone, turned off the speaker and put it to his ear, waiting for Jesse to do the same.

After AJ and Matt left the room, he spoke, "Kelly and I plan to stay in Montana. We'll come home and wrap up our lives in Baltimore, but we'll live here."

"What will you do?"

"I'm going to become a rancher. Have some cattle. Breed some horses. Muck out some stalls. That kind of thing." He chuckled, which surprised him considering he'd been pissed off a second ago. He'd chosen right for his new life.

"We've still agreed to make you a partner in the business. You just need to sign the paperwork."

He shook his head and then remembered Jesse couldn't see him. "I'll pass."

"We'll work out your not being involved if that's

what you're worried about."

"I appreciate that, but it's not that. I just can't." He didn't want anything that showed he'd accepted being Senator Hamilton's son. He'd already acknowledged the man's other children as his siblings. That was enough.

"Okay." Jesse paused. "If you change your mind, we're here."

"Thanks, man."

"I wish you luck at what you're doing. If you ever need anything, and I mean anything, you just call. We'll be there for you without fail."

His eyes misted at the deep sentiment from Jesse. Trent knew that he meant it and that built a love in his heart for his brother that he'd never expected to feel.

Jamie had been right about so many things. He wished she'd been here so he could share his breakthroughs with her. Of course, she'd still be after him to settle with the senator. As far as he was concerned, that door could remain closed.

Chapter Thirty-One

Kelly folded a sweater from the laundry basket while Trent folded a pair of jeans. Her mind tried to focus on the good things, like her wedding, but it wouldn't settle on anything but problems. Although glad HIS had some information, her story about Adrian—and how it may have been inaccurate—also bothered her. "Do you really think he set Adrian up for the arson charges?" she asked Trent.

Having heard all the team had found, she wished Adrian had HIS when all the trouble went down. Then again, everyone assumed him guilty, so no one went to too much effort to help him. Losing his money hadn't helped either.

Trent shrugged and reached for a pair of black socks, matched them, and rolled them together. "We don't know him, so anything's possible. It could just be a coincidence the two cases met, but I'm not a big believer in coincidence between cases."

With a snort of agreement, she placed the sweater on a pile when Ashley decided to give her a swift kick. "Oh." She rubbed her hand over her belly.

Trent dropped the socks and rushed to her side. "Are you okay?"

His frantic concern made her laugh.

Taking his hand, she placed it over where the baby had been moving. "She's just making herself known today."

A smile spread on his face when she kicked again. "That's our girl."

To know that this man would be raising Ashley without holding her time with Brian against her brought a stronger love into her heart. With Roger McKenzie as a great father role model, Trent had explained that while the girl would know all about Brian, he wouldn't deny her anything, including the Hamilton brood. Minus Blake, of course.

She'd tackle that in a few minutes. At the moment, the thought of Reggie Brightmore bothered her.

The link to Adrian Copeland astonished her. Coincidence or not, if Reggie had truly set him up, a deep sadness for what the man had endured hit her gut. Even she'd almost crucified him in the public eye. She was glad he'd taken her advice and hired HIS to find out the truth.

With a heavy heart, she hoped it helped him get released. It wasn't too late to recover all that he'd lost.

Worrying her lip with her teeth, her mind shifted again. "Do you think Reggie will come here?"

Trent reached his arms around her and pulled her close to him. With a confident grin, he said, "Even if he does, we'll be fine. Just promise me that you'll stick with one of us, preferably me."

Panic tried to seize her, but she tamped it back—somewhat.

It must've shown in her eyes because Trent kissed her lightly on the lips. "Promise me, angel."

"Oh, that's an easy promise." And it was. If Reggie had been the one to have someone try to kill her, she didn't want to run into him, especially alone. "What if it's not him?"

"Then we'll cross that bridge when it happens."

His assurance didn't stop her flutters of worry. To think this could be over soon and they could start their new life. Her heart soared. They'd be married. Finally, she'd be with her Mr. Right forever. And to be near her family…life didn't get much better than it was, with the exception of someone possibly trying to kill her.

Putting her arms around Trent's neck, she leaned up and kissed him for what had been meant to be a peck but turned into a passionate embrace once he took control. As her tongue played with his, he leaned his pelvis into her so she could feel the beginning of his arousal.

Butterflies fluttered in her stomach at the thought she could do that to him with only their lips connected. Yet he also got her wet with only a kiss, sometimes even just a hint of one.

Breaking apart, he looked at her and smiled. "I love you."

She'd never tire of hearing those words from him. "I love you, too."

Separating himself, he reached back for the discarded socks. "Let's get this done and maybe get to bed early." He winked playfully.

That sounded like an amazing idea, so she picked up something to fold. Tamping down her desire enough to get through the task, she thought of the other topic she'd meant to introduce. Now or never. "When are you going to see Blake?" She started. *Was that a growl from him?*

"I don't want to talk about him."

"You accepted the men as your brothers and Emily

as your sister."

One of his shoulders lifted in a shrug. "That's different."

"How?"

Running his fingers through his hair, he sighed. "They're blameless. Besides, growing up, it always felt like they were at least cousins. I couldn't hold anything against them."

"Your parents?"

"I've finally let that go. They were good to me, but they lied. I had a hard time with that. Then I figured they were up against the powerful Senator Hamilton. They probably didn't think they had any choice."

Somehow, Kelly didn't think that to be the case—completely, but she refused to say so.

Closing the distance between them, she placed her hand on his arm. "Look, I'm not saying what he did was right or wrong or that you must accept him as your father. But this is bothering you, and before we marry, you must resolve your relationship with him"—she held out her hand to stop his interruption—"no matter what it turns out to be."

The scowl on his face had her taking a step backward.

Lord, she hoped she didn't just postpone her wedding indefinitely.

Chapter Thirty-Two

Ned Tyler—a fairly new ranch hand—had missed Friday night in town with the other hands because he was sick. Kelly wanted to check on him in the bunkhouse. She understood the warnings and potential threat to herself, so she asked Trent to accompany her. With the way he carried on, you'd have thought she'd asked for the world.

"I'd rather you didn't leave the house," he told her.

"I'm just going to the bunkhouse, and if you come with me, I'll be perfectly safe, not that I wouldn't already with both AJ and Matt patrolling." She couldn't be any safer. She gulped. Famous last words in a movie. But she really was safe. "I just want to bring some chicken noodle soup and check his fever."

"Why? You can't do anything for it."

She sighed in frustration. "No, but if it's too high, we'd need to get him to the hospital."

Trent grumbled something under his breath she couldn't make out, but she smiled. It meant he was coming around to her way. "Okay, but you listen to everything I say."

With her sweetest smile, she said, "Don't I always?"

He tossed his head back and laughed. "Like that would ever be the day."

Kelly opened a can of soup while Trent talked to

AJ and Matt through his earpiece. She liked that he didn't have to track down the men to tell them their plans. If Ned still felt poorly tomorrow, she'd make him a pot of homemade soup. That should've been what she'd done in the first place, but she hadn't counted on whether Trent would agree or not. She wouldn't go behind his back when her and her daughter's lives were at risk.

While stirring the pot as it heated on the stove, strong arms wrapped around her from behind, and Trent's head leaned down beside her ear. "You look good enough to eat." Then he ground himself against her backside where she could feel the distinct beginnings of an erection.

She giggled. The man was insatiable. Then again, she pretty much felt the same way every time she saw him. It'd be a sad day when her hormones went in the other direction as some women's tended to do because she couldn't fathom not having sex while pregnant.

She set the spoon down, turned, and wrapped her arms around his neck. "Then go ahead," she teased.

After that statement, and from the lust in his eyes, she braced herself for a bruising kiss and to be swept off her feet in ecstasy. Instead, he nibbled on her lips as if really tasting her. A string of warmth made its way through her body, resting at her core. Damn, the man could turn her on like no other.

Using his tongue, he outlined her lips before he licked the seam and slid it into her mouth. Her tongue greeted his in welcome. Just knowing the things that man can do with that tongue sent delightful shivers coursing through her. They'd have to hurry their visit and get into bed—but not to sleep.

With a slight tug to pull her closer, he deepened the kiss and Kelly moaned in pleasure. God, she loved him. And to know that he finally loved her back could've given her an orgasm on its own.

Trent pulled back, breaking the kiss. "That sounded like you enjoyed it. But—" He gave her lips another quick kiss. "—I think you'd best stir that boiling soup."

She jumped. "Oh." Spinning around, she picked up the spoon and stirred the soup, then turned it off.

Humming while she prepared a tray for Ned that included the soup, crackers, and juice, Kelly wondered how she'd help Trent resolve things with the senator. He'd said things were fine the way they were, but she knew it'd eat at him if he didn't speak with the man—even if just to tell him off—which she hoped he didn't.

As much as she'd like to resolve it for him, she knew he had to do it. All she could do was gently push him to get this clear of his mind. And that meant not avoiding it.

Turning with a tray in her hands, she smiled at the man leaning in the doorway with his arms crossed over his chest. Trent had already put on his jacket. Damn, he looked relaxed. And that grin. He'd been watching her ass. That made her secretly smile. "I'm ready."

He stepped forward and accepted the tray from her, then followed her through the house to the front door, where he waited while she put on her jacket before they went into the cold. People said cold was cold, but there was a difference between the cold in Baltimore and the cold in Reed Point. She figured the air coming through the mountains instead of off the bay might have something to do with it. It would just take a little longer to get used to, but she would once again.

She stepped off the porch in the direction of the bunkhouse and nodded to her future brother-in-law, knowing he would follow. "Hi, AJ." Pulling her jacket closed tight and zipping it, Kelly looked around nervously even though she felt safe with the Hamilton men—including Trent—with her. The bright night surprised her, so she looked up to a nearly full moon and too many stars to count. She sighed in contentment. She loved it here.

"This soup is going to be cold by the time we get it to him," Trent said, walking abreast of her.

"Why do you think I put a lid on the bowl?"

"Don't know how much it will help."

She playfully swatted him on the arm. "Quit. It's not that far to the bunkhouse."

When they reached where the ranch hands slept, Kelly knocked on the door and announced herself, giving time for Ned to cover himself if he'd been naked. Pushing past her, Trent entered the room first, took a look around, and then allowed her to enter. She wanted to grumble but left it since he was just protecting her.

They walked through the front room that doubled as a place to entertain visitors. In the next room, Ned lay in a bunk near the back. Kelly had only been in the bunkhouse once before, and it'd been empty and cleaned up. The men sure hadn't rushed to clean everything up before they left for town. This room hosted a dozen bunks, many empty due to the size of the staff. She knew through the next door to be a game room where the men spent most of their off-time hanging out. Plus, there was a kitchen in the back.

Ned lifted his head weakly and greeted them. He'd

only been there a little more than a week, hired as one replacement for those two lowlifes who'd quit before they'd arrived. It sucked for Ned that he'd come down with a cold so quickly. Being new to a job was bad enough, but to end up not being able to keep up on a ranch was awful.

Placing her hand on his forehead, Kelly felt for fever. It didn't occur to her until after she'd done it that she hadn't asked permission. At the heat of his face, she frowned. "You're still pretty hot."

"I'm fine," he croaked out.

Kelly worried her lower lip. "I don't know."

"Kelly, if the man says he's fine, he's fine. We men know these things." Trent's frustrated voice did nothing to deter her.

"Well, we should check it. Is there a thermometer in the bathroom?"

"No," Ned said forcefully.

Taken aback, Kelly decided to go a different route. The man's high fever bothered her and she had to find out if it was high enough for the hospital. "I brought you some soup and juice. Are you keeping anything down?"

He nodded against his pillow. "Yes, ma'am."

While Trent spoke with Ned, Kelly excused herself, pleading her pregnancy made her have to pee. Although feeling like an intruder, Kelly rifled through the medicine cabinet looking for a thermometer. She didn't have any success, so they'd have to return to the house, then come back. She shivered at the thought of going back out in the cold so much. But if she and Trent would eventually run this ranch, it'd be her responsibility to help take care of the men.

A sense of foreboding slapped Kelly as she walked back into the room with the men. The heavy weight of her feet made her feel as if they were weighted with lead and slowing her progress. Back in the room, she went to Trent's side, planning to hurry him along.

She didn't have a chance. Her heart stilled for a brief moment when a man entered the room pointing a gun at them. Terror flooded her system and her body stiffened in fright. Recognizing the face from a photo Trent had shown her on his phone, she whispered in a shaky voice, "Oh God. Reggie."

Trent shoved her behind him, and she grabbed the back of his shirt with trembling hands in a death grip. Her heart pounded mercilessly against her rib cage. She'd brought them to this end. Just the thought of the potential death of Trent or Ashley had her screaming inside, *No!* She wouldn't allow it. There had to be something she could do to help them escape with their lives. Reggie hadn't been ballsy enough to shoot them right away, so she had hope. *Flee,* her mind sang. With a pounding pulse that could be heard in her ears, she tried to draw Trent backward, toward the exit, away from the threat.

"Brightmore," Trent said, and to her utter relief, he took the micro-step back with her.

In the midst of her mind seeking escape, she suddenly remembered that Trent kept an open mic—except when they were in bed—so help should be on its way. An ounce of relief flowed in. Enough to steady her ragged breathing. Peeking around, she caught sight of Trent tightening his jaw, and that relief fled, and her fear skyrocketed. Maybe it shouldn't have, but he'd have been more relaxed if AJ or Matt were on their way. *Please don't let us be alone.*

Ned struggled from the bed. "Boss, are you sure we have to go about it this way? The old man seems reasonable. We can convince him to sell."

"Shut the fuck up and go take care of him."

A rock dropped in her stomach and broke into small stones that bounced around painfully. Christ, they were going to hurt Mike. Hell, it looked like they might hurt them too, but with Trent, they had a fighting chance. She trusted he'd figure it out if she couldn't get them scooted to the exit. But Mike was alone. *Where are AJ and Matt?*

"I'm not killing him."

"I don't want him dead—yet. Just out of the way until we deal with her." He waved his gun at her and Trent.

Kelly gasped and quickly covered her mouth.

"What about the other two men?"

"River, Tim, and some men I brought are taking care of them as we speak." Reggie grinned, and it twisted her insides. River and Tim were the two men who'd worked for Mike and left unexpectedly. They'd probably done those things to hurt the ranch as had been suspected.

And, they were taking care of AJ and Matt. *No,* she chided herself. *The Hamilton men are tough.* But she had no idea how many men Reggie had brought.

"What's this all about?" Trent asked, hostility oozing into his words.

Why would he ask such a stupid thing? He'd told her everything about Reggie, the silver, and their fear he'd come after her.

Reggie narrowed his eyes. "I will have this land."

"Why are you after Kelly?"

"Because she's carrying the heir to the place," Reggie said.

"That doesn't make sense since Mike still owns it."

"Once she's dead, he'll change his will to that useless son of his, Luke, and then Mike will have an untimely accident leaving the land clear for Luke to sell to me like we'd agreed."

So they'd been right in their assumption Reggie had been the buyer to approach Luke when he'd been drunk.

"Luke agreed to all of that?"

"Of course not. He just agreed that if the land became his, he'd sell it to me for the right price. I can always pay the right price."

Without skipping a beat, Trent continued to pound him with questions while they took another step back. "What about Brian? Did you have him killed?"

"Of course. He found out about the silver. He'd never have sold or would've asked too high a price."

"Tell me about Copeland." Trent's words grabbed her attention, even though she wanted to grab Trent and sprint for the door.

Reggie spat. "That stupid bastard wouldn't sell his business to me. Me!" The man jammed a thumb into his chest. "So I kept going until he paid for denying me."

"I thought you wanted the property."

"I changed my mind. Setting him up was more fun." His malicious grin sickened Kelly. Adrian had been innocent all along. And she'd gone after him in the beginning, thinking him guilty like Reggie had planned. She bit her tongue because she wanted to ask questions, her journalist instinct told her to, but she had to believe Trent asked these questions for a reason. She trusted him and interfering was something she promised not to do.

"Did you have anything to do with Copeland's ex-wife's death?"

"Not personally, of course. I don't kill." A maniacal chuckle left his mouth. "I just hire for it. It's not as hard as one would expect."

Another sprig of hope surged through her. He didn't kill. He'd just said it. Then the hope sank like a stone. He had others here. Someone would probably do it.

Not giving up, they took another micro step back, putting more distance between themselves and Reggie. They hadn't moved far when the door opened. Kelly jerked her head around in eager anticipation of help, but at seeing the newcomer, she wanted to cry.

It wasn't a savior.

Ned entered and nodded at Reggie. "He'll be out for a while."

"Did you tie him up in case he wakes?"

"Yeah."

The two men put their heads together, and Trent took advantage of their distraction. He turned his head and whispered, "When I say go, you run for that door and get to the house to Mike and call Jesse."

Her gut clenched at what could happen to him alone. "No. I don't want to leave you."

"Please. You promised to do as I say until this is over. I'm going to make sure it's over."

She swallowed against the lump lodged deep in her throat and agreed. Tears formed in her eyes, and she wiped them before any could flow. If only Trent had an advantage, at least a—Wait, his gun. She felt down his shirt and touched the handle of the weapon in the back of his pants.

"No," he bit out.

Snatching her hand back as fast as if she'd been bitten by a snake, she had a sliver of hope that now he could hold his own against the man. Trent just wanted her out of the way and safe, and based on what Ned had said, Mike was alone. Safe.

"Good, get a fire started in the kitchen," Reggie said loudly as he inclined his head to a room behind them that adjoined the game room.

When Ned left the room, Trent shouted, "Go," and reached behind him for his weapon.

Kelly stepped away to rush to the door. A gunshot rang out, and she stopped in her tracks. Fear laced through her veins. Fear for Trent. With her only thought of him, she disobeyed the order she'd been given and turned. Her heart fell. Turning back, she took two steps when Reggie stepped toward Trent, who was on his knees, doubled over, clutching his stomach. *Oh God, how severe is it?* Christ, he'd just healed from the knife wound.

Aiming the gun at Trent's bent head, Reggie looked at her. "Stay right there until I say otherwise."

Frozen in her tracks, her fear for Trent almost a living, palpable thing, she could only nod. With her eyes refocused on Trent, she noticed him sinking lower to the ground. *Oh, Trent.* She wanted to rush to him and make sure he was okay. Assure him that he'd be okay.

Reggie kicked the gun that had fallen from Trent's hands out of the way and waved her over. "You can see to him now if you want." Laughing, he stepped back and called to Ned.

Terror clawed at her, and her heart plummeted to her stomach at what she might find, but she rushed forward and dropped to her knees more nimbly than she'd expected with her condition.

"You should've...left." Trent's broken words over his harsh breathing tore at every fiber of her being. They had to have help. Now.

Her eyes watered, and her vision blurred. "Help him!" she cried up to Reggie, even knowing in her heart that no help would come from the man. Hell, he'd asked Ned to set the place on fire. *Please, God, don't leave us in here.*

"I wouldn't have shot him if he hadn't tried to draw on me."

"You're a monster!" she shouted, her pulse raging through her veins.

"I'm a man who gets what he wants."

Trent collapsed on the ground, unconscious as tears ran down her face in rivulets. She pulled his head into what lap her bulging belly didn't hide and stroked his face. "Oh, Trent. I love you." It was up to her to figure out how to save them.

Something struck her on the back of the head, and before she could question it, blackness crept into her mind.

Chapter Thirty-Three

"You've got a fire out there," the helicopter pilot informed Jesse.

"Let me see." He stepped to the front of the chopper, looking out the front view. "Fuck! This can't be a coincidence. Get us as fucking close as you can."

With a nod, Brad unbuckled his seat belt and pulled a rope from the bag he'd carried onboard. Picking up the bag, he launched it at Jesse's feet. "Put on a harness."

As the men in his helicopter dug through their equipment and put on repelling harnesses in the event they needed them as their fastest exit, Jesse lifted binoculars and watched the smoke billowing out of the back of a building. They were still too far away for him to make out much else. Thank God he'd added repelling out of helicopters to their training program. Although he'd expected to use it in some hot zone, not fucking freezing Montana.

The more he scanned the area with the binoculars, the more he knew they'd be repelling out of this and the other helicopter as the choppers would have to land too far away.

His gut did a somersault. Something told him one of his brothers, or Kelly, was in that fire. If it hadn't taken so long to hand off Hogan to the proper US authorities, they could've been here sooner. Thank the fuck they'd finally caught the sicko. The FBI had been almost salivating when Jesse had told them who they'd be bringing back from Belize. No doubt they'd ignore any laws HIS had broken since they finally had their hands on Hogan. Apparently, there was a long list of charges awaiting him.

Now, he could focus his efforts here but feared it might be too late. Not being able to reach anyone in Montana on a cell didn't sit well. The team prepared themselves to walk into an all-out war if that happened to be the case. It had to be close to that for no one to respond to his repeated calls and texts.

Turning to the team members on his helicopter, he hailed the second chopper with more HIS men and women—to include his wife—over the radio. Then, on an open mic, he spoke to them all with a plan. It might not be the entire team, but there was enough personnel to do the job.

Thank the fuck they'd all seen the plans of the grounds and had pictures of workers so no innocents were caught in the crosshairs. "Danny and Steve,"— who they'd picked up along the way—"you've got the main house. Clear it as quickly as you can." He paused. "Rob and Joe, you've got the outbuildings and corralling any workers. Find my brothers and see what the hell is going on in the area." Another pause as he went through the list of who remained. Shitty time for Jake to have a team in the UAE. "Kate and Rylee, you've got perimeter. Don't let anyone in or out. Brad and Dev, you're with me on the burning building." He'd rather have his wife with him, but he might need his brothers' strength to lift anyone who needed help. Plus she was a crack shot. With all seriousness, he asked, "Dev, do you think you can make it down the rope?" Devon hadn't failed at his repelling training, but he hadn't been a big success either. Jesse wouldn't have asked him to participate if he didn't think he needed every available hand on deck for this. Whatever it was. A rich kid with endless funds could buy anything…and anyone.

"You can count on me," Devon replied firmly.

Fuck, how he wished he knew more. Going in blind sucked, but so did waiting around to see what was happening.

"I can't get any closer, or I'll fan those flames," the pilot said. "And I can't land here if you want both of us to land at the same time. You'll have to go from here or wait for me to find a larger landing spot."

Not willing to wait, the men stood ready to jump out of a perfectly good helicopter on a rope for the sake of family. While he hated they tended to be in trouble lately, the men would do anything—without pay—to keep any of them safe. Admittedly, he'd try to compensate them, but in the past, every member of the team refused anything in exchange. The Hamiltons were their family also.

"We're going from here," Jesse stated forcefully. After connecting himself to the rope with the clamp on his harness, he slipped on a pair of leather gloves, leaned back into the cockpit, and covertly snagged two cylinders, slipping them in his pants side pockets. He didn't need the pilot telling him no. Successful in his hopefully forgivable theft, he stepped to the open door. "Hurry your asses down," he told the team. Then he stepped out of the helicopter into nothing, working the rope with his gloved hands to reach the ground as quickly and safely as possible.

Once on the ground, he cleared himself, then stepped back so others could begin their descent.

Brad, who had exited out the other side of the helicopter, approached him with a grim expression. "We'd best hurry our asses if what is happening is what we both think is happening."

Jessie nodded. "I'll breach the back. You and Dev clear and help me out the front. Maybe we'll be lucky and the building is clear." Without waiting for the rest of the team to hit the ground, he pulled up the rifle he'd stashed across his shoulder and hustled toward the house and outbuildings with Brad beside him. Even though fieldwork wasn't his thing, Jesse felt confident that Devon would catch up from the other helicopter. He'd come through when Rylee had been in trouble; he'd come through again.

Before they reached the house, a group of men and women with weapons had spread out in support of finding Trent, Matt, AJ, and Kelly while stopping Reggie and any cohorts he might have active on the ranch.

The assholes didn't know what they'd done. No one fucked with a Hamilton. No one.

Chapter Thirty-Four

Trent came alert with a sudden sharpness, assessed his situation, and steeled himself. His side hurt like hell, and he could tell by the dampness of his shirt that he still bled. The noticeable absence of his earpiece and microphone—his hope of rescue—sank his heart. *Fucking Brightmore.*

It felt like a mile, but Kelly lay only four feet from him, tied and unconscious. A deep gash appeared in his heart at the impact of her position. *Please let her be unconscious and not dead.* Pushing away the pain as best he could, he struggled against the ropes tied around his hands and feet. His heart pounded almost painfully in his chest. Pure panic flooded his system, but he just as quickly squashed it with the calm needed to see this through. He had to save Kelly and the baby. He *had* to find a way.

Coughing as the smoke from the fire made its way to them, Trent thought frantically. They were both bound and tossed on their sides, just waiting for the fire to make it in their direction. The fucker hadn't even had the balls to kill them outright.

Already sweating from the heat, he didn't want the added challenge of the actual flames. Knowing the pain associated with severe burns, he'd do everything he could to protect Kelly from suffering a similar fate.

His mind firmly resolved that they would not die

like this. AJ and Matt had to know they were still in there. What the hell was taking them so long to take care of the men they'd said jumped them when he'd announced Reggie's presence over the open mic? Knowing the two men had needed time, he'd tried to keep Brightmore talking, but they hadn't come, which meant they'd had more than they could handle. *Shit. Fucking shit.*

Moving his body like an inchworm to get closer to Kelly, he stopped at the initial move, almost crying out. The pain in his side seared through him. Thank God the fucker couldn't hold the gun still and that Trent had been shot in the side and not the gut. But Reggie had still hit him, and a gunshot wound was nothing to play around with.

The room darkened as the thick smoke filled the space and began to slip lower. His eyes burned from just blinking in the air. Coughing again, Trent's heart clenched because Kelly hadn't been coughing. Christ, was she even breathing? Praying again—more than he could remember doing in his lifetime—he silently pleaded. He couldn't lose them, not now, not ever.

He tugged against the restraints holding his arms behind his back again and wanted to scream in frustration. *Check on Kelly*, he told himself, *while you work the ropes*. Ignoring the pain and resulting oozing of blood, he inched toward her until his head touched hers. Tilting this head until his nose was sideways beneath hers, he held his breath until he felt hers. Immense relief washed through him. She was alive.

Shifting his head near her ear, he breathed a heavy sigh when he made some leeway with the knot on the ropes at his wrists. "Kelly, angel, I need you to wake up."

While coughing hard enough to burn his throat raw, he almost rejoiced when she began to cough, even though she hadn't woken yet. *One step at a time.* Panic seized him, though. Flames licked on the doorframe from the back. They didn't have much time. *Please let Brightmore have underestimated Kelly and left her restraints loose enough so I don't have to fight to untie her.*

After more of what seemed to be futile straining again against his bonds, the snap shocked him. Bringing his hands around, he stretched and moved them to regain bloodflow.

As loudly as he could speak, he said, "Kelly, please wake up," but it came out more of a hoarse whisper with the burning in his throat.

Another coughing fit seized him. Tears left his eyes, and he didn't know if they were from the smoke or from the potential loss of his and her life. *No.* He was one step closer. He could save them. Adrenaline surged through him.

He positioned himself to a sitting position so he could untie the bonds at his ankles. As he leaned over, a moment too late, he realized someone had snuck up behind him. Not that he could do much to defend himself in his current situation. Maybe swing out his weak arms, but that'd be about it since he couldn't stand and get a good purchase. Surprisingly, the culprit put a mask over his face. Over the roar of the flames and creak of the building as it burned to cinder, he heard Jesse say in his ear, "Breathe slow and steady."

Not needing to be told twice, he took a gulp of air, then inclined his head to Kelly. He had to get the air to her…and to the baby.

"I'm way ahead of you." Jesse produced another mask with a small canister, like the ones pilots used, and knelt beside Kelly before carefully placing it on her face. His heart sank when she didn't wake. What the hell had they done to her? She needed medical help. *So do you, buddy.* He shrugged that off. Not until he knew Kelly was okay.

Crouched down to avoid the smoke drifting lower, Jesse turned back to Trent and pulled a vicious-looking knife from his combat boot and stepped over him to slice through the bindings on his ankles.

Removing the rope while watching Jesse cut through Kelly's restraints, hope flared in Trent even though his hands and feet stung like a bitch from where they were regaining circulation. God, he hoped he could walk. Who the hell was he fooling? He'd crawl his ass out of here if he had to—as long as he had Kelly with him.

He stripped off his jacket against the sweltering heat, the stretching of his arms and torso ripping at his wound. Shifting his mask away long enough to speak as clearly as possible, he asked, "How did you get in?" A deep hacking cough hit him, and he covered his mouth. Once again, he displaced the mask to speak. "Can we get out that way? I don't know where they've gone." They being the assholes who tied him and Kelly up, but he figured Jesse understood that.

The smoke lowered again, so they remained down on their hands and knees. Trent worried for a moment about Jesse not wearing a mask but knew he and Kelly needed the pure oxygen more than his brother did…at the moment. They had to hurry.

Jesse shook his head. "No can do. I came in the back since we weren't sure what was going on. It's not passable to go back." He nodded to the connecting archway to the game room with flames licking around the edges. "We're going out there." He pointed to the front door.

"That door is going to be hot as fuck to get out of. In case you didn't notice, it's metal."

"It'll be opened for us." He surveyed the area. "One of us is going to have to carry her."

"I'll do it," he said through the mask, not caring if he'd been understood. She was his. His responsibility. His love. His life. He'd do whatever it took to save her.

"Then keep the masks because you're going to have to do this standing—No, do it on your knees. It'll be slower but less of the blinding smoke. I'll crawl beside you where I can see our path and guide you by holding onto your shirt."

Trust. A whole lot of trust went into what needed to happen. While he knew Jesse wouldn't lead him astray, carrying an unconscious Kelly—hell, even a conscious one—into thick smoke, knowing that if he went the wrong way it could mean death, frazzled his already fraught nerves.

Ensuring Kelly's mask was fastened and the bottle rested on her chest, while on his knees, Trent lifted and cradled her to him. His wound screamed, but he ignored it for her sake. He'd never tell her, but dead weight with a baby made her incredibly heavy, but he'd lift the world to rescue her. Jesse adjusted where Trent's oxygen bottle rested, dropped down on all fours, then, as promised, reached out with his right hand and held Trent's shirt.

Moving on his knees was excruciatingly slow. He couldn't get her to safety fast enough for his liking. Sweating from the heat, exertion, and not to mention pain, he wondered if he'd end up with ice on him once they walked outside to the freezing cold.

With Kelly nestled in his arms, he blindly trudged forward with Jesse's hand tight on his shirt. Even with his eyes closed tight, tears slid down his face from the thick smoke. He couldn't even imagine if he'd tried to stand tall and walk her out.

The clank of the front door opened, and a whoosh went through the place as oxygen fed the fire, rushing the flames forward until he felt the searing heat near his body.

Before Trent could surge forward, someone grabbed Kelly from his arms, and someone else grabbed him, both men wearing masks similar to his and Kelly's. Eager to follow the man who held his woman, he rushed behind him, almost bumping into him when he slowed outside the door. But the man didn't stop until they were well away from the building. Brad knelt down and gently laid Kelly on the grass. Beside Trent, Devon removed his mask.

Glancing around, Trent noticed the activity of HIS as a couple of team members pulled out a large hose and watered the buildings around the bunkhouse, catching flying embers before they could connect with the roof. Obviously, they'd written off the ranch hands' space.

In contrast, most of HIS wasn't watching what was happening; they focused on keeping the area clear. Their injured—AJ and Matt—were being scrutinized by Rodney—a new team member who'd been a medic in the Marines. AJ's wrist hung at an odd angle. Whatever the damage, it looked painful. One of Matt's eyes had swollen, and his clothing was torn. Trent guessed they had one hell of a time themselves.

"Don't worry about them," Jesse said. "They'll get spoiled once Kate and Rylee come off point and can give their attention to the men."

Those two women behind assault rifles still awed him. They were strong and didn't flinch when most women would. It was why they are so good as part of HIS.

Kelly still hadn't moved, and he worried even more. How long could she and the baby be deprived of good oxygen? Had it been too long? Mike would know how long the ambulances would take to get all the way out here.

Mike. Fear sliced through him. Where the hell was Mike? He wanted to run to the house but wouldn't leave his angel. "Has anyone checked on Mike yet?" he yelled, although it came out as a raspy whisper with the rawness of his throat.

"The old man in the house?" Brad asked, then continued when Trent nodded, "He's got a head wound. He's conscious, but we've kept him at the house until EMTs arrive. Danny and Steve are with him."

Kelly coughed, and he leaned closer to her and removed the mask. That was probably idiotic as she needed pure oxygen, but he had to be close and hear her. Once she stopped coughing, she blinked a few times, as if trying to bring him into focus. His eyes watered, but he figured it was because of the residual smoke effects. "Trent," she croaked in a low voice.

He smiled and kissed her lips as happiness and

relief shot through him. She was the most beautiful woman he'd ever seen, even more so with her face a sooty mess. "Hello, angel. You gave me quite a scare. You okay?"

"I'm alive." Panic filled her eyes. "The baby? Do you think the baby's hurt?"

Brushing some hair from her face, he smiled. "I'm sure she's fine." He felt like he'd lied since he had no ability to predict that information. "There's an ambulance on the way, so we'll have you checked out. Just in case."

"Where's Reggie?" she asked. "Some bastard hit me on the head."

Jesse stepped forward. "He got away, but there's an APB out for him, so you won't have to worry about him. Devon was busy while we were traveling, and we've enough to help the police put together a nice case on him."

Matt stumbled toward them and slapped his twin on the shoulder. "Thanks for helping with the fuckers who jumped us."

As large as Matt's shoulders were, it was hard to believe anyone could get a jump on him. But crazy shit happened all the time.

"You're bleeding," AJ said to Trent when he ambled over.

He'd all but forgotten about his wound even though it pained him fiercely. Kelly's safety had consumed him. Only now, that he knew she was safe, did he feel himself slipping. He placed a hand down to his side. "Gunshot."

Rodney rushed over to him. "Let me see." Probing and looking at both sides of the wound, he frowned.

"It's a through and through. I'd say since the bleeding has mostly stopped, nothing vital was hit—at least not enough to notice. But, you'll have to go to the hospital to have the wound checked for minor damage and stitched. I could stitch it, but I don't dare lift the shirt because it looks like you've some dried blood around the edges of the wound, and I don't want to start it bleeding more. Plus, there might be bits of your shirt in the wound that need to be cleaned out."

At the pain from the probing, Trent dropped to the ground beside Kelly, unable to hold himself upright any longer. The wound seared his side and wrenched his stomach.

As the sirens approached, Jesse spoke of how they'd flown into the airport but had rented transport helicopters to get there as quickly as possible.

"By the way, Jesse, the pilot and copilot were pretty pissed when you lifted their oxygen masks without asking. But, I think they'll get over it when they hear how the apparatuses helped save lives," Brad said.

"Funny, they were bitching about it in our chopper when Kate did the same thing." Rodney laughed.

Trent looked down at the mini-oxygen tank he held in his hand and smiled, thankful they'd had the foresight to swipe them. Whatever it took to accomplish the mission.

He could've lost Kelly and Ashley. Sure, he could've also died, but he couldn't imagine his life without them in it. Someone had been looking over his shoulder to bless him with the Hamilton men as brothers and friends.

Holding Kelly's hand, Trent leaned over and whispered, "We're going to be okay, angel."

Chapter Thirty-Five

Reggie was captured at the Billings airport while attempting to leave Montana, despite having recently attempted to murder a couple of people. Both he and Kelly suffered no lasting effects from the smoke. With Reggie in custody, Trent set off to attend to any remaining tasks. What he'd promised two women he'd do. Set right his past, present, and future with one man.

Trent stood on Senator Blake Hamilton's doorstep in Washington, D.C. and raised his finger to press the doorbell but dropped it before he completed the act. With his heart pounding loudly in his chest, he spun away from the door. *I can't do this.* Two women's voices mixed in his head telling him he had to. That no matter how things turned out, he wouldn't be completely free until he did. *Jamie and Kelly.*

He hated when they were right.

Taking a deep breath, he steeled himself, then turned back and raised his finger again. He pressed the doorbell button before he could talk himself out of it. He would tell the old man to leave him alone, and then it would be done.

Yet he wanted to know all the details. Not *all* the details, but the what and why of Blake's relationship with his mother.

To his surprise, the senator, dressed in dark slacks, a white button-down shirt, and a red tie, answered the door. Trent guessed he'd dropped his jacket to relax after a long day at the senate. Worry and a bit of fear tinged the man's expression. "Trent, is something wrong?"

With his hands stuffed deep in his black leather jacket pockets, Trent forced out, "Kelly won't marry me until I resolve things with you." Damn if he didn't sound like a petulant child.

Blake appeared to bite on his inside lip before he spoke, yet the corner of his lips still tipped up a twinge. "Well, I guess you'd best come on in then." He stepped back, leaving a wide space for Trent to enter.

Glad to get out of the cold, Trent nodded and stepped inside the brownstone, then followed Blake to the man's office. Rich wood paneling covered the walls, with burgundy and gold used in the decorative pieces. The essence of the room made him feel important and that his meeting with a U.S. Senator in his office occurred every day.

Trent's tense muscles relaxed. He could do this. He needed to do this.

Blake offered him a beverage, which Trent declined before settling in the burgundy armchair beside him. Sitting in front of a small fire, Trent focused his gaze there. It hypnotized him and made him think of almost losing Kelly in the fire. Pulse racing, he willed the thought away to finish this business and marry the woman he loved.

Loosening his tie and unbuttoning the top button on his shirt, Blake broke the silence. "What can I do for you to…resolve this?"

Arms folded over his chest, Trent caught himself before he simply shrugged. Growing up, he'd looked up to and respected this man. It still sickened him to think it'd all been a big secret. "I just want you to know that I don't want anything from you. I had a father—one who actually acknowledged and raised me."

Blake winced but nodded. "I deserve that."

Turning to the man, Trent saw the pain in his eyes. He'd never thought of this from the other man's perspective. What must it have been like to see someone else raise your son and you not be able to say anything? Instead of feeling anything for the man, he fired a shot. "You cheated on Mrs. Hamilton." They'd always seemed to have the perfect marriage. He prayed that he and Kelly wouldn't go through what they did. At least he'd know not to fuck around, even if she threatened divorce.

"Yes, I did. I can't be sorry, though. True, I'm sorry for what it did to my marriage, but you were created."

Frustration welled inside him. Frustration for the life his mother had led. Frustration for the life he now had to lead. "Did you even love my mother?"

Nodding, Blake spoke softly, "I did love her."

"Then how could you have done it?"

Blake shook his head and sighed. "Weakness and despair will drive us to do things we normally wouldn't. I was a new senator—the youngest the state had ever elected. And, I thought I'd lost my rights to my kids. Then your mother made me feel like I was someone again. It was wrong, but it happened."

"Did my mother love you?" *Please, God, say no.* He wished he hadn't asked, but he had to know.

His father nodded. "I think she did. But she loved the man who raised you more."

Air released from his lungs on a rapid exhale. He'd needed to hear she loved Roger more. Only, he didn't have nearly enough information to process everything to his satisfaction. And what would that be? *No fucking idea.* Gut-wrenching pain exploded for his mother and her living so close to a man she loved while raising that man's son as someone else's. "Why did you push her to stay here? Didn't you think it would be awkward for my mother and father?"

Taking a typical politician's stance, he asked a question in lieu of answering. "Did it feel awkward growing up?"

He thought about it as far back as he could remember. "Not that I noticed, but I was a kid. I didn't pay attention to things like that." The vise clamped around the part of his heart reserved for the love of his family tightened. "Why didn't they tell me?" he croaked in palpable despair.

"Your mother didn't want you to think less of her or Roger. The man loved you as if you were his own."

As far as Trent was concerned, he was Roger's. This man may have given him life, but Roger, his father, made sure his life was everything he needed. His heart swelled with love for Roger. Had he been put in that situation without a choice? No matter. Trent was glad he'd been there. No finer man would bear the title of father.

He clenched his hands into fists. He didn't need Blake Hamilton or any fucking closure. There'd be no relationship.

Finding no need to forgive the other man who called himself his father, he lashed out, "You should've done like she asked and taken it to your grave."

"Do you really feel that? Can you not forgive her for her own moments of weakness?"

The son of a bitch had no right to talk to him about forgiving his mother and her lie. "It's none of your business how I feel about my mother. You don't deserve that right."

"Okay. Fair enough." Blake cleared his throat. "Trent, I've watched you grow into a strong man, one I am proud to call son, even if you aren't ready to do that. I'll announce it to the world if you ever accept me. But you are going to get one father-son talk whether you want it or not." He held up a hand to stop Trent from interrupting. "I'm sure if Roger was here, he'd deliver it."

Unease crept up his spine.

"I understand you might be suffering survivor's guilt."

"I've conquered it," Trent said quickly, too quickly. Hadn't he conquered it? His talk with Mike had been a breakthrough for him. Yet something still seemed to be wrong.

Blake raised his eyebrows. "Really? I'm glad to hear it, but you're still going to hear from me because your not wanting to tackle this problem between us might tie in. Before I was in politics, I spent a few years in the Marines. I understand all about the emotion of survivor's guilt as I suffered from it myself after returning from my first real campaign overseas. This was years before the war broke out. We were on the ground—special forces—quietly trying to prevent an all-out war. We ultimately failed. There were always the questions, 'if I had done this,' or 'if I hadn't done that,' that stream through your thoughts. One thing someone told me once that stuck was what if by doing, or not doing, what I'd done, would things have been worse?"

How worse could it have been? Les died.

The senator shrugged. "I always figured they couldn't be since I survived and my friends didn't. Then, someone else told me something that I eventually took to heart. 'Nothing can change what happened. You were given a second chance. Don't let your friends' sacrifice be wasted.' Now, none of that will fix you, but it's something to consider. From what I understand, Les willingly chose to tackle the terrorist, knowing the outcome. Sure you guys couldn't talk it out, but he knew and acted. I met the man a couple of times. I think he'd kick your ass for not living a full life because he did what was necessary to save my granddaughter."

Trent's heart sat lodged in his throat. He could only sit and stare blankly at the fire. He wouldn't allow Blake to be the reason he finally released all the welling turmoil of emotions within him. Rising abruptly, he said, "I have to go. I have something I need to do."

Blake nodded and led him to the front door without speaking a word.

With nothing left to say and the stinging of tears at the back of his eyelids, Trent turned and left Blake standing at the doorstep while he briskly walked to Kelly's car. Once there, it took two tries to select the right button to unlock it with the remote. He was so angry that once he'd settled into the driver's seat, he slammed the door shut.

Emotion after emotion stormed through him—fear, pain, heartache, loss, love. Dropping his head in his hands, he allowed the tears to slide down his face.

Before today, he'd never cried over what had happened to him, to Les, or at learning his parents had lied to him all his life. Was this him finally grieving? Finally letting everything go? Whatever it was, he hated it.

It had to be more than that because he'd already made his peace with Les. At least he thought he had. Did living his life fully include trying to form a new relationship with Blake? It was the only other thing lying painfully in his heart.

Maybe it wasn't the guilt. Maybe it was just finally knowing the truth about his conception. Sometimes being an adult sucked balls.

After swiping his face with the backs of his knuckles, he slapped his hands against the steering wheel in frustration and then exited the car. Senator Hamilton stood on the doorstep as if he'd been expecting Trent to return.

"All right," Trent said, "I'll give you a chance, but you won't replace Roger McKenzie so don't even try."

A slow smile spread across Blake's face. "I'd like to know what you're going to name that new grandchild of mine?"

Bewildered, Trent asked, "You do know that's not my baby, don't you?" It was his child as far as he was concerned, just not in the way Blake meant.

"But she'll be your wife, won't she? That makes the baby a Hamilton."

Acceptance bled into him and repaired his heart. That had been the missing key. Whether he and Blake became close or not, he could return to Kelly ready to live a full life.

Chapter Thirty-Six

He'd finally done it. Trent and Kelly were meeting at the altar. However, they'd almost not been able to get married at the church where she'd grown up attending because neither was attending a church nor had been. He'd felt helpless when Kelly had cried the entire day the pastor had to consider their request. In the end, he'd agreed as long as they sat through his counseling and attended church in the future. He could live with that since it made Kelly happy.

Standing with AJ by his side, at the front of the church, he waited for the love of his life. He'd been such an idiot not to notice her as anything more than a friend sooner. The light she brought into his world filled him with love, need, desire, and all the good possible. In his heart, he knew that he'd survived so they could be together. So that she could be his wife, and he could be a father to Ashley.

Both prospects excited him and improved his life, making him feel like the luckiest man on earth, one not to be tangled with because Kelly and Ashley were everything to him, and he'd do anything to keep them happy.

He almost laughed out loud. Love did strange things to a man.

His heart swelled with love and belonging as he gazed over the guests. The entire Hamilton family had flown in for the event. Jesse and Kate sat with a cute Reagan and their fourteen-year-old adopted son, Jason. If the boy could keep his leukemia under wraps, he was destined to be a great quarterback. Trent wondered what Jesse would do once Jason was old enough to make his own decisions because while the boy loved football, he wanted to be part of HIS.

With Megan standing up with Kelly, Emily held a three-month-old Alex for AJ and Megan while Amber squirmed between her and Jake—who'd made it home from the assignment. Somehow, Trent doubted they would be there for the entire ceremony. He expected they'd be toting one or the other children outside when the little ones became too unmanageable to be still that long.

Down the pew from them, it still seemed odd to see Devon and Rylee together, but the love they shared bled into the room. He'd have never paired the two of them together since they were so different. It went to show what he knew about love.

The twins rounded out the guests on his side of the church. He wondered when love would hit them. The rest of the family was falling like flies. Not that it was a bad thing. Everyone seemed happy in their new lives. In fact, he couldn't imagine his life without Kelly.

The men and Em had accepted his refusal to join them at HIS well. They'd, of course, left the door open for him, but after a few weeks of grueling ranch work, he knew he'd made the right decision. He loved working with the animals. Well, the cows weren't too friendly, but riding with the herd to bring them to new pastureland hadn't been so bad. Cold as fuck, but not so bad.

The ranch hands had taken well to his greenhorn ass soon to assume control.

As if on cue, AJ ribbed him. "I heard you got thrown from a horse." He chuckled quietly.

Yes, he'd been thrown, and the ranch hands had laughed their asses off. They'd also helped him corral the horse and get back on it. "Fuck you." He blanched and glanced at the altar to make sure the pastor hadn't heard him.

"And the roping?"

Damn him. How the hell had he heard this? Mike. He'd forgotten they already knew each other. Damn him, too. "So what? I can't rope a calf yet. I'm just starting." Another thing the hands had laughed about, but they'd also been there ready to give instruction and advice.

He wouldn't give up. This was the perfect life for him and Kelly, who'd taken to writing a journalism book or something like that.

Still in awe that his little Ashley would own the ranch, he worked hard every day to make sure she'd have something worth being proud of. Although Mike's health seemed steady, Trent felt it had to do with the impending grandchild being born and Luke's return. His son had come back, hat in hand, with an apology and a plea to accept him for who he was. Trent had no idea what they'd discussed, but Luke had been brought back into the fold with the understanding the ranch was Ashley's. Since Luke had been settled in to help manage the silver operation—and it appeared to be a big strike—he seemed happy enough. He'd been friendly with Trent and offered to help him however he could. Trent saw no reason to worry about him, but he'd still keep a wary eye out.

A hush came over the crowd, and Trent stiffened.

"Oh shit," AJ said quietly, obviously not giving a shit he'd just cursed in church like Trent had.

Oh shit was right. Blake Hamilton slipped into a back pew. Once settled, he looked at Trent with a plea in his eyes.

AJ shifted beside him. "Do you want me to ask him to leave?"

Trent hadn't invited Blake, so he'd be within his rights to have him asked to leave. Blake being so bold as to assume he was welcome irked him. But he'd promised to try, and he guessed as a father, he'd go nuts if he couldn't watch Ashley get married. He and Blake would never have a close relationship, but he wouldn't deny the man a simple request that cost him nothing to give. "No, let him stay."

To show his agreement to allow him to remain, Trent nodded at Blake. The man visibly relaxed as a smile spread across his face. Would Trent look so happy when Ashley stood up here? He sure as hell hoped so.

Music began to play, and the church doors opened. His heart pounded in excitement. Finally.

He didn't pay much attention as Megan walked down the aisle in a lavender dress, carrying some flowers he couldn't identify. He only knew daisies and roses. What man knew them all? Besides a florist.

With a bright smile, Megan's eyes didn't leave AJ's except for when she passed little Alex. She leaned over and gave him a kiss before she continued down the aisle. Once in place, she spun around and faced the door.

His palms turned sweaty, and his pulse rate increased. Was he truly nervous? He couldn't be. He'd been waiting for this day ever since he realized he'd fallen in love with her. In truth, he'd imagined them being married before, but those had only been snippets of a fantasy. The great thing was the fantasy was coming true.

Somehow, in the back of his mind, he caught a change in the music, but his entire focus was on the doorway and a beautiful Kelly on the arm on her father. His breath caught at the stunning vision walking toward him.

Her belly had ballooned this past month, and she looked adorable in her white gown with lace covering the bodice. The rest of the dress in white silk or satin—how the hell was he supposed to know the difference?—flowed down over her belly and to the floor.

As she passed her family—her mother and six brothers and sisters and some assorted spouses and children—she leaned down and kissed her mother, who'd taken to sobbing as soon as Kelly had appeared in the doorway.

Stopping beside him, Kelly smiled, and he couldn't stop himself. He reached over, lifted the veil, and kissed her amidst gasps, laughs, and claps. It hadn't been the soul-searing kiss he'd wanted to give her. Instead, it'd been sweet, soft, and without tongue. Holding back hadn't been easy, but he'd somehow managed.

Her taste was something he'd never tire of, nor that of her soft lips. Nipping on them, he reached his hand up to cup her neck. When he heard a man clearing his throat, he froze.

"Mr. McKenzie," the pastor said.

Realizing what he'd done, he pulled back, not ashamed, but a bit contrite for disrespecting the pastor. The smile and dreamy look on her face made it all worthwhile. "I'm sorry. She's just so beautiful."

"Let's get this moving."

Yes, he was ready to marry the woman he loved with all his heart.

Chapter Thirty-Seven

The changing weather drove Kelly nuts. At least today, she didn't have to squeeze back into her jacket that she feared was done for the season. Her belly had stretched to the size of an over-inflated basketball. Each night, before they slept, Trent had a talk with Ashley. Well, he talked. The little girl would sometimes kick, but Kelly didn't hold her breath the baby understood what her new father said.

Leaning against Jesse's SUV, outside the North Branch Correctional Institution with her husband and Jesse, Kelly swelled with pride. With her and Trent's testimony of Reggie's confession, plus the help of HIS investigations, Adrian had been cleared of all charges. They'd come to congratulate him on his release.

"How's married life?" Jesse asked.

Kelly smiled and leaned closer to Trent. "It's fabulous."

Trent put his arm around her shoulder and kissed her briefly on the lips. "I couldn't agree more."

Jesse smiled but shook his head. "And you're sure about this Montana thing?"

Grinning at Kelly, Trent answered his brother, "Yes, we are."

They couldn't get back there fast enough. But they wanted to settle this for Adrian. She wanted to be here.

"Kelly, make sure to take some video of Trent

doing ranch work, especially after he's ridden all day."

She laughed. "I think I can do that." The men had been all over him about his becoming a rancher, all stating they wanted to be present the first time he attempted to break a horse since he'd put that task off until necessary. That was an aspect of the business she didn't look forward to him learning. But Mike said he'd learn everything to include mucking the stalls, which sucked, but he'd done it. A smile spread across her face. She'd definitely send back a picture of him mucking stalls.

"We'll miss you here." Jesse leaned around Trent to look at her. "Both of you."

She'd miss her friends here also. Megan had been about as close as her sister had been growing up. "We'll miss everyone also. You're all welcome to come to the ranch."

Nodding, Jesse leaned back against the SUV again. "I can't say much for the others, but we might take you up on that. Kate and I think Jason and Reagan would love a few days there. After the fun Reagan had at the ranch after the wedding, that's all I hear about." It'd been great to see Jason riding a horse and enjoying himself at the ranch. Mollie and the other dogs and kittens had loved it when Reagan played with them.

Trent snorted. "I doubt Devon and Brad will want to come out for the horseback riding."

She'd heard about how the two had been thrown while on a trail ride led by Les and had sworn off horses. That explained why they'd avoided the animals when they'd come to visit for the wedding.

Jesse laughed. "Trying to get them back on horseback will be an epic chore."

Learning more about Les and how Trent had suffered from survivor's guilt, the more she liked the man.

The door opened and in the outer gate, they witnessed Adrian with a younger version of him exit. Paul held the door open and gave Kelly a wave before closing it back. The two men walked through the outer area and went through the gate opened by a different guard.

Adrian approached them and went straight for Kelly. "I feel like I should hug you. You gave me my life back."

With tears sliding down her face, she opened her arms and hugged him. She didn't care if it bothered Trent. She owed this man after almost crucifying him in the papers. Pulling back, she said, "A hug is good." Wiping at her face, she continued, "This is my husband, Trent McKenzie."

He stuck his hand out to greet Trent. "This is my son, Jeffrey."

"And, this"—Kelly gestured to Jesse—"is Jesse Hamilton, head of HIS."

"I'm pleased to meet you." Adrian shook his hand and nodded. "Thank you for taking on my case and proving my innocence."

Jesse smiled. "I think you've got Kelly and Trent to thank more than us, but we were glad to help."

"I guess I've got a bill to settle with you."

"Get squared away," Jesse told him. "Then we'll worry about it."

Adrian turned to Kelly. "I did right getting you to help me."

"I'm glad I could help." She reached out and

squeezed his hand. "And I'm sorry I was wrong about you in the beginning."

Adrian shrugged. "It's okay. Brightmore did a good job of setting me up."

"Well, he's behind bars now. We'll see how much he likes it." Doing something good warmed her soul. Correcting a wrong felt righteous, and pride infused her veins. Maybe she'd find a way to work cases such as this from the ranch.

She was writing a journalism instructional book, but she wanted to investigate. Maybe the local paper would take her on. Well, not local as they didn't have a paper for their couple hundred residents. But, the next town over might. The larger her belly became, the less she enjoyed driving. Once Ashley was born, she'd have to leave her little girl at home while she worked. That idea didn't appeal to her.

Special cases it was. She'd find them and work them as best she could because she wouldn't give up helping others.

Chapter Thirty-Eight

Panic seized him, grabbing his balls and squeezing so hard he thought he'd vomit. This was so much worse than he'd imagined. "Do something for her!" Trent screamed at the nurse. "She's in pain."

"Mr. McKenzie," the woman said calmly, "Mrs. McKenzie is in labor. She's going to hurt some. That's natural. But don't worry, we'll give her an epidural, and she won't be hurting any longer. It'll be a piece of cake for her."

She looked kindly at Kelly and smiled.

He tightened his hands into fists at his side. "She's supposed to have a C-section tomorrow. This can't be happening now." He wanted to pull his hair out. The baby was upside down and backward, so she couldn't have it naturally. Couldn't. He would not allow them to try something that could cost his wife or his daughter their lives.

"I assure you, it is. Don't worry. She'll still have a C-section—"

A small portion of relief flowed through him Why the hell couldn't they have said that earlier? Maybe they did and he missed it, but still, emphasis or some shit. But he couldn't feel fully relieved because she still had to have the surgery. He wouldn't relax until both of them were safe.

"—but it's happening now. We're prepping her for

surgery."

No. No. No. His mind fought to reconcile this was happening now. Would he have still been this way tomorrow when it had been planned? Maybe, but this happening a day early scared the hell out of him. They weren't ready. She wasn't supposed to be in labor.

"You need to put on the protective outerwear, Mr. McKenzie. I'll take her into another room to have the epidural administered. Don't worry, she's in good hands."

Let her leave his side? He'd promised to be by her side the entire way. He couldn't leave her.

"It's okay, Trent," Kelly said weakly. "I'll be fine. Get changed, and you can come meet me."

Leaning down, he gave her a light, lingering kiss on the lips. Pulling back only slightly, he breathed in her cherry scent. God, he loved that on her. "I love you."

"I love you, too."

"Mr. McKenzie, we need to get her moving."

Realizing he was the one holding up things and prolonging her pain, he kissed her on the forehead and told her he loved her once more before begrudgingly watching as they wheeled her from the room.

He dressed in the protective outerwear in what had to be record time. But the wait for them to come get him seemed extremely long although it could've been as simple as a few minutes. Yet, for all he could tell, it could've been an hour. His anxiety level peaked because it just took too long for him to be near Kelly again.

When he arrived in the room where she got that monster shot in her back that was supposed to numb her from the waist down, his wife had transformed from the woman screaming in agony to a mild, relaxed mother about to give birth as if it was nothing more than a typical shopping trip.

Thank the fuck for that damn shot.

He hadn't looked forward to seeing her writhe and cry out with each contraction. In the future, she was getting one of these damn shots as soon as they arrived at the hospital. Anything to prevent the woman he loved from being in pain.

"Come here, Trent," she said softly, extending a hand toward him.

Eagerly, he strode to her bedside and clasped her hand. He gently wiped at hair that had matted to her forehead when she'd been sweating through the pains. "How're you feeling?"

Kelly chuckled. "It hasn't taken full effect, and I feel small contractions, but nothing I can't handle."

"I wish I could take this pain from you. I wish you never had to suffer through it."

"Oh, Trent," she said lovingly, "if I didn't, we wouldn't have any children. Once you hold Ashley in your arms, tell me it wasn't worth it. The pain is temporary. Besides, I wouldn't give it up for the world."

He figured they'd have more to say about the subject when she wanted to get pregnant again. He'd leave it for now since she was relaxed.

They chatted about the ranch and the family they knew had overfilled the waiting room. The Hamiltons had flown in, en masse, and he figured it had to do with the problem of how Ashley rested and Kelly having a C-section. From his side of the family, Blake was the only one missing, and they figured he didn't want to intrude on something so personal.

When the nurse came to collect them, Kelly had no pain, and relief surged through Trent. Now, he had to get her through the operation. Who the fuck wanted to be awake while they cut you? He just didn't understand that part. Or even the partner watching it.

In the operating room, he stood near her head, with a fear so great it screamed through him that he wanted to snatch her away to safety. So much could go wrong.

Trent was asked to step away from her for a moment. As the surgeons began their job, he looked down at his wife to support her. He also didn't wish to see what was happening. Sure they'd put up a screen that started below her breasts and wrapped around somewhat. But, he was tall enough, he could see over it. He fought to keep his eyes averted.

When Kelly didn't flinch as the first incision was made, he relaxed, but only a little. They allowed him back close to her, and he stroked the part of her face not covered by an oxygen mask and rubbed her head to soothe her. Hell, it was to soothe him just as much.

Looking up, he watched the doctors and their faces. When he saw what could be considered worry on the obstetrician Dr. McGill, he moved to Kelly's side and slid a hand into hers that had been tied down to keep her from moving it and disrupting IVs and shit.

"She definitely didn't want to turn," Dr. McGill said.

That snapped his gaze to what was happening with his wife. He froze, transfixed and ready to pass out. His heart pounded at the sight of the insides of his wife that weren't all inside her. Terror gripped him. Could they fix this? Had Ashley's position done damage to Kelly that couldn't be repaired? He took a deep breath to try to calm himself although that didn't help much. This was too much to take in.

"There she is." Dr. McGill pulled a yucky mass out of his wife's stomach that couldn't be the baby. Yet, her legs kicked. She didn't make a sound, and that ratcheted up his pulse. Was she okay? Why wasn't his baby crying?

Two nurses, or some position dressed in scrubs, took Ashley off to the side and began to clean her body and her mouth, and it wasn't long before a hearty scream raced around the room.

Relief like he'd never known took over his body. His fear evaporated. Now they just had to put Kelly back together.

"Mr. McKenzie, it's time for you to leave," the nurse who'd escorted them to the room said.

"But—"

"She'll be fine. This is routine, but you don't need to be here for this. Why don't you go out to the waiting room and tell everyone about your baby girl?" she suggested.

He nodded, not really sure what to do. He stared at the baby and then his wife. His vision blurred as he fought tears of happiness and relief. A deep love for her seeped into every bone, every muscle, every pore. He leaned down and kissed her forehead. "I love you," he whispered.

Although he couldn't be sure what she said under the oxygen mask, he'd bet it was that she loved him also.

He left the room and disposed of his outerwear

with no other choice. God, he wanted to go back in there and hold her hand while they sewed her back up.

His relief at their making it through the birth okay—because he believed the final step was routine and he wouldn't worry—turned into excitement and joy. Funny how that wasn't the first feeling he had when Ashley had been born. Every man must fear for the mother of his child during that process and be relieved they made it through okay. He couldn't believe it any other way. The excitement and joy came after everything sank in.

He was a father. The enormity of that statement slammed into his chest, and worry whether he could be a good one tried to grab hold. He fought it back. He was a father. Saying it the second time eased into his heart. "I'm a father," he said aloud. A grin split his face.

Opening the door to the waiting room, he thought his smile might break his face because it was so large.

"I have a loud baby girl," he shouted to the room's occupants.

Amidst a chorus of cheers, clapping, and sounds of congratulations being shouted, everyone seemed to want to personally congratulate him at once. Instead, he sought out one person.

Going to Kelly's mother, he knelt on one knee and took her hands. "She's going to be okay."

Mrs. Williams wiped the tears from her face and nodded. "Good." A smile replaced the worried look. "I have another granddaughter."

"And she's beautiful." Trent released her hands and stood. Nodding at Kelly's father, he moved to the side where his family sat and stood since there wasn't enough room for everyone.

"Trent, you look," Kate said and paused. "—ridiculously happy."

"I saw inside her." He shuddered. "No one should see that."

Several people laughed at this, and Jesse slapped him on the back. "Brother, you'll survive this. Congrats on the baby."

AJ came up beside him. "Congrats, bro."

"They still have to sew up her. What if something goes wrong?" He didn't understand why this worry crept back in when he'd resolved it was routine. If only he could be there for her. That'd make it better.

"Dude, chill," AJ said. "That's the easiest part. Now, do you have a horse already for her?"

Horse? Had he lost his fucking mind? Ashley couldn't ride a horse. She'd be too small.

"Yeah," Matt said, "I hear they start riding when they're babies on a ranch."

"She probably should be a toddler first. Don't you think?" Kate asked.

AJ shook his head and laughed. "No, that's when they start breaking horses."

They were trying to keep his mind off what was happening since his mind had switched back to a bit of fear for the unknown of what was happening with his wife.

"I'll have to come up here and teach Ashley the good places to hide like he did with Reagan when she was younger," Jesse promised.

Surprisingly, a chuckle erupted from his chest, and he knew they'd won. His attention was properly diverted. He had shown a four-year-old Reagan the places they'd learned to hide while growing up. Sliding in certain cubbyholes made great hide-and-seek locations. Apparently, they also made great hide from Mommy and Daddy locations. "You will not." Trent figured the ranch hands would do enough of that. They'd taken to Kelly like she'd been a part of the family forever. The baby was part of the package, and they asked about her every day.

"I can't wait until she's ready for boys." AJ laughed.

Trent growled. "There will be no boys before she's thirty."

Laughter rang out, and he felt it deep in his bones. And so the ribbing went until the nurse returned and called for him. "She's being moved to recovery if you're ready to join her."

Blood rushed through his veins, and his pulse skyrocketed as he shot up from his seat. "I'm ready." He would sit in recovery with her until all was well. No matter how long it took for his wife to feel as normal as she could again. Hell, she'd had her stomach opened up and all but turned inside out, he wasn't sure how normal she'd feel after that.

"We'll sneak off to the nursery and see Ashley, but we'll be here when you need us," Jesse told him.

He'd been alone so long, and now he had this amazing family. When he needed them most, they'd been by his side as promised. Add in their spouses, and it made for a huge group of people to love and care for with all he had in his heart.

And he knew the size of the family would grow because, according to Kelly, when the Hamilton wives had spoken, they'd decided they needed to concentrate their efforts to get Matt and Brad married. Considering how his other siblings had ended up with their spouses, Trent had a feeling that a couple of dangerous adventures would have to occur first.

A word about the author...

Sheila Kell writes about the romantic men who leave women's hearts pounding with a happily ever after built on memorable, adrenaline-pumping stories. Her debut novel, His Desire (HIS Series #1), launched as an Amazon #1 romantic suspense bestseller, later winning the Readers' Favorite award for best romantic suspense novel.

As a Southern girl who has left behind her days with the U.S. Air Force, and as a University Vice President, she can usually be found nestled on the Mississippi coast, where she lives with her cats and all the strays that magically find her front door. When she isn't writing, she has her nose in a good book, is dealing with the woodland critters who enjoy her back porch, or is wishing she had a genie to do her bidding.

https://www.sheilakell.com

Thank you for purchasing
this publication of The Wild Rose Press, Inc.

For questions or more information
contact us at
info@thewildrosepress.com.

The Wild Rose Press, Inc.
www.thewildrosepress.com